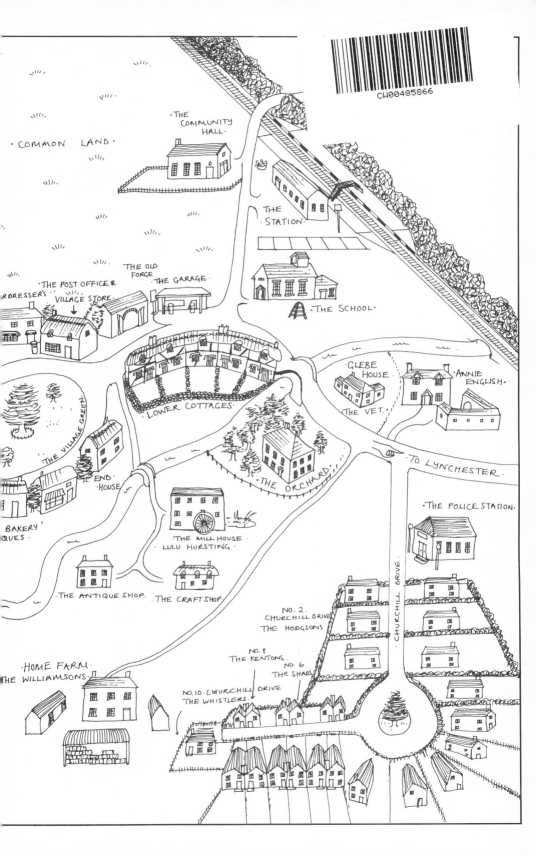

TALES FROM SARSON MAGNA

TALES FROM SARSON MAGNA

1
MOLLY'S FLASHINGS

ANNIE LEITH

Chatto & Windus
LONDON

Published in 1991 by
Chatto & Windus Ltd
20 Vauxhall Bridge Road
London SW1V 2SA

A CIP catalogue record for this book is available from the
British Library

ISBN 0 7011 3671 5

Endpaper maps © Kate Jackson 1991

Photoset by Rowland Phototypesetting Ltd
Bury St Edmunds, Suffolk
Printed and bound in Great Britain by
Mackays of Chatham PLC, Chatham, Kent

For James Leith with love.

Extract from Eldridge's Guide to Rural England

SARSON MAGNA, LYNSHIRE

Village of exceptional beauty. There are some good examples of Elizabethan thatched cottages. Recent development of 'executive' houses does not blend in happily. **The Dower House** *(formerly the Manor) Listed Grade 2. Elizabethan perhaps around a late medieval core. Good panelling.* **The Hall** *Listed Grade 2*. Grand Palladian mansion, little altered, in a park of 80 acres laid out by Repton. Mouldings in the ballroom are of special note. Viewing by appointment – Tel. Sarson Magna 671422.* **Church of St Mary.** *Medieval W. tower. Font, Square, Norman. Particularly fine monument to Sir Hubert de Parminter, Kt 1567 (recumbent figure on a tomb chest).*

Lynchester 7 miles. London 130 miles.

Pop: 380 EC Wed. Hotel, Parminter Arms (3dbl,2s) AA** Tel. Sarson Magna 671225. Garage, The Green. Tel. Sarson Magna 671336.

Contents

Chapter 1

Molly's Thursdays

THE ELECTRIC PLUG, with two further adaptors sprouting from its side, looked like a plastic, lop-sided, armadillo, as it crackled in the middle of the chipped skirting board. The paint was 'eau de nil' gloss. It should have been Adam Green but 'eau de nil' was the nearest in colour that Mr Lambert's store in the village could provide.

'That colour reminds me of caravans, they're always painted in it,' Lulu had said as she watched Molly laboriously applying the paint the year before.

'What you know about caravans could be written on a pin-head.' Molly had laughed at Lulu, perched on the edge of the chair, gold bangles jangling, long silk-hosed legs twined around each other – like an elegant, beautifully turned out, stick insect.

'It won't stay on, you realise. It'll chip in no time, you should have sanded it down first. Preparation is most important,' Lulu had told her sagely while studying well manicured hands that had never so much as touched a piece of sandpaper.

'I should think your knowledge of decorating is about as extensive as your knowledge of caravans.' Molly patiently picked at a long black hair from her brush which was embedded in the new paint. She cursed, mildly, as her hands stuck together and she left a perfect fingerprint behind.

'I've watched decorators a thousand times. Why don't you get the professionals in instead of getting into that pickle? Just look at your hands!'

'I'm saving money, if you must know.'

Lulu snorted with derision. 'Making a rare old mess more like, while depriving some poor man of his livelihood.'

Lulu had been half right. The paint had begun to peel within six months, the least knock and it flaked off. But when it flaked, it brought the paint of centuries with it, leaving large multi-coloured holes all along the skirting board. Lulu had been wrong about the caravans though; all last summer Molly had made a point of noting their colours as the holiday-makers poured into the area – cream was in the ascendancy, not eau de nil.

Molly offered up a silent prayer as she plugged in the two-bar electric fire, virtually on her knees in supplication as she added the radio. Provided only the table lamp, the radio, and the fire were turned on simultaneously, the plug usually crackled; if another lamp was added, it sparked. But if a third bar of the fire, or the black and white television were added, then, because of the increase to the load, the whole of the ground floor of The Hall was liable to be plunged into total darkness. It was one of the reasons that she was regarded so highly by Mr Lambert at the hardware store – she bought fuse wire cards by the dozen.

The wiring of The Hall was one of the crosses that Molly Parminter had to bear. She had several crosses but none with such potentially dire consequences. She understood a little more about electricity than her husband and explained with depressing frequency the importance of not overloading the system. But Hector, since he could not see the electricity, refused to comprehend it and blithely, and regularly, fused everything.

If she had not known Hector so well and understood his passion for his ancestral home, she would have thought that he lied and, in fact, knew exactly what he was doing – hoping for a convenient fire with a handy insurance payout to follow. There were days when she herself could contemplate a ruined hall, and the where-withal to build a nice small modern house in the park, with interest. Especially those days when another leak appeared in the roof, another sash-cord went, the cesspit overflowed or Mrs Hodgson's legs were playing up again and she had not arrived to help clean.

There was nothing Molly could do about the electricity or Mrs Hodgson's legs. The former since the last estimate to rewire the house, several years ago, had been £20,000 and with inflation was now no doubt more like £30,000. A sum they would never find – especially while there was urgent need for lead flashing on the area of the roof which increasingly resembled a colander.

What exactly was wrong with Mrs Hodgson's legs was a mystery. In truth, they were rather nice legs with no mottling and not a hint of a varicose vein. But at regular intervals the mysterious ailment that beset them would strike, disabling Mrs Hodgson to the point where she could not clean – but not seriously enough to prevent her from catching the bus into Lynchester to shop. Molly often fantasised the scene where, with a well chosen phrase, a studied coldness in her voice, she would point out this discrepancy to Mrs Hodgson. She never did, of course. She couldn't, for Mrs Hodgson was the only cleaning woman left in the village to help her. Once she had had a pool of six women to call upon, until four years ago when five of them had decamped to jobs at the executive housing estate which had been built at the end of the village. Executives could afford to pay a better hourly rate than the landed gentry, it transpired.

The house was a problem. It was neither one thing nor the other – too large for a family home but far too small to be classed as 'stately'. So they had all the expense, hard work and worry but could never open it up to trippers for money to help defray the cost. Since it was listed Grade 2 with a star – how often they had cursed that star – there was no question of their knocking part of it down to make it more manageable. So it stood in Palladian splendour in its park as if smugly aware that it had trapped them and that the whole of their lives was dedicated to its maintenance. The house absorbed money as rapidly as a compulsive eater absorbed food but, unlike the eater, it never went on a diet. As soon as one part of the roof was repaired, another demanded attention. As soon as one drainpipe was replaced, another one fell down. As soon as the woodworm were eradicated in one section, they started munching merrily away in another. As to the drains – there was a subject that gave both Molly and Hector nightmares. Truly the house was awesomely selfish.

Consequently, the main part of the house with its fifty-foot drawing-room, forty-foot dining-room, with the library that she'd never measured and the ballroom with its spectacular mouldings, was used only on high days and holidays. Since they were in Pevsner's guide to the buildings of England they were occasionally approached by people interested in viewing old houses. The Parminters did not mind. Both Molly and her husband felt strongly that they were privileged to live there and that The Hall should be shown to anyone who cared to ask. In any case, all the minor grants they had managed to squeeze from the authorities would cease if they did not fulfil this duty.

So within the huge house they had contrived two flats. One for Hector's garrulous mother, Cuckoo, and her companion Hope Trenchard, a permanently depressed woman of fifty-five who had long given up on hope. And there was their own five-bedroomed quarters which were furnished with the rejects from the main house and which were never repaired or decorated unless Molly did it herself – hence the chipped skirting board.

Molly tuned in to Radio One. She loved pop music, the louder the better, but could only listen when Hector was out. She poured herself a cup of tea from the heavy silver teapot, helped herself to sugar from the crested bowl and from a domed muffin dish she took two crumpets. She speared the crumpets on to two separate forks, knelt on the carpet and waited for the elements to heat up. She pulled her cardigan closer. It had been hot all this month, unusual for May, but today was chilly . . .

She looked across the wide room to the long, casement windows and glanced anxiously at the sky. It was going to rain, for certain, and Hector would be sure not to have an umbrella, he would catch cold and then he would be the fearful nuisance he always was when ill.

At last she felt the warmth from the fire and began to toast her crumpets, leaning back against the sofa, its seat sagging, its tassels unravelling and with stuffing beginning to sprout from the arms as if it were beset with a fungus.

Beside her, a picture of dejection, lay Rufus, Hector's labrador. Rufus loathed Thursdays, convinced, she was sure, that he would never see his master again. He lay, his black head between his paws, soulful eyes watching her every move, and whined. Some-

4

times Rufus' reaction worried her as if he knew something she didn't about Thursdays: that, if not today, then on some future date something awful would happen to Hector. She patted him, as much to comfort herself as the dog, at such a thought.

Molly didn't have a dog. Not since the day, ten years ago, when she had buried her pet cocker spaniel. The grief she had felt for her canine friend was so deep, the void left so large, that she had vowed never to repeat the experience. She had a cat, instead, called, rather unoriginally, Tiddles. The cat and she liked and respected each other but there was not that intensity of love and devotion that only a dog can give.

Molly could not agree with Rufus; she loved Thursdays. On Thursday her mother-in-law was driven to Sarson Parva to spend the whole day with her bedridden friend Agatha Trenton, and as Thursday was market day in nearby Lynchester Hector was always away by nine. Once the market was over he would lunch at the Black Bull and then attend the weekly committee meeting of the local Conservative Association, of which he was chairman. It was the day of the week that Molly could regard as her own. She had no need to bother with lunch, she could have tea when she wanted, she could do whatever she liked – conscience permitting. Her conscience was a bane: Molly would have liked to be idle, but invariably the day was spent in catching up with jobs that needed doing.

'Why don't you set aside Thursdays to do your own thing?' Tabitha, her daughter, had suggested.

'I don't even know what doing my "own thing" means.'

'Doing whatever you want and not thinking about anyone else.' Tabby had sat on the kitchen table swinging her legs back and forth, tapping at the leg of the chair with her heavy lace-up shoes – ward maid's shoes, Molly had called them, much to Tabby's annoyance.

'You mean being selfish. . . .' Molly laughed as she mixed the pastry in the bowl. 'What would I do? I'd like to curl up with a Jackie Collins and read it from cover to cover in one go. Buy a David Shilling hat. I'd like not to have to weed the herb garden because Flint refuses to tend it. I'd like . . . to go to the cinema in

5

the afternoon with the sun shining – such a decadent thing to do.'

'Going to the cinema?'

'When the sun's shining, yes. Wicked!'

'Ma, you're pathetic. Honestly, apart from the hat, what a dreary load of things to want to do.'

'I don't think so. Would you mind moving . . .'. She waved her hand at her daughter who, with her customary lethargy, slid from the table as if in slow motion. Molly opened the large flat drawer at the end of the table and searched for her pastry cutter. She wiped her marble pastry board, dusted it with flour and began to roll the dough.

'Then why don't you do all those things?'

'I can't – there's too much else to do.'

'You're a martyr, that's your problem.'

'I'm not,' Molly said indignantly.

'Yes you are. You've just admitted it – doing boring things when you'd much rather be doing others. What is it about mothers makes them like that?'

'I don't think I am. Aren't martyrs supposed to moan all the time, make sure everyone is noticing their martyrdom?'

'So?'

Molly ignored that 'so'. She sometimes felt that Tabby set up conversations such as this just to annoy, hoping an argument would ensue. This invariably meant that Tabby was bored. Then she could stay bored as far as she was concerned, Molly thought, as she expertly wrapped the pastry around the rolling pin and transferred it to the pie dish. She had sharply told her daughter to go and tidy her room. Tabby had sloped off but it was unlikely that she would tidy anything, least of all her room. Molly had long ago stopped even opening the door to it, for the shambles inside offended her too much. Why her daughter should choose to live in such chaos mystified her, as did much about the girl. Doing anything to the room herself only led to further arguments and accusations of 'snooping', so now the room festered away above her.

She turned over the crumpets to toast the other side. In fact,

Tabby, that day a month ago, had been closer to the truth than she realised. Molly did not know why but recently she had begun to question many things in her life. It was too restricted. Her whole life revolved around this house, the village. These days, if she went to London she suffered a culture shock from the crowds, noise and mess – last time she had walked through Leicester Square she had had an insane urge to pick up a broom and sweep it clean herself. There was a dreadful sameness to her year. No doubt she could say now what she would be doing, month after month, in ten years time. That thought she found particularly depressing.

When her children had been at home, life had been so full. First James had gone to university and then the city and last year Tabby had left. Now there was just Hector to look after. These days, she felt she was becoming distanced from her children. James was like a stranger to her. The little boy she had loved and nurtured had disappeared completely, as if he had never existed, remaining now only in her memory, to be replaced by a self-centred young man of twenty-six, whose pomposity gave him the air of a middle-aged man. There were times now when Molly felt she was the younger of them – a ludicrous state of affairs.

And herself? Thinking about herself was becoming an increasingly depressing exercise. In the past Molly had always advocated never thinking about self, convinced that it only led to deeper problems. That had been easy to say when she had had the children to think about; now she found she spent more and more time thinking about herself. Physically she had weathered pretty well: she had not reached the point of cringing when she saw her reflection in the mirror. But, mentally, she feared she was rapidly becoming boringly middle aged. Why else would she do things she did not want to do, all the time? Nobody ever asked her to; it was always presumed that she would. And she did, as if she had no will of her own.

For a start there was the Conservative Association. As the chairman's wife many duties were expected of her. The various jumble sales, fund-raising tea parties, chivvying of other Conservative wives were very much her responsibility. It was also her job to collect the subscriptions of the party faithful and to approach all new people in the area to ensure they joined and paid their dues.

The problem was, no one had ever asked Molly what her politics were. When she had returned home from honeymoon it had been assumed she was Tory – wasn't everyone? But she wasn't and never had been. Not that she felt strongly about any other party – she didn't, she didn't feel strongly about anything to do with politics. She supposed she should have said something right at the beginning. But at twenty-two, newly wed, afraid of her own shadow let alone her imperious mother-in-law – she had said nothing.

But just recently . . . She knew what had made her stop and think. In the past, new people in the village were a rarity but nowadays they came and went at an alarming rate. Once she had known everyone, whom to approach, whom to avoid – now she didn't. Then, last week, she had been alerted to more newcomers in the village by Mrs Hodgson, who knew everything that went on. She had pottered up to the new estate, Wood Close, to introduce herself and, she hoped, sign up new members for the party.

Jill Martin had opened the front door of her house, The Larches and had said, 'Yes.' Not a 'yes' that ended in an upward friendly tone but a flat one, a most unfriendly one. Molly had introduced herself. She was normally invited in by people but Mrs Martin did not offer her the courtesy so she stood in the drizzle, conscious that her hair was rapidly turning into rats' tails, and explained why she was there.

With no warning, a long, red-painted nail was stabbed in her direction. Molly stared at its length, fascinated, and resolved never to eat pastry in this house, goodness only knew what organisms could lurk under such a length of nail. The woman's hair, streaked like a tiger's, bounced aggressively on a head that was thrust menacingly forward. Molly backed down the step as she found herself being criticised, personally, for all of Mrs Thatcher's policies – not one but all. After rounding on her over the state of education and the health service, Molly was given a stiff lecture on the plight of the homeless and, inevitably, the Poll Tax was included in the diatribe. Since she wasn't truly Tory she had, reasonably enough, felt it was unfair that she should suffer such verbal lashing. But worse was to come: as the young woman ranted on, Molly found there was much with which she found herself in agreement. Not that she could get a word in edgeways to say so. Instead she backed further away, knocking over a Wendy House and with confused apologies turned on her heel and walked briskly out of Wood Close, vowing never to do that again.

She had been thoughtful on her return home and had been thinking on and off ever since about what the young woman had said. She began to butter the crumpets. She was going to have to tell Hector that she was no longer willing to canvass for funds. The problem was that she had never taken a stand in her life and didn't know really where to begin — well, she wondered, would insisting on the swathe of Michaelmas daisies in the long herbaceous border when Hector couldn't abide them, could that be classed as a stand? And then there was the time she'd refused to allow Flint to prune the clematis. She bit into a crumpet. But, no matter how you looked at it, such rebellion could hardly stand comparison with telling Hector she might just want to join the SLP, SDP or the SLD or whatever they called themselves these days.

Chapter 2

The Petition

TWO WEEKS LATER, Molly hadn't told Hector anything. She was not surprised she had not — it was all just Thursday dreaming she told herself: no doubt she would never say anything.

She had not spoken, not out of weakness but out of consideration. The news that she wished to desert the party would have made Hector very unhappy. Not only would he have been shocked but he would, she knew, have felt humiliated at the Conservative Club. In a minor way, within their circle, it would have been the equivalent of Denis Thatcher doing the same thing. And she was far too fond of her husband to do that to him. What was the point of making a fuss? She could always vote whichever way she wanted in the ballot box — no one would ever know. And she could, perhaps, get someone else to collect the subscriptions — she would have to think of someone suitable.

It was a perfect June day, as she let herself out of a side door. As she walked around the side of the house she automatically looked up, checking the guttering, the pediments, to see if anything was about to fall off — one could never be sure. She crossed the semicircle of gravel in front of the house, newly raked by Flint. She stopped at one of the great lead urns, removed a couple of weeds, admired the hydrangeas, and set off down the long avenue, guarded by the rows of limes which cast dappled shadows in the bright sunlight. They'd been lucky in the hurricane a few years ago, they had lost a beech and an oak in the park, but not one of the limes in the avenue. Lulu's son had lost two hundred beeches on his estate just ten miles away. Strange how selective the wind was.

She walked confidently until she had almost reached the end of the drive and then her footsteps faltered. She paused by the gatehouse where Flint, her tyrant of a gardener, lived. She looked down at her bright pink track-suit trousers, as pink as a liquorice allsort and wondered, not for the first time, if it wasn't a mistake – not the suit but its colour. Two years ago when she had discovered track suits, they had revolutionised her life: never had she worn anything so comfortable and practical. Normally she had stuck to safe grey; it was Tabby who had persuaded her into buying this one, and a yellow one. Well, bullied might be a better word: she had been quite put out when Tabby said she looked like a boring country mouse in her old grey one. She had felt quite jolly when she put on the pink suit this morning but that was in the privacy of the house. Now she was not sure if it were suitable garb for the lady of the manor to be seen in. Then she chided herself for being a coward and purposefully stepped through the large iron gates which stood open. There was no one left alive in the village who could remember ever seeing them closed. Percy Barnes had been the last, remembering when he was a small boy seeing the gates being closed when Hector's great-grandfather had died – but now Percy himself was dead. She doubted if they could be shut now; the hinges were firmly rusted up.

A large lorry roared past, alarmingly close, dust swirling up and enveloping her in a choking cloud as she entered the main street. There never used to be as many lorries thundering through the village, something ought to be done about it before someone was killed, she thought.

The cottage gardens were ablaze with roses and larkspur, delphiniums and daisies. Everyone who lived here was justly proud of the village that, year after year, won Lynshire County's Most Beautiful Village competition. What would happen if some-one moved in who did not take a pride in their cottage and garden, Molly shuddered to think. No doubt deputations of inhabitants would descend on poor Hector, and ostracism of a high order against the offender would take place, if not murder.

Molly strolled slowly. She had not always been able to do this: time was, if she dawdled, then her passage through the village took her hours, as everyone stopped to pass the time of day and to gossip with her. For in those days she had known everyone in the old houses – understandable, since Hector had owned most of them. But now if she knew a quarter of the villagers she would be surprised.

She had lived here for twenty-seven years and had witnessed the change, the inexorable alteration, to the village's life. She crossed the road to the other side where the pavement was wider and passed the row of thatched Upper Cottages – called upper because they were at that part of the village where the road rose sharply, and to differentiate them from Lower Cottages across the Green. Once they had been called by numbers from one to five; now they all had names, Myrtle Cottage, Box Tree, Honey Pot and so on. Each had its name on the gate and again on the wall, some carved in wood, others in ceramic. With their artificial shutters and front doors cut in half like stable doors, they no longer looked like the Lower Cottages, which was not surprising for they did still belong to Hector and had escaped gentrification. She liked that word 'gentrification', which she had read in a magazine when she had visited the dentist in Lynchester. It had just the right ring of disapproval, of falseness. She sometimes felt quite sorry for the cottages not being allowed to be themselves, as if they had had a face-lift forced upon them. She really did prefer Lower Cottages, which still looked like genuine cottages.

She paused in her step, noting with interest a large pantechnicon parked outside Bakery Antiques. She crossed the road and peered into the shop, which was almost completely stripped of its contents.

'Mr Appleby.' She stepped into the shop. 'I'd no idea you were leaving,' she said sadly – time was when she would have known everything.

'Dear Molly. I should have told you, naughty me.' He playfully slapped his own wrist. 'In fact I told no one, not until I knew everything was going through. I'm opening up in Lynchester – bigger premises, Molly love.'

'I'm very sad you're going, Mr Appleby.' He always called her Molly but she could never bring herself to call him Quinton. And yet oddly she'd never minded his familiarity with her name; normally she abhorred the modern practice of instant first names.

Tabby said it just proved how old-fashioned she was; maybe so, but to Molly the use of a Christian name was a serious matter not to be undertaken lightly and one which denoted friendship. Consequently she did not wish the insurance man who had called about a pension plan last week, to presume so easily he was her friend. Nor did she wish her hairdresser to do so, or the army of people who, these days, assumed they were on such terms with her. The use of her Christian name was a gift which it was her pleasure to bestow. But Quinton, as in so many things, was different. She had enjoyed the odd chat with him and his friend Terry.

She moved out of the way as two removal men manhandled Quinton's Welsh dresser out. 'I wonder who'll replace you. I suppose there's no chance of it being a baker?' She laughed as she spoke, realising that the chance of a baker returning to the village was too remote to contemplate.

'I'm afraid not, Molly, but no doubt it'll be someone as charming as me.' He pirouetted, his glance darting from right to left, as he watched the workmen like a hawk, and hitching up his red corduroy trousers, he smoothed his pink shirt down into the belt which with its heavy silver buckle was slung around his hips instead of his waist. With his long blond hair scattered now with grey he looked like a character from a history book – a history book of the sixties, though. It was as if the past two decades had never been, as far as Quinton Appleby was concerned. 'I'll give you a card and then when you finally decide to sell some of your treasures you'll come straight to Quinton, won't you?'

'Of course, but I shouldn't hold your breath – Hector would die rather than sell anything.' This she said with feeling. Without doubt The Hall was a treasure house – Chippendale, Hepplewhite, Wedgwood, Minton, silver from the seventeenth, eighteenth and nineteenth centuries. A painting that might be a Gainsborough, another that some thought was by Millais and one they hoped might be a Turner – experts had been arguing over that particular painting for years. Admittedly, things needed restoring, re-covering, regilding, cleaning, but still The Hall was a microcosm of English heritage – not a piece of French, Flemish, German furniture or porcelain marred its perfection. So crammed was the house, and the value of its contents so high, that for the past twenty years they had been able to pay the insurance premium, only on the building itself. Another reason why the wiring worried her. It would be devastating if the contents went up in smoke; she did not feel the same way about the house, however – it caused too much hard work for her ever really to love it. If only Hector would sell one painting or the odd piece of furniture, their worries would be over. But he never would; he regarded it as a sacred duty to hand over to their son James the contents of the house intact.

'Well, Mr Appleby, I wish you luck in your new shop.'

'Thank you, Molly, I've enjoyed my time here – it's a nice village.'

'Is it?' she said vaguely, for she was no longer sure.

She blinked as the bright sunshine momentarily blinded her when she stepped back into the street and bumped into a woman standing on the pavement.

'I'm collecting signatures,' the woman's very upper-class voice informed her. So upper-class it sounded like metal grating against stone. A voice which brimmed with confidence, the confidence of a person who was used to being obeyed.

'How nice for you,' Molly said nonplussed, peering up at her and wondering who she was. Despite the heat, she wore a green sleeveless padded jerkin over a cashmere jumper and pleated tweed skirt. A scarf was tied severely round her head – in just the same way as the Queen tied hers – and she wore brogues that shone with new ferocity, yet her face was heavily made up, with bright red lips and black-mascaraed eyelashes. A *newcomer* Molly decided. You could always tell: as soon as they arrived they were decked out in tweeds, brogues, Barbours and green wellies. It was one of the reasons that she had branched out into her track suits: she didn't want to be taken for one of *them*. Lulu had gone as far as throwing out her green Hunter wellies and buying bright red ones.

'These lorries. Something's got to be done. Don't you agree?', the woman barked out.

'Yes,' Molly replied obediently, mesmerised by the voice.

'Are you a resident of the village?' The black-lashed eyes glanced down her track suit to her sneakers. And Molly wished she were safely back in her country-mouse grey one instead of this lurid pink.

'Yes,' she said, and wished she could think of something else to say.

'From the estate?' The woman nodded down the street towards the council estate.

'No, from The Hall.'

'Ah, I see.' The woman looked down her long nose at Molly with the look of one who is talking to a servant. Molly began to feel herself bridle. Who was she? Why had she not met her? She was supposed to sign on all newcomers – Mrs Hodgson hadn't told her about this one.

'How long have you been living here?' she asked. 'I can't understand why I haven't met you.'

'I beg your pardon?' The woman huffed at what she obviously felt to be impertinence.

'I normally meet all the newcomers – signing them up for the party. I must have missed you. Very perplexing.'

The woman stood back clutching her clipboard to her broad chest as if it were a shield. 'Did you say you lived at The Hall?' she said rather breathlessly.

'Yes. I'm Molly Parminter.' She smiled brightly, held out her hand, quite enjoying the woman's discomfort – that would teach her to jump to conclusions.

'Mrs Parminter, I'm so sorry. I should have realised . . .' she blustered, no longer the haughty creature of a moment before.

'So what is it you're collecting signatures for?'

'Well, Mrs Parminter, it's the lorries. The noise is unbelievable. Our cottage shakes, literally shakes sometimes. I'm sure it's only a matter of time before someone is killed. We need a bypass.'

'I sympathise Mrs . . . ?' She looked enquiringly.

'Potter-Smythe.' Mrs Potter-Smythe announced her name with just sufficient pause to signify the all-important hyphen. 'We've just moved into Honey Pot Cottage, two weeks ago tomorrow.'

'As I say, I do sympathise with you. But it's not that simple, you see. A bypass would suit us fine but not the shopkeepers, nor Mr Blunt at the local inn. Where would their customers come from?

Even the vicar says that without the tourists the offertory box in the church would be almost empty. Sadly, so few of the villagers even go to church these days and those who do aren't over-generous.' She didn't laugh, she didn't even smile, for she was angry. Who did this woman think she was, less than two weeks in the village and already taking control? It seemed extremely presumptuous to Molly.

'But you will sign?'

'I'm afraid not. My husband is chairman of the local Parish Council as well as our member on the County Council – it wouldn't be proper of me, would it?'

'I understand . . .' Mrs Potter-Smythe said stoically, and looked so disappointed that for a moment Molly felt sorry for her and nearly changed her mind. 'Perhaps you can help me, Mrs Parminter, you would know. Where can I find a scut?'

'I beg your pardon? A what?'

'You know, a scut, a cleaning woman.'

Her initial dislike returned with a vengeance. 'You'll find that extremely difficult, Mrs Potter-Smith . . .'

'Smythe – with a y,' she hurriedly interrupted.

'It's been pleasant meeting you, but I must be going, Mrs Smythe,' Molly said spitefully, and moved quickly on before the woman had a chance to invite her for drinks, as no doubt she planned to.

Once, Molly would automatically have called on any new-comers, left her card, and invited any suitable ones to drinks at The Hall to meet other local people. She did not make such social calls these days – only on party business. And she bided her time before inviting new people into her home. For the newcomers were rarely her own or, more importantly, for he lacked her patience, Hector's sort of people. For the most part, they had not lived in the country before and her idea of country living was not in tune with theirs. She had, in the past, endured the most upsetting attacks from people who knew nothing about the subjects, on hunting, shoot-ing, fishing – all the while handing around canapés of game pâté, ham, smoked salmon and the like. Invariably they had dogs that sat on the sofas and covered one with hair and slobber. With astonishment she had heard one couple complain about the noise they had to endure and which they intended to do something about; the noise, it transpired, was the dawn chorus and the lowing of the cows in Farmer Feather's lower field – the one closest to the village.

Their cottages were awash with frilled and pleated curtains in bright, shiny, floral glazed chintz. Lace curtains, similar to the ones that Molly had thrown out years ago, were draped everywhere. Dried flowers and herbs abounded and brand new Agas gleamed in every tiled kitchen with copper pots and custom-made butchers' blocks, all of which made Molly feel she was between the covers of one of the magazines in the dentist's waiting-room. She remembered the cottages as they once had been, when the old-timers had lived here, when black ranges glowed, geraniums bloomed, where every chair had its antimacassar, where a piece of Staffordshire took pride of place. The cottages had been fusty, warm and welcoming and exactly as cottages should be, in Molly's opinion. Of course, she realised that she preferred conveniently to forget the lack of sanitation, the damp, the outside wells that her husband's former tenants had had to endure. Sad how reality rarely matched the dream.

She could have signed the petition. Hector's position need not have stopped her but this woman was so like many of the new people. They were here only a few days, it seemed, before they were organising committees for this, committees for that, getting themselves on the council. It nurtured resentment within the diminishing real population and she did not blame them. She found she felt quite miffed herself.

As she arrived at the Green, the true centre of the village, a coach squealed to a halt outside the Parminter Arms. Its door hissed, like an enormous fart, she thought, as it opened and the passengers poured out on to the Green. The village was neatly divided in its attitude to the tourists. Half – and Molly had to admit that half tended to be the incomers – resented them bitterly. The other half welcomed them with open arms, seeing work and money in each car and coachload that appeared. And that half was made up of the real indigenous inhabitants. Molly was with the latter group. She felt they were lucky to live here in one of the most perfectly preserved English villages in the country. They had it all to themselves in the winter, so it seemed only fair that they should share it with others for the rest of the year.

She skirted the Green, past the doctor's fine Georgian house, called Pooldown (though no one knew why for it had no pond or pool) and down the lane leading to Lulu's. Lulu was her best friend. Not only had they been débutantes together but they had both met their husbands at the same ball and those husbands had served in the same regiment. Their joy at finding they would be spending the rest of their lives as near neighbours, if they accepted their young men's proposals, propelled both into marriage. Molly could no longer remember a time when Lulu hadn't been part of her life.

Lulu lived at the other end of the village in what had once been a mill but had been converted into a beautiful four-bedroomed house, with a long drawing-room, with large picture windows looking out on the millstream and with a kitchen by Smallbone for which Molly would have given her soul.

Lulu was a widow. And although Molly felt nothing but sympathy for her loss of Wilton – a dear man – she did envy her having left their large mansion over at Hursting, for her son and his new wife to take over, and her move to this excellent, convenient house.

Though they were friends they were very different – life had seen to that. Molly realised that life, despite the lack of money, had protected her, whereas Lulu, rich as she was, had been hurt by it. Lulu's husband had died after too short a time; she had weathered several disastrous love affairs; she now had a daughter-in-law she could not stand. And Lulu suffered from the curse of all beautiful women alone in the world – men pursued her and women feared her.

Lulu was one of those women who could fly around the world and still step off the aeroplane bandbox fresh. Whereas Molly would dress, approve her image in the mirror, knowing full well that within the hour the dress would be crumpled, her nose shiny, her lipstick eaten and her smooth, straight blonde hair would already be in need of a brush.

They differed in experience, too. Molly had only ever loved one man in her life whereas Lulu had lost count of the men in hers. Molly had lost count, too, and frequently had to be reminded who Lulu was talking about by the production of a photograph. Lulu was never discreet – it was not in her nature – and she always wanted everyone to meet the latest love in her life. In normal circumstances she would have been ostracised by the local community. But Lulu was not normal. Lulu had a title, and so disapproval and censure were set aside. An eccentric aristocrat, she was benignly called, never immoral, and so her position in local society never altered a jot.

'Molly, what a pretty colour.' Lulu held the door open wide for her. Lulu had a wonderful way with doors. She never peered round them anxiously as Molly was prone to do but flung them expansively open, always making Molly feel important and very welcome.

'I fear it might be a mistake. Not only do I think I'm too old for it, but I've just been taken for a servant.'

'By whom?' Lulu laughed as she led the way across the parquet-floored hall and into her drawing-room where coffee and cake awaited them.

'A Mrs Potter hyphen Smythe.'

'Oh don't forget the hyphen! Never forget the hyphen!' Lulu shrieked.

'Don't be such a snob, Lulu. She can't help having a hyphen.'

'We are snobs, Molly, both of us.'

'Are we? I didn't think I was.'

'Of course you are. Everyone's snobby about something. Whether it's hyphens, Dralon-covered furniture, plastic, literature, or family trees. I'm sure I'm a snob about all of them, but not garden gnomes, I love garden gnomes. Was it the lorries?'

'Yes. You know about it?'

'I got caught this morning. Did you sign?'

'No. I didn't think she was the right person to be organising the petition. She's only been here a couple of weeks.'

'You can get very tired of lorries in a couple of weeks.'

'Don't be so dreadfully understanding, Lulu. The woman is

presumptuous. That sort of thing should be left to the true inhabitants.'

'What true inhabitants?' Lulu snorted as she cut a slice of cake for Molly. How many people live here, four hundred? Three hundred? I bet half of them are new, and what are you left with? None of them is interested in doing anything. Be honest, Molly, we need people like Mrs P-S. At least they're doing something.'

'Oh you're probably right. I suppose I resented being asked if I lived in the village. It seemed to underline just how everything is changing, and so fast.'

'Poor Mrs P-S. She must be mortified. Now she'll think her chances of being invited to The Hall are doomed for all time.'

'Did you know Quinton's moving?'

'Dreary, isn't it? I liked Quinton – gave us some exotic colour. I expect it will continue as an antique shop.'

'Undoubtedly. You know, as I was walking here I counted up – we've got four antique shops – it's ridiculous.'

'At least it brings shoppers in.'

'True, but how I long for a baker's, a fishmonger's, a decent greengrocer's . . .'

'Have you heard Steve and Betty Trotter are giving up the shop? She says she can't cope any more and wants to move nearer her daughter's in Swindon.'

'Oh, no! Oh, Lulu. How awful – no general shop, that means the Post Office will go. We're going to be left with the hairdresser and the pub at this rate.'

'Certainly no Post Office will be a nuisance, but there's still the one at Sarson Parva.'

'That's all right for us with cars. What about the OAPs and the mums with small children – how are they to get their allowances? It will be a catastrophe for the village. It can't be long before Lambert gives up his hardware shop now that ghastly DIY place has opened in Lynchester. I told Hector, they should never have allowed it planning permission.'

'Probably you'll be seeing a fifth antique shop opening up any day – how do they all make a living?'

'I think they just sell everything to each other.'

'Probably.' Lulu laughed. 'I'm giving a drinks party by the way – next Friday – to welcome the new people from Dower House. Can you and Hector come?'

'There, you see – even new people there. I really thought that the Clements were going to stay, but no, they do it up and sell for a small fortune. Doesn't anyone want to stay in one place any more?'

'Evidently not. Let's be absolute gluttons and have another slice of cake, shall we?'

Chapter 3

Lulu's Party

'LULU, IT'S MOLLY. I hate to be a nuisance but may I bring Tabitha and a friend of hers who has just arrived?'

'But of course. How can bringing dear Tabby be a nuisance?'

'Easily,' Molly laughed. 'The friend most definitely is. He's probably a communist.'

'Why? Has he said?'

'No, but he looks as if he might be. His clothes look belligerent; denim, unwashed and holes.'

'What fun! I should think Hector loves him.'

'He hasn't met him yet but I'm sure I'm in for a thwart weekend. I think Tabby chooses her young men just to annoy us.'

'Probably. That's the whole point of being young surely?'

'I had better warn you, parts of Tabby's hair are orange.'

'How quaint!'

'She pinched my moustache bleach and her hair has come out bright orange.'

'What about your moustache?'

'Dreadfully heavy,' Molly laughed, looking in the mirror over the telephone table and pulling a face at the offending fluff on her upper lip.

'Then avoid any Greeks or they'll fall all over you, they think it's sexy. See you later – moustache and all.' Lulu chortled as she put the phone down.

Hector was grumbling; he always moaned at the thought of any social gathering not organised by himself. Molly took little notice. He would have a wonderful time when he arrived, he always did.

'Damn cocktail parties. I hate them,' he fumbled with his collar.

'I know you do, darling,' Molly said in the sympathetic tone of voice that she also used at sickbeds and funerals. 'But you'll love it when you're there.' The voice changed to one of relentless brightness, which she also used at sickbeds but never at funerals.

'No I shan't,' he sulked. 'Everyone shouting at each other to be heard. Legs aching from all that standing about. It's a bloody uncivilised way to entertain; give me a dinner party any day.'

'You hated the dinner we went to at Annie English's.'

'She always serves foreign muck to eat, that's why.'

'But we have to accept Lulu's invitation, don't we? And sweet of her to give it for the newcomers.'

'It's nothing but bloody newcomers these days. The whole village is being taken over by aliens.'

'Who are these new people?' The question was tinged with anxiety. For who these people were, who were moving into the Dower House, was of more importance to Molly than who lived elsewhere in the village. Not that it had been a Dower house for years – the last incumbent having been Hector's grandmother. When she had died his father had sold it with 20 acres of the parkland, and had planted a screen of trees so that one could no longer see it from the main house. But still, whoever lived there were their closest neighbours.

'I haven't met him.' He reknotted his tie, sighing with exasperation as he always did when he battled with his black tie. 'I know about him though from various planning applications and from complaints about noise. He owns that DIY emporium outside Lynchester.' He patted the tie, finally satisfied with it, and smiled at himself in the mirror.

'DIY? Oh dear. Oh Hector, how awful, you never said. They're unlikely to be p-l-u, are they?' She looked up anxiously. What she meant was that they were undoubtedly 'common' but it was not a word she cared to use, for Molly was not an unkind person, and instead she hid behind that upper-class euphemism – people like us. Molly patted powder on to her nose. 'He won't make it all plastic and gnomes will he?'

'We'll keep an eye on him – it's listed after all. I'll tip the wink to the Historic Buildings coves and the Rural England lot, they'll make sure he doesn't get up to any nonsense.'

23

'It's so sad that the Clements left, they were such suitable people to have as neighbours. I thought they would have stayed for ever. Why they wanted to move to the Dordogne of all places from Lynshire . . . !' She peered into the mirror fearing she had over-done the green eyeshadow.

'Capitalising on his assets, that's why they went. Robbie told me he could buy a property out there and still have 50 per cent of the selling price left to invest. But they'll be back. Some things are more important than money, and living in England is one of them,' he stated confidently, thrusting his cuff out to Molly to thread his cufflinks for him.

Molly checked herself in the cheval-glass, and smoothed down the skirt of her black taffeta cocktail dress. She smiled at her reflection. She had bought this dress in 1960, never dreaming that one day the little black taffeta dress would come back into fashion. Tabby had begged her to give it to her but for once she had refused her daughter.

Tabby's request had taken her by surprise. Normally, anything that Molly wore – apart from the track suits – made Tabby sneer, which was hard to take, or reduced her to hysterical mirth, which was even worse. Molly's confidence in her appearance had begun to melt away with the advance of middle age. Having a daughter whose assurance in her looks was beginning to blossom, as hers was disappearing, had led to many a scene of hurt and puzzlement.

Tabby's interest in this dress was, she hoped, an indication that perhaps life might be returning to a stricter normality. Life had once been so simple: rules abounded, you knew where you were, who you were and most important what to wear. None of this had been the case since the mid-sixties, she supposed. Certainly she had floundered through the seventies and eighties, invariably wrongly dressed. But style, it seemed, was back in fashion.

'You look very pretty, Molly.' Hector never failed to tell her she looked nice, it was one of his more endearing qualities and was one of the reasons he was still easy to love, after twenty-seven years of marriage. Not that he could not be annoying; he could, frequently, but then what man wasn't?

'Why thank you, and how handsome you look too, my darling.'
She smiled up at her tall slim husband whose black hair was now
totally silver and whose face these days was lined to one of great
distinction.

'Who's this friend Tabby's invited for the weekend?'

'He's called Sebastian, she did not say his surname. I barely had
time to meet him before she dragged him off to the folly.' She had
already decided not to say anything about the young man's
appearance. Telling Hector would only send him into a tizzy, and
since he'd be sure to have another one when he met him she was
saving him the trouble of having two.

'Ready?' He offered her his arm and together they went
downstairs.

Molly sensed Hector's shudder rather than saw it. She willed
him to say nothing. Tabby, when reacting to anything she regarded as a criticism of herself or any of her friends, was likely to
fly into a tantrum which invariably led to doors being noisily
slammed and a twenty-four-hour sulk.

Tabby sat on the arm of the sofa in a large black baggy sack of a
dress that ended at mid-thigh. She wore thick ribbed black stock-
ings and the heavy laced shoes which were the ugliest things Molly
had ever seen but which were her daughter's proudest possession –
this month. She had cut the front of her long dark hair: Molly had
quite liked the ensuing fringe, but could not admire the resulting
orange hair that was now plastered with what looked like lard and
that stood up in greasy spikes. What was more, the colour clashed
with the cyclamen of her lipstick and the maroon blusher which
she had slashed across her cheeks. One would have thought an art
student would have a more developed sense of colour, was Molly's
prime thought. From one ear dangled three earrings, from the
other two, and through her nose was a small diamond stud. On her
hands, incongruously, were a pair of fine black lace gloves.

His daughter's appearance was a continual, sad puzzle to
Hector who still fondly remembered her as a pretty little thing
dressed in a frilly frock or neat skirt and jumper. She had been
content to look that way until last year, when she had announced
she was not going to Oxford but wanted to be an artist. Overnight

she had changed into an apparition which would have frightened the horses had they had any left to frighten. If anything, it was probably all Hector's fault for, right at the beginning of her transformation, he had made the catastrophic parental error of objecting to her appearance. This of course had merely fuelled Tabby to greater flights of outrageousness. A punk, Hector mournfully called her. This wasn't strictly true for Molly had seen real ones in Lynchester. Tabby was more 'designer punk', Molly said.

But tonight Molly thought her daughter looked quite respectable – for her. Hector had always nurtured a fond notion that she might study law and would thus save him a fortune in lawyers' bills. Molly, on the other hand, thought it was probably a good idea she hadn't. She couldn't imagine any judge being overimpressed with the orange hair. No, Molly knew it wasn't his daughter's appearance that made Hector shudder, he had adjusted quite well in the circumstances – it was the friend Sebastian.

Sebastian leant indolently against the mantelpiece. He looked as if he hadn't shaved for several days. His black trousers were baggy as if he'd put the wrong ones on by mistake. Under a black jacket which was also at least two sizes too big for him could be seen a fine leather jerkin and a lot of dark, curly chest hair; he wore no shirt or tie. Neither trousers nor jacket had been pressed in years. His black hair was greased close to his scalp, which made both Hector and Molly think of gigolos, and was caught back in a surprisingly neat little pony-tail. In fact compared with how he had looked upon his arrival – jeans more holes than fabric, a T-shirt with DEATH inscribed on it in lurid red and black and spotted with stains rather like an unfinished Pollock painting – in contrast to that, he now looked quite smart.

'Aren't you going to change, young man?' Hector asked as soon as introductions had been made.

'I'm changed, Sir,' he said half-apologetically. Having prepared herself for him to speak in any accent but standard English, Molly looked up with surprise at the pleasant, cultured voice.

'Not to my standard, you're not, young man.'

'I do apologise, Sir. I'd no idea we'd be going out. Tabby said it was to be a quiet, relaxed weekend.'

Hector frowned, he had expected an argument, unpleasantness, not apologies. He paused and rocked on his heels. Tabby and Molly waited – Tabby coiled like a spring to leap to her friend's defence, Molly just anxious.

'It's insulting to your hostess,' he said finally, not prepared, after all, to give in to the apology.

'I quite understand, Sir. It would perhaps be better if I didn't go.'

'If you don't go, Seb, neither do I,' Tabby sulked, and Molly's heart sank, it always did at the prospect of her daughter sulking. If she were honest, Tabby's moods frightened Molly rigid. The fact that one could never be certain when they were going to descend frequently made her feel insecure in her company.

'That's silly, Tabby. Of course you must both come. Lulu could not care less what either of you wear. She'll just think you're very bohemian,' Molly said brightly, hoping to defuse the situation.

'Mother!' Tabby said through her teeth, her upper jaw rigid with irritation. 'Seb wouldn't be anything so naff as a bohemian, would you?'

'Well, I'd prefer not.' He smiled charmingly and Molly found herself smiling back. He really was rather handsome, she thought.

'I'm sorry Sebastian,' she said, wondering why she was apologising. When young she would have loved to be a bohemian – a very sophisticated thing to be but one that she had never had the courage for. 'Ah well, whatever, Lulu won't mind. Come along everyone, we're already late and you know how your father hates that.'

'Punctuality is the politeness of princes . . .' Hector began to intone, as he often did, but had only just started when Tabby and Sebastian chanted it in unison. Hector looked put out and busily filled his cigarette case from the large silver box on the table. While Tabby and Sebastian both broke into uncontrollable giggles, Molly, behind her husband's back, pulled frantic faces at her daughter to stop – which only made her giggle more.

'Stop being silly, Tabby,' she said as sharply as she dared and, with a no-nonsense sweep of her hands, ushered her party out of the room.

Lulu did not flinch a centimetre as she swung her door open to their party. Molly and Hector lurked with embarrassment but Sebastian and Tabby swept past into the hall, brimming with confidence.

'Darling Tabby, I love the hair.' Lulu planted a kiss in the air either side of Tabby's cheeks. 'And this is?'

'Sebastian. Seb, this is Lady Hursting.'

Molly waited, convinced that Sebastian would not approve of a 'lady' and would either be rude or sneer and feel contaminated by meeting her. It was a perfectly reasonable fear, since that was how all Tabby's London friends reacted. Molly was glad Hector didn't have a title. She had seen the reaction of people time and again upon meeting her titled friends. No one, it seemed, could approach a title without reacting. They either tripped over their feet with an embarrassing obsequiousness, or they displayed bolshiness or deep suspicion.

'Lady Hursting, how kind of you to allow me to come,' Sebastian said smoothly, to Molly's continued confusion, as Lulu shepherded them through towards the drinks like a fussy hen.

Armed with their drinks — which at Lulu's were always of a lethal size — they moved into the drawing-room to meet the guests of honour who stood, rather self-consciously, in front of the huge picture window. The millpond with its weeping willows formed a dramatic background, rather as if they were on a stage set, and Molly felt an almost uncontrollable urge to call out 'Anyone for tennis?'

Neither Colin nor Sue Mann, owners of such an enterprise as theirs, were quite what Molly had expected. She supposed she had expected Mrs Mann to be a peroxided blonde encased in crimplene of a livid pattern. Instead, the very pretty, tiny, bird-like woman was dressed in an exquisite silk dress of stunning simplicity. The pearls at her ears and around her neck, with their incandescent glow, pronounced their genuineness. The only sign of vulgarity that Molly could see was the size of the solitaire on her finger — like a film star's, she thought.

Colin Mann was six feet tall and impeccably suited, a shade too impeccably, was Molly's initial impression. He was dark and handsome in a Clark Gable sort of way. Molly invariably compared people she met with film stars from the past – never from the present. She no longer went to the cinema: she found the rustling of sweet papers and the chewing of popcorn too much to bear and since they did not have a video machine she had no idea these days who was or wasn't a film star. She did not mind the lack of a video; if they had one undoubtedly neither she nor Hector would be able to work it. Their son had once given them a radio alarm clock which neither of them had been able to set with any certainty that it would call them when they wanted and so they had returned with relief to their old wind-up clock from Woolworths.

Lulu fluttered about her guests of honour possessively, proud of them as if they were a personal acquisition.

Hector harrumphed behind Molly. It was the noise he always made when confronted by a pretty woman. Once it had annoyed her – of course she'd been younger then – but over the years she had become accustomed to it. He did it anywhere – on the street, in a restaurant, on a train. Silly middle-aged goat, she thought.

Colin was smooth, too smooth – Molly was fully aware of this but still he charmed her immediately. Tabby, having decided he was an 'old' man of at least thirty-six, was prepared to turn away. Instead she found herself melting at the smile he switched on her, making her suddenly feel the most beautiful, interesting, adult woman in the room.

Hector was reassured by Colin's firm handshake but most of all by the Old Harrovian tie and, in any case, was far more interested in talking to Sue, who had the female version of her husband's smile. Hector was being reduced to putty by charm. Had Molly not been so involved with Colin she would have wanted to kick Hector for making such a fool of himself.

The group around the Manns was growing. They were joined by the vicar and the doctor, as well as the retired General, Squadron Leader and Rear-Admiral who made up Sarson Magna's armed forces, as everyone joked. Finally the vet and two local farmers, all with their spouses, were standing in the group about the Manns.

With subtlety and skill, honed by years of ascertaining if people were 'one of us' and not that dreaded breed of social climber who did not know how to behave and who must be repelled at all costs, the Manns were plied with significant questions of the most harmless-sounding kind. But by finding out their interests, the names they had given their children, even the breed of their dogs; by listening with sharp ears to the sound of their vowels, they could in seconds place them. The company relaxed; the Manns enjoyed tennis, bridge, hunting, they had interests – not hobbies, that most feared word. Their children were Charlotte, William and Rupert – no worries there. And their dogs were a Jack Russell and a retriever – excellent. The Rolls-Royce was a bit of a worry, but at least it wasn't a Jaguar or a Porsche. There was concern over a certain rigidness in their speech. But wasn't it rumoured that even dear Mrs Thatcher had had elocution lessons? At least it showed a desire to fit in, and times were changing. Everyone had been worried by Colin's profession, but these people prided themselves on their adaptability – a total myth – and trade, they supposed, could be accepted these days – but only if very successful.

Provided the Manns were willing to live by the rules, which they appeared to be doing, a certain degree of social climbing could be forgiven them. Provided, that is, that they never expected to be totally accepted – that could never be. But with their wealth and given the right education it was conceivable, these days, that their children might marry well and by the time their grandchildren arrived on the social scene undoubtedly the initial stigma of their origins would have been conveniently forgotten.

And then the company, collectively, began to hang on Colin Mann's every word. For, if not from the right drawer, Colin had that intangible magic of a rich man. That aura that head waiters and railway porters could recognise at a hundred yards. He did not so much smell of money, he reeked of it. Closer they all crowded round: was it in the hope that some of his expertise might rub off on them? Or his luck? Or whatever it was that made him a millionaire while they all seemed to struggle, no matter how hard they worked or how index-linked their pensions were.

By now there were a good twenty-five people in the room but with all the will in the world one could hardly say the assembled company was a cross-section of the village. Lulu's choice had been highly selective: the Manns were meeting the cream of Sarson Magna's society.

Williamson and Jenkins, though calling themselves farmers, had never seen the inside of their milking sheds at dawn. Nor did they harvest. Nor did they clean out sties. Daily they rode their land – on good days on horses, on bad days in their Range-Rovers. Both men had had the wisdom to make their fortune – one from banking, one from law – before embarking on farming life. Both had farm managers who saw to the routine of the farms, but neither of those had been invited by Lulu.

There were two vets in the village practice. Timothy Tenterden, born at Lynchester, Marlborough educated, was here with his Roedean wife. Peter Brown, his junior partner, from Lancashire and his local grammar school, had not been invited.

Had anyone asked them, both Lulu and Molly would have regarded themselves as liberal, tolerant and modern-thinking women. They were – within limits. Those limits were the restrictions imposed on them by the society they moved in. And since neither of them wanted, or had ever attempted, to move in any other sphere so they remained, confident in the attributes they bestowed upon themselves, but which were rarely put to the test.

So engrossed had Molly been in the assessment of the Manns that she had quite forgotten Sebastian, who having shaken Colin's hand had turned his back, quite rudely Molly had thought, and moved away from the circle. She looked around the room for him, concerned. Since she did not know him, she had no idea what opinions he might be expounding, or who he could be offending. And since he was her guest it was up to her to see that no one's sensibilities were hurt. She saw him moving about the room, glass in hand, in a way which, uncomfortably, reminded her of a prowling animal. General Naughton approached him which was a worry, for on closer inspection – she couldn't swear to it – but she had a suspicion that Sebastian was wearing mascara. The General's views on sexual deviants were well known about the village. Molly herself was not happy about the idea of men who were not men, but on the other hand she did think talk of castration or exile to the Outer Hebrides rather extreme. So, excusing

31

herself from the Manns, Molly endeavoured to join them.

She had expected Porky Naughton to eye Sebastian suspiciously and his high colour to deepen dangerously. She did not expect him to shake Sebastian's hand enthusiastically and within a minute to be joining him in laughter. She saw the Squadron Leader approaching with the Rear-Admiral on his heels but her path was blocked by the vicar's wife, her face screwed up with peptic anxiety about the forthcoming church fête. It was five minutes before she was able to sidle into earshot.

'Do you also have to appear to be a member of the alternative society?' Bat Rogers asked, his handlebar moustache lifting and falling in rhythm with his words. Surprisingly this question had been asked in the pleasantest of tones, when everyone knew the fearful fuss the Squadron Leader had made when a party of 'bus people' had camped outside the village. All three military men had petitioned and ranted and roared and had begun to sound like the Gestapo they had spent such critical years of their lives endeavouring to destroy.

'Not likely, too uncomfortable, Sir. No it's all to do with image you see. The right image is essential.'

'Quite,' Porky said knowingly, fingering his tie.

'Mrs Parminter.' Molly swung round to find the hyphened lady of the petition anxiously looming over her. Reluctantly Molly had to turn her back on the men and smiled as coolly as she could manage. 'I can't apologise enough for not recognising you the other day but Lady Hursting said you just laughed at my mistake.'

'It was unimportant, Mrs Potter-Smythe, why should you have known who I was?' But with a start she realised who Mrs Potter-Smythe reminded her of – Joan Crawford to a T, no wonder she had, at first, felt intimidated by her.

'I hope you didn't think it was presumptuous of me. I mean only just having moved in and then organising everyone. So silly of me,' she chortled in a deep laugh.

'Good gracious no,' Molly lied. 'The village needs such enthusiasm,' she compounded the lie. 'Do you like organising?' she said innocently.

'Well it's more of a habit. I've been an organiser all my life so it's difficult to give up. Reginald, my husband, says it's my greatest strength and weakness. My husband was Headmaster of Trundalls – so you see . . . .' She waved her hand expansively and in that wave indicated all the work and all the bossiness required in being the wife of a headmaster of a minor public school – so minor Molly wasn't even sure she had ever heard of it.

Quickly Molly pounced. 'I wonder if you could help me then. I'm finding it harder these days to keep up the subscription list of the party.' She arched her brow questioningly.

'I should be thrilled to help out. Thrilled to bits,' she said excitedly.

'Wonderful. Then maybe you could come to tea next week and I can explain everything to you?'

That arranged, a glow of satisfaction settled on Molly and much to Mrs Potter-Smythe's regret she introduced her to the vicar's wife, made her excuses as quickly as possible and sidled back into the party and in the direction of Jolly, their Squadron Leader's wife.

Of all the armed services' wives, Jolly was Molly's favourite. She lacked the relentless snobbery of Hyacinth that was so fine-tuned it risked being twee. Nor was she, like Twink, always alert for implied insults, for Twink took seriously her position of wife of a member of the *senior service* and was always alert to any deni-gration of that status. Jolly was far more relaxed, presumably from being married to a member of the *junior service* and thus unencumbered by centuries of pretension.

Latterly, Jolly was far from jolly, and had become a permanent bundle of nerves. Quite recently Bat had reached that age when some men become obsessed with young girls. He seemed blissfully unaware that his conversation, spiced with constant references to 'pretty girls' and endless innuendo, was bordering on the salacious. Molly knew that Jolly's constant nightmare was that one day he might be arrested lurking in the bushes outside Lynchester Girls' School. Hector, with his usual heavy-handedness, had jokingly offered to find him a dirty raincoat. Poor Jolly quite understand-ably had failed to see the joke and had burst into tears. Bat was rapidly becoming a liability to the community and it was only because of his position that nothing had been done so far. Jolly had confided to Molly that in truth the pretty girls were perfectly safe since Bat could only talk about such matters these days and was quite incapable of *doing* anything. He really ought to have his glands seen to, was Molly's advice.

Having heard Bat going on, Molly could only thank God once again that she was female. Men and their preoccupation with sex had often mystified her. When she had been young they would travel miles across the country at the rumour that there was a girl who would *do it*. Once safely married they were frequently to be found peering and snooping into other fields, imagining sexual delights they were missing. They risked marriage, children, money for a romp in an illicit bed – extraordinary. With luck, after forty or so their hormones settled down for a short time and there was a degree of contentment but then there were those who in later middle age, like Bat, became once again obsessed with the silly subject. Truly it was far more comfortable and dignified to be a female, Molly had long ago concluded.

The party continued, to the formula of all such parties in English villages. There were no voices of dissension for there was nothing to disagree about. To a man and woman they voted Tory, were C of E, were unanimous in their total disregard for racial harmony; all had trouble with their drains – that eternal topic of conversation of all country gatherings, and the one which raised the most excitement. They were so totally attuned to one another, they were like mental clones. Their voices rose with time, excitement and alcohol to the loud baying normal at such functions. They were content in the knowledge that in each other's company they could safely speak their minds. Despite her new awareness, Molly, with the social hypocrisy of her class, nodded and agreed with everyone. She knew her companions well and knew that to say anything of her recently formed views would only lead them to the conclusion that she must be unwell.

'The government should insist people take the jobs on offer, that would solve the problem. Can I get a second gardener? No, I can't . . .'

'All this fuss about the homeless. In my opinion, most of them choose to be . . .'

34

'Wasn't dear old Enoch right . . .'

'Bring back the birch . . .'

'Who is this Rushdie fellow? I ask you, calling himself British . . .'

'He went to Rugby . . .'

'Good God, he didn't, did he . . . ?'

'It's a media plot . . .'

'Poofters and Commies, that's the BBC these days . . .'

'Pinkoes . . .'

'Leave it to Maggie . . .'

'Good old Maggie . . .'

The doctor did limply attempt to bewail the state of the National Health Service, but after a fearsome look from his wife was soon forgotten as they compared notes on the new BUPA hospital in Lynchester.

The economy was discussed but more in relation to the FT index. A forty per cent top rate of tax suited them fine. No one had a mortgage and so increased interest rates hardly worried them. They gloated about their dividends and advised each other which shares, which unit trusts to move into for a higher yield. But the wave of higher wage demands by the workers was put down to greed.

They were unanimous in preferring Mr Major as Chancellor of the Exchequer, not on matters of policy but on the grounds that a lean Chancellor, imposing restrictions on the nation, was more acceptable to the electorate than a fat one.

As one, Molly's neighbours considered the Poll Tax a good thing. Their houses were large and, unlike Molly and Hector, they did not have a Cuckoo and a Hope to account for.

Greenness was a subject that interested them not one jot, apart from considering it as interference from townies ignorant in the ways of the countryside. Their reaction to the recent spate of health scares in relation to food had led them only to eat more of each suspect food. A new kind of machismo, thought Molly, who recently had found herself looking at Farmer Feather's cattle with a wary eye.

One faint heart did draw attention to the findings of the latest opinion polls. They were rubbish, unscientific, mid-term wobbles, she was assured. There was plenty of time to get things sorted out. Maggie would do it, good old Maggie would see them right. Mrs Thatcher would have glowed with pride at the exaltation of the faithful and Mr Kinnock would have hanged himself in despair.

All was well with England, the party guests unanimously agreed, even if they were somewhat worried about the Channel Tunnel and a united Germany.

By ten, Molly noticed a distinct drooping of Hector's eyelids which would quickly lead to his falling asleep. After a certain amount of alcohol Hector could sleep anywhere, and had done – at a Lord Mayor's banquet, on a horse, in a hot air balloon. This particular habit was her constant worry and greatest source of embarrassment. Expertly she shepherded her small party together to make their farewells.

The Parminters walked home under the clear, star-studded sky. Hector weaved somewhat and Molly gave him a steadying hand. Tabby and Sebby loped off ahead. Early in the evening Molly had decided that Sebastian must come from a good family. Not once had she heard his voice raised in argument with his elders. A good sign that. Several of their friends had children who pursued a different lifestyle to their parents, but, when out in society, as this evening, the training of years rose to the surface. They were respectful, charming and polite, just like these two had been.

No doubt Sebastian was having a last fling before settling down in a nice merchant bank somewhere.

At the house Molly quickly peed and watered the dog, then put the cat out, checked the fuel in the Aga, the locks, the lights. She showed Sebastian his room – pointedly single and as far away from Tabby as possible. She could live in hopes that nothing untoward would happen, even if it was a doubtful hope. On the other hand she could have been right about the mascara and have nothing to worry about, or was mascara the latest rage? – oh it was difficult keeping up with the young.

She found Hector asleep in his study. Sprawled in the chair, his mouth open, snoring. She switched off the light and shut the door quietly. She smiled to herself; he'd wake up eventually and think he'd gone blind – that would teach him.

Chapter 4

Sebastian to the Rescue

CUCKOO PARMINTER WAS being difficult. This was nothing new of course, but sacking Hope Trenchard for the third time this month was going too far.

Molly climbed the stairs towards Cuckoo's flat. She had no idea why her mother-in-law was called Cuckoo when her real name was Joan. She often wondered if it was a secret reference to the woman's past. Had she had a penchant for flitting from lover to lover, often in some other woman's nest? It was possible. Cuckoo often hinted obliquely at a racy past. But Molly had never had a sufficiently cosy relationship with her mother-in-law to pry further. It was only in the past ten years that Cuckoo had even allowed her to call her anything but Mrs Parminter.

Molly's head was throbbing. Each time she went to Lulu's she vowed to have only two of her friend's legendary 'depth charges', but she always succumbed, and this head was her legacy. Hector was in an even worse state, and she was praying that he hadn't discovered what she had feared – that Tabby and Sebastian had spent the night together. Given his mood this morning, sparks would fly if he found out. As it was, he had driven Molly mad in bed that morning with his endless complaining about Sebastian. It was no good Molly pointing out how well he'd behaved or voicing her theory that he must come from a good family. Hector saw none of this. To him Sebastian was a threat, a drug addict, no doubt a criminal, a corrupter of daughters. 'Tell him to leave,' he had instructed Molly. 'Tell him yourself,' she'd retorted, sliding out of bed and padding along to the bathroom in a bid to get away from Hector's hectoring.

Soaking in her bath she had realised how differently she and

Hector regarded their daughter's sexuality. Obviously Hector dreamed of Tabby as a virginal bride being led by him to the altar. 'Hypocritical old twerp,' Molly muttered as she searched for the soap. Certainly she had been a virgin when they had married – but only just. The only reason she was had been their fear of an unwanted pregnancy. Had the pill been invented she and Hector would undoubtedly have leapt into the first available bed. As it was, the heavy petting they had indulged in, in motor cars parked in isolated fields, windows totally steamed up with condensation, was as near to the real thing as they could go. She would not wish the cricked necks, the battles with gear levers that she had suffered, on Tabby. Provided the girl was not promiscuous and did not become pregnant she was happy for her to be happy with Sebastian. And yet Hector ranted and roared about the selfsame thing. Where men, sex, women, wives and daughters were involved, a lot of hypocrisy was involved, she thought as she towelled herself dry.

She knocked at Cuckoo's door and entered. These rooms always reminded her of a cross between an Edwardian drawing-room and a bordello. Reduced to a sitting-room, dining-room and bedroom after a lifetime of thirty or so rooms to call her own, Cuckoo had conspired to crowd in as many of her possessions as would physically fit, hence the clutter of a bygone age. The bordello aspect came because of Cuckoo's penchant for the colour pink and frills. Frilled curtains, pelmets, cushions and round tableskirts were all pink, and all twisted, twirled and ruched. She had also, over the years, amassed a hideous collection of dolls from other countries so that kilted Scots dolls leered at flamenco dancers who simpered at Welsh witches who looked malevolently at German lederhosen-clad dolls. Molly felt sorry for Hope, who had to dust the rooms; Mrs Hodgson had long ago announced, 'I ain't going up there to get the verbals from her, no way!'

'This woman has to go, Molly, see to it,' Cuckoo said imperiously from the mound of pink silk pillows. A bedraggled heap sniffed from the large wing chair. 'Oh shut up, Trenchard, do!'

'Cuckoo what's happened? Oh, poor Hope, don't worry.' Molly fished in her pocket and drew out a clean handkerchief which she handed to the weeping companion.

'I broke a doll,' Hope blew noisily into the handkerchief. 'My favourite what's more – my Carmen Miranda doll.'

'I'm sure it was an accident, Cuckoo.'

'Of course it wasn't. She did it out of spite,' the old lady hissed. Cuckoo had been a great beauty in her time but was sadly refusing to acknowledge the fact that her beauty had faded. Her face was heavily made up. The eyebrows plucked ruthlessly, long ago in the twenties, never to grow again, were sharply pencilled in. The rouge glowed redly on her pale skin and the pink of her lipstick had settled into the myriad cracks about her lips so that it looked as if it had been applied vertically. On her head was a fair, curled wig – too blonde and too curly for one of her age. 'She knew I loved that doll best of all. Hector's father gave it to me,' and she too burst into tears. With no more handkerchiefs in her pocket Molly crossed to the dressing table, took one from the pink hankie sachet and handed it to her. Cuckoo was lying; this penchant for these hideous dolls had not beset her until years after her husband had died but if she wanted sympathy she always mentioned him, tearfully, though Hector had confided in Molly that his parents had fought like demented creatures. Cuckoo cried into the fine linen. 'And I want my lawyer. I'm changing my will,' at which announcement Hope Trenchard blubbered anew.

Cuckoo's will was a constant thorn in Hector's side. His mother changed it monthly. Given the chance, she would have changed it weekly. The point was that she had little of any value to leave. Apart from the odd piece of furniture, a couple of pleasant Victorian watercolours and her silver-backed hairbrushes, there was nothing. Everything in the house had been left to Hector. Her jewellery was paste. What family jewellery she had had passed to Molly. Not that it had done Molly any good for Hector did not have the same passion for preserving the family jewellery that he had for the house and its contents. So Molly had only enjoyed it for a few short years before, piece by piece, it had all been sold. Now all hers was paste too except for her pearls and her Georgian diamond brooch which her own mother had left her and was not Hector's to sell. No one had the heart to tell Cuckoo that the furniture, stocks and shares, the cottages, and everything else she constantly juggled in her will were hers no more. But each month Hector received a bill from the family lawyer for, if they were lucky, a codicil or, if they were unlucky, a complete new will.

'There, there, Cuckoo. Don't upset yourself. Where's the doll? Maybe it can be mended?'

Hope proffered the broken doll. 'Oh really Cuckoo, what a fuss, It's only some of the fruit knocked off. That can be easily mended.'

'Do you think so?' Cuckoo brightened up considerably. 'She still goes though, I hate her.'

'No you don't, that's silly talk. Hope isn't going anywhere. What would I do without her? I've enough to do without having to run up and down the stairs to you every time you want something. There's no question of her leaving.' Molly surprised herself with how strong she was being. Normally she would be pleading with Cuckoo, not telling her – maybe it was because of the hangover or perhaps she had finally had enough of her increasingly irascible mother-in-law. Irascible was Hector's word; she personally thought the old woman was batty.

'Oh, Mrs Parminter, thank you,' Hope gushed, brightening up too.

'I suggest you both have a nice sherry and make it up.' Molly crossed the room and went into Cuckoo's drawing-room, equally pink and equally cluttered, and poured two glasses of sherry, shuddering at the smell of alcohol. It was a miracle to her that Hope stayed. There had been a succession of companions too numerous to remember before Hope had arrived five years ago. For the first year Molly had lived in terror of Hope handing in her notice – but she hadn't. Despite the rows, despite being shouted at, despite being handed her notice at depressingly regular intervals, the woman continued in their lives. Hector's theory was that Hope was a mental masochist and lived for his mother's abuse. Molly's was that both women were bored to tears and used their fights to prove to each other that they were still alive.

'There, sherries for you both. Give me the doll and I'll take it to that nice Quinton Appleby to have mended.' In exchange for the sherry, to which she was more than partial, Hope relinquished the doll. 'In any case the fête's next weekend, now how on earth could

I manage without both of you to run the raffle stall?' She smiled
brightly at them through the thudding of her head and, before
Cuckoo could argue with her, slipped from the room and back
down the stairs to her own kitchen where Mrs Hodgson, with
her own particular idea of cleaning, was 'having a go' at the
cupboards.

'Trouble?' she smiled at her employer.

'Mrs Trenchard broke a doll.'

'Good God, and she's still alive?' Mrs Hodgson laughed. 'Did
you know, Mrs Parminter, that you've got twenty-five tins of
sardines and fourteen of tomatoes?'

'Have I?' Molly asked vaguely.

'You could put some of them on the food stall at the fête.'

'What a good idea. Yes, I will.'

'You don't seem yourself, Mrs Parminter. At Lady H.'s last
night, weren't you?' Molly did not reply. 'Ah, I see,' Mrs Hodgson
said sagely. 'I expect the whole village is feeling under the weather,
truth be told.'

There was no point in denying this. Not only was Lulu's
reputation as a hostess well known but somehow Mrs Hodgson
would have known Molly had been a guest even if she had gone in
an all-enveloping cloak, a Venetian mask, and had approached
Lulu's from the fields at dead of night.

'Coffee?' she asked in a solicitous voice and slid the large kettle
on to the Aga. The sympathy might have been genuine, but it was
far more likely that Mrs Hodgson had decided it was time for
coffee.

Molly allowed herself to be waited upon and decided she might
just risk a dry digestive biscuit or two.

'Tired out I am, Mrs Parminter. One of them nights,' she nodded
her head in a conspiratorial way.

'Oh really?' Molly looked up, sat up, and leant forward with
interest.

Mrs Hodgson's nights were a continual mystery that both Molly
and Lulu were determined to solve before they died. But still, after
ten years with the woman, they were no closer to knowing the
truth of what went on – for Mrs Hodgson 'did' for Lulu too.

What little they knew about these nights of Mrs Hodgson's, it had been a slow, laborious process to garner. At first both had presumed that it was an indication of Mr Hodgson's libido. But the mystery was darker than that. It was only when Mrs Hodgson, a few years ago, had announced she'd had enough, that she was going to get a divorce, that the extent of the magnitude of the problem emerged. Mr Hodgson was a sexual pervert – that they knew for she had told them so. What the perversion was remained the secret, and neither woman, despite many patient hours of listening, had been able to solve it.

They presumed the doctor must know. But, of course, he would never tell them, never break a professional confidence. All Mrs Hodgson had said upon her return was that Dr Linklater had never heard of such a thing in all his medical years. This was stated with a marked degree of pride only to be surpassed when she returned from the lawyer to say 'he'd never heard of it neither.'

To their shame both Lulu and Molly rather hoped the divorce would go through. Even if they didn't attend the court hearing, surely they would be able to read about it in the *News of the World*, which Hector took every Sunday without fail and which he pretended he never read.

But for some reason, never explained, Mrs Hodgson had decided not to go through with the divorce and still lived with Mr Hodgson. Both Lulu and Molly found themselves looking at the man with very nervous eyes – a neat unprepossessing man of barely five feet eight who worked on the railway, as bald as a coot but with a large and lugubrious moustache.

Lulu was sure the moustache was the key to it all – but what could be done with a moustache was outside their experience, and imagination failed them. Lulu had one day begged Mrs Hodgson to tell her what the mystery was.

'If you could just give me a hint.'

'Oh, Lady Hursting, you'll make me blush. I'll tell you this. I'm not safe nowhere . . .'

'You mean?'

'Yes he's doing it everywhere – anywhere there's a plug – the garden shed, the hall. If there was a plug on the roof he'd be doing it there.'

'Good gracious!' exclaimed Lulu, her head reeling at the possibilities.

But Mrs Hodgson was saying no more.

'One of them nights?' Molly asked, with what she hoped was a sufficiently sympathetic voice.

'I guess he won't stop till he's in his coffin and that's a fact.' She noisily sipped her coffee and dipped her biscuit in the cup. Her unreliability, her legs, were a great nuisance to Molly but how could she ever sack her? – then she would never know.

'Any chance of breakfast?' Tabby clattered noisily into the room in her large shoes.

'Good morning Mrs Parminter,' Sebastian smiled, following close behind.

At that point a strange gurgling sound issued from Mrs Hodgson. She swallowed and began to choke, she stood up, her chair clattering on the tiled floor. She clutched at her throat.

'Oh my gawd,' she shrieked pointing a finger at Sebastian. 'Oh my Gawd. Whatever next! It's him!' And she fainted dead away.

Hector was on the telephone in the study, his face creased with a worried frown. General Naughton was on the line. A brother General, whose recently published memoirs had, surprisingly, gone straight into the bestseller list – not because of their military content but more from his indiscretions about the sex lives of various world leaders – had written apologising profusely, but since he'd fallen out of an apple tree and broken his leg in two places there was no way he would be able to open Sarson Magna church fête next week, as promised.

'What was the bloody fool doing up an apple tree in the first place?' Hector barked.

'Picking apples, I presume.'

'You don't pick apples in June,' Hector snapped.

'True. I don't know then. Inspecting them probably.'

'Now what the hell do we do? We'll get no one of any importance now.'

'But, old boy, he's done us a favour. Ask that young man and we'll get them here in thousands. He's a very nice fellow. I'm sure he'll oblige.'

'What young man?'

'Tabby's friend – that Sebastian chappie.'

'Sebastian? Opening a fête? You gone barking mad, Porky?'

'Good God Hector, you don't know, do you?'

'Know what?'

'He's famous. He's a pop star,' Porky said, his voice full of awe.

'A what?'

'A pop star. Sebastian and the Drones – that's what they call themselves, seems they're partial to Wodehouse. He was explaining it all to us last night – about his image. The image is all-important. Fascinating life they lead.'

'Good Lor'.'

'Two number ones in the charts this year alone. And he's big in America.'

'Good Lor'.'

'Oh yes, he's got a new, now what did he call it? A new LP out next month.' The General imparted all this new information with self-importance brimming in his voice.

'Have you ever heard of him?'

'No, but Hyacinth says she saw him on *Top of the Pops*.'

'What's that when it's at home?'

'It's an important television show.'

'Oh I see. Never watch it myself, only the news. Molly watches more than me but she's not recognised him, or she would have said. Right, leave it with me old boy.'

'You haven't heard the best bit. He's Viscount Featherhead's son and heir.'

'Good God!' Hector's eyes were glazed as he replaced the receiver and rushed off to find Molly.

He found her in the kitchen where she was busily fanning Mrs Hodgson, who was propped up in the Windsor chair and looking very pale.

'I just loved "Wolfman in the Day",' his astonished ears heard Molly saying to Sebastian. 'Better than anything the Stones ever did. Mind you I've never seen you perform, I've only heard you on the radio, you're wonderful.'

'Why thank you Mrs Parminter.'

'Molly . . .' Hector started.

'Hector it's all so exciting, Sebastian is dreadfully famous.'

'So I hear. Hyacinth says you were on *Top of the Pops*, Sebastian.'

'Yes Sir.' Sebastian looked embarrassed and modest at the same time.

'We shall have to watch it now, Hector, won't we? – instead of the News on Four which you always insist on.' Molly, he noticed, was quite pink with excitement.

Hector did not know quite what to say, so instead shook Sebastian's hand. It did not seem to matter what he wore any more.

Chapter 5

The Morning of the Fête

EVERY YEAR IT was the same – chaos, endless rows and rain. It did not matter that this was the hottest summer for years: when Sarson Magna held its fête, it rained.

Molly stood despondently in the middle of the large lawn at the back of the house where the annual fête was always held. Her wellingtons were sinking into the grass which was becoming alarmingly soft, the rain dripped relentlessly off her brolly and plopped on to the large plan she was studying with a worried frown. She flicked the water from the sheet of paper and glanced up at the lowering clouds, massively pregnant with more rain, and loathed everything. She loathed the fête, the arguing villagers, the weather and Hector who was behaving like Attila the Hun as he strutted around bossing everyone unmercifully. On these occasions, as on most, Hector never actually *did* anything; he saw himself more in a supervisory capacity – unfortunately his efforts generally caused more chaos rather than less and without doubt created a great cloud of resentment, of which he seemed blissfully ignorant.

For the umpteenth time this morning Molly was studying the stall plan. It was always the same and had been for as long as anyone could remember – the white elephant stall was situated at the bottom of the steps that led to the upper terrace, on the left of it was sited the cake stall, and on the right jams. But this year Flint, for some peculiar reason known only to himself, had put the coconut stall there instead and the white elephant to one side of it.

Reg Whistler was standing his ground. The white elephant stall had always monopolised the best position, unfairly, in the opinion of many. But this time his coconuts had been given it and it was a site he was not going to relinquish, no matter how much fuss Mrs Naughton made. Reg hated the likes of Hyacinth Naughton. Five years in the village and they behaved as though they owned it and everyone in it. 'Bossing here, bossing there . . .' he muttered to no one in particular. The way she had spoken to him one would have thought she was the General and not her husband. 'Who the hell does she think she is?' he moaned to his neighbour, Fred Hodgson, who was in charge of the hoop-la stall. (Molly and Lulu had years ago contemplated the hoop-la as a possible explanation of Fred's 'peculiarities', but had rejected them for the simple reason that they could not think what he could do with a hoop-la.) 'Stuck-up cow,' he said to his mud-grimed boots. Resentment hung thick in the air as the group about Molly grew larger.

Molly summoned Flint who, before anyone could say anything, held up his hand as if in benediction.

'Now, before any of you start it's got nothing to do with me. Mr Parminter, 'twas him said as to put the coconuts there.'

'Then where is my white elephant stall to go, tell me that, my man?' Hyacinth spoke shrilly, stabbing at the air with her umbrella. 'And stand still when I'm speaking to you,' she added, stamping her feet with rage, as Flint turned away.

Oh, dear, thought Molly. That was a mistake. No one called Flint 'my man', not even Hector. Flint was the sort who, at the least hint of disrespect to his person, real or imagined, was quite capable of downing tools. Then where would they be?

'Hyacinth . . .' Molly stepped forward waving her hands in a placatory way.

'Don't you "my man" me. I ain't your man and I pity the poor bugger what is,' Flint stared belligerently at Hyacinth, straightening his stooped shoulders and standing upright to his full five feet five.

'Well, really! How dare you speak to me in that way!' Hyacinth's face mottled with anger.

'I speaks as I find. You're rude to me I'll be rude back, fair's fair.' There was a groundswell of voluble approval at Flint's stand. Reg clapped him encouragingly on the back. 'Tell the truth, I don't give a monkeys where your stupid white elephant stall goes, so there!' he shouted, emboldened now by his friends' tacit support.

'See, I told you, Squire himself said to put my coconuts there,' Reg added his halfpennyworth.

'You keep your nose out of this,' Hyacinth snapped.

'Don't you speak to my Reg like that or you'll have me to answer to.' Maggie, Reg's fifteen-stone spouse, elbowed her way to the front of the crowd.

'Please, please everyone, let's calm down, it's only a stall . . .' Molly pleaded.

'ONLY!' The whole group swung round, momentarily united, and eyed Molly with amazement at such an outrageous statement.

She couldn't summon Hector, not today of all days, when he was having his annual change of personality. Instead she went in search of him, followed by Hyacinth Naughton and her three helpers, all red-faced with indignation as if suffering from a communal hot flush, a muttering Flint, the Whistlers, Fred Hodgson and half a dozen others who'd joined in, out of curiosity, to see what had happened – after all, the placing of the stalls was an important matter.

'Hector, darling,' she cooed, smiling sweetly. 'We've a problem. Hyacinth's stall's been moved.'

'I know. Essential. Can't be helped, Hyacinth. Sorry.' Hector spoke with all the clipped urgency of a Field Marshal about to launch a major offensive.

'But Hector. The white elephant is always there. We can't have the wretched coconut shy anywhere near – the balls could fly at a tangent and damage things.' Hyacinth's eyes, as blue as her name implied, widened and the spiky eyelashes fluttered at Hector.

'Crowd control,' he barked.

'Crowd control?' They echoed in unison. Crowd control was not a customary problem at the annual fête. One virtually had to bribe people to come, not control them.

'Darling, this is hardly the Royal Lynshire County Show. I mean . . .'

'Sebastian. With Sebastian here everything's changed. He's got to be protected from the crowds, you see. Top of the terrace is the only safe place for him to stand. The white elephant's tent would prevent the crowds getting a good view of him. But the coconut shy's back board can be lowered, and the ropes can still keep them back.'

'But we've such lovely stuff this year – Sue Mann alone gave three very valuable and pretty figurines – what if they were smashed? Tell me that, Hector. And the cakes and jam would be at risk too. Who will be willing to accept responsibility?'

'I take your point, Hyacinth. Let's see the plan, Molly. Let's solve this problem.' Hector studied the now sodden plan with deep concentration. Apparently he had given up his Field Marshal's baton for the time being and was now behaving like a captain of industry studying a factory layout plan.

'Move them over the other side of the lawn, Flint, move cakes and jams too. Put the coconuts, the hoop-la and the apple dunking at the bottom of the steps . . .'

'Hector, you can't!' Hyacinth was wringing her hands in anguish. 'We've always been there.'

'No longer. Sorry. Now, I've things to see to . . .' and in mid-sentence he strutted away, obviously imagining himself a Field Marshal again.

The rejuggling of the stalls upset everyone except Reg and Fred, who went to find Bert Shad and his apple dunking. Of Hector there was not a sign as Molly valiantly tried to calm various indignations.

'Mrs Parminter, come quick, the donkey's died!' Chip Whistler ran towards her and skidded to a squelching halt. The Whistlers seemed to be everywhere.

'What do you mean, Chip?'

'It just keeled over, Mrs Parminter. It was standing there munching and then, wham, it was on the ground and wouldn't get up.'

With Chip she ran to the donkey ride. Candy the donkey lay on his side. He was surrounded by a weeping crowd of little girls and women. At sight of the donkey Molly felt a lump form in her throat and tears begin to well. At least he died happy, she thought, at the sight of grass sticking out of the dead donkey's mouth. She purposefully sniffed her tears away – time for that later.

Candy, now forty-seven, had always done the donkey rides. He'd done them when Hector was a child. In fact Candy had come as stable companion to Hector's first pony – Hector would be heartbroken and so would most of the village, for dear gentle Candy was part of all their lives. He had only been known to misbehave once and that was years ago when he took part for the first and only time in the primary school's nativity play. It was a mystery still why he had taken such an instant dislike to little Poppy Kenton who was playing the Virgin Mary, and had bitten her so hard on the bottom that she'd cried herself sick all over the kneeling shepherds and the whole play had had to be stopped. There were those in the village who said that the donkey had only shown sense – Poppy and her mother Glad were not popular. And heads nodded even more sagely when years later Poppy had turned up as a Page Three girl known as Poppy the Pout. Molly, studying the photograph in Mrs Hodgson's copy of the *Sun*, had gone so far as to get the magnifying glass that Hector used for his stamp collection the better to see if Candy had left a scar on Poppy's very pretty rump – but he hadn't.

'Get Flint, quickly,' Molly urged Chip.

Flint, summoned once again, assessed the situation, did not mutter but called for reinforcements. Four of the largest men in the village could not lift Candy – a dead donkey is a formidable weight.

It was Chip, so called for his penchant for fried potatoes, who had the brainwave of asking Mr Mann if they couldn't borrow the JCB that was in his driveway. It was undignified, but no one could think of a better solution as Candy was scooped up and borne away.

Molly, mercifully, was not given time to grieve nor to tell Hector before a new row began over the price of tickets. It had been 30p, 15p for children and OAPs, for ages. Now Hector had boards painted 'Entry £2, children & OAPs £1.'

'Sebastian,' he said in explanation. His voice seemed to take on a special tone when he said the young man's name.

'You sound like a besotted groupie,' Molly said sharply.

'What's that?' he huffed.

'Never you mind,' Molly snapped back, pleased she knew something he didn't. But she'd read a biography of the Beatles and he hadn't, so she knew about such things.

'We'll get thousands here with Sebastian to open it.'

'We haven't got room for thousands. Where would we put them all? Do the police know?'

'Of course the police know. That's why the price is up, to pay for them.'

It took her ten minutes of heated argument to get him to agree to villagers being admitted free. At last she was able to escape to the house to change before she could be asked to sort out any more problems.

She had presumed, with Sebastian stepping in at such short notice, that no one would know he was here and that the fête would falter on in its usual way. She hadn't reckoned on Hector's, to her unknown, entrepreneurial talents. He had managed to get the editor to run a special feature in the weekly *Lynchester Gazette*. That day's *Lynshire Morning News* had carried a half-page advert and Lyn Sounds had been broadcasting the news all week. Certainly huge crowds were expected. All Molly could hope for now was an enormous thunderstorm to keep everyone away and, better still, have everything cancelled.

At the house she made a quick call to Pat Jenkins to borrow her donkey. She bathed in five minutes flat and a further five minutes later changed into her cotton shirtwaister covered in pink cabbage roses which she always wore, whatever fashion dictated and whatever the weather.

In the kitchen she found Tabby and Sebastian, his manager Thin O'Connor – a stupid name for one so fat – and two enormous men with biceps like footballs and very rough looking who were, it transpired, Sebastian's minders. She wondered if she should lock up the silver. The sight of them was of no comfort at all and her mind raced, wondering how long they were all staying and if she had enough food.

'Mummy, Sebastian says that Colin Mann is a fraud.'

'Really dear?' said Molly, glancing across the kitchen to see how many eggs were in the basket.

'You're not listening, Mummy,' Tabby said in the clenched-teeth voice which she reserved exclusively for Molly.

'Yes, I am.' At least she'd got that tin of ham.

'What did I say then?'

'That Colin Mann's a fraud. I do hope none of you are vegetarians?' She voiced her sudden thought, apparently oblivious to Tabby's fury and the sound of Tabby's feet banging noisily against the table leg.

'All carnivores, Mrs Parminter,' Sebastian smiled.

'Don't you want to hear?' Tabby banged the table again.

'Oh, yes, tell me all, my darling.' Molly allowed herself to sit down for a minute. 'I'm all ears.'

'Sebby says he's not an Old Harrovian, that he's pretending. I knew there was something fishy about him.'

'Rubbish, you were as charmed as the rest of us. What makes you think that, Sebastian?'

'I can recognise an Old Harrovian at fifty yards. But I didn't actually say he was a fraud, Mrs Parminter, just that he didn't go to my school.'

'How interesting. Then maybe he's an Old Etonian.'

'No, Mrs Parminter,' the largest and roughest looking of the bodyguards interjected. 'Like Seb here, I can recognise a fellow OE immediately.'

Molly knew she looked surprised and she tried hard to remove the expression from her face. Why, oh why was nothing and no one what they seemed any more? 'Well,' she said, standing up purposefully, 'I'm not sure if it matters that much,' though she knew full well that it would, that it would be a scandal of monumental proportions in the village. But she had decided not to say anything – not until after the fête.

'Any chance of lunch, Ma?' Tabby asked from her vantage point on the kitchen table. What was it about her daughter that made her incapable of sitting on a chair like other people?

'Oh, really Tabby, can't you get your friends something?'

'You invited him,' said Tabby aggressively.

'But I've so much to do,' Molly said, beginning to feel flustered again.

'Just tell me where everything is, Mrs Parminter, I'll rustle something up.'

'Dear Sebastian,' Molly beamed.

'I'll do it, I suppose,' Tabby complained ungraciously, slithering from the table and clumping across to the fridge. 'Ice-cream everyone?' she said brightly.

'Make everyone ham, eggs and chips,' Molly shouted over her shoulder and hurried from the room before Tabby's venomous look could reach her.

She raced up the stairs. With this rain the buckets in the attic would be overflowing, she thought, as she hurried up to the top of the house. It was as she had feared, the rainwater was slopping over the top of the buckets and bowls that littered this section of the attics. On such days she knew that if the Devil appeared she would give him her soul if only he would get the flashings fixed for her.

Chapter 6

The Fête Opens and Closes

THERE WERE TIMES when Molly could quite happily throttle Hector. Descending from the attics with almost overflowing buckets, she was far from happy to be told that he'd just invited Jib and Twink, his wife, to lunch but had warned them it would be 'pot luck'.

'Pot luck! What pot luck? I've a tin of ham, or did have if Tabby and her friends haven't demolished it. Sometimes Hector, you can be so inconsiderate . . . !' she snapped, as she hurried into the back regions of the house still muttering, leaving a perplexed Hector in the middle of the hall wondering what on earth it was he'd done wrong.

Rear-Admiral Walters and his wife were the last people she wanted to entertain at this moment when she had so much else to do – anyone else she could have invited into the kitchen to eat, but not them. Once, soon after they had moved into the area, they had unexpectedly dropped in. Molly prided herself on being a very relaxed individual where hospitality was concerned, but 'dropping in' without an appointment or prior phone call was not for her. She regarded such casual behaviour as rude, lacking in considera- tion, and something she would never do herself even though, in the way of the English, she frequently invited people to do just that.

However, she had smiled as graciously as her irritation would allow, and since she was cooking and since they were such 'relaxed' individuals to drop in the first place, she had ushered them into the kitchen and offered them coffee.

One did not have to be as sensitive as Molly to realise she had committed a social *faux pas*. Both Jib and Twink had looked at each other with eyebrows almost imperceptibly raised and nostrils slightly flared as if a bad smell pervaded her kitchen. Smells *could* frequently be detected in Molly's kitchen – the cat was often responsible and Hector's aged labrador could drop the most malodorous and insidious farts at times. Then there were the drains, which could be particularly noxious when the mood took them. But today was not one of those days, instead her kitchen had the warm yeasty smell of baking. So their expressions annoyed her to such an extent that she decided not to apologise and suggest the drawing-room instead. She crossed to the dresser and took down three mugs and collected cream and sugar.

At sight of the mugs Twink's eyes grew double in size.

'Oh Molly dear. Forgive me, but Jib can't abide a workman's cup, can you Jib?'

Jib grunted and Molly returned to the dresser. What stupid names some people give themselves, she thought with a mental snort. She replaced two of the mugs, and took down two cups and saucers. Undoubtedly they would much prefer real coffee – so she put it away and got the 'instant' out instead.

She couldn't wait to tell Hector of this episode.

'Going a bit far, weren't you? Entertaining an Admiral in the kitchen?'

'They called uninvited, and he's only a Rear-Admiral.'

'I wouldn't fancy their kitchen – I wouldn't fancy anyone's kitchen. Kitchens are for family and intimate friends,' he announced pompously, as if he were an expert in the daunting and confusing waters of modern etiquette.

'You wouldn't have called unexpectedly, you'd at least have telephoned first.' She wished she hadn't told him now, Hector had such an annoying way of disagreeing with her when she least expected it. 'But fancy being so silly about mugs – in this day and age, it's too ridiculous. Everyone has mugs these days,' she said. Even Hector was very attached to his mug with 'Property of Dartmoor Prison' on the side and he became very angry if anyone else dared use it.

'I think I agree with Jib. I like a cup and saucer myself, improves the taste.'

'You never said.' She felt and sounded very affronted as she always was when he suddenly sprung such information upon her – one of his particularly annoying habits.

'I don't *mind* mugs – they're more convenient, I see that. I've never mentioned it before since, you know me, I don't like to make a fuss.'

This last comment rendered Molly speechless – Hector was always making fusses. He was fussy about his clothes and how they were ironed, the objects on his dressing table and how they were placed, about his shaving gear in the bathroom. He could explode with rage should he find that his *Daily Telegraph* or *The Field* magazine had been read first by someone else. His biggest and most successful fusses, however, were over food. He claimed he was the easiest man in the world to feed – this from a man whose list of the food he refused to eat was endless. He was fond of claiming he could live on fish. Oh yes, thought Molly, when he made this particular boast – provided it was crab, prawns, oysters or lobsters. Cod and whiting were fit only for the cat, was Hector's opinion.

But then, Molly had long ago noticed that when people made a statement about themselves it was generally safer to take the opposite point of view. Her own mother had been fond of boasting how much she loved the company of the young – Molly had never been aware of this, since all her friends were banned from the house. When she heard someone say they were tolerant she waited for the bigotry; when someone told her they had an acute sense of humour she knew she was in the company of a depressive. Those who said they were mad as hatters were invariably boringly dull and ordinary; and when she heard the claim 'I never speak ill of anyone' she knew she was in for a good gossip.

But here she was, in the midst of preparations for the fête, flying dementedly between her crowded kitchen and the cavernous dining-room, laying the table with the second-best silver and hating herself for being such a coward in not bundling the Walters into the kitchen again.

'Ah! A cold collation,' Twink had cried, clapping her hands with pleasure at the sight of ham, tomatoes, salad and a hastily pre-pared potato salad with the steam still rising from it. And Molly wondered why she bothered with anyone who could say 'cold collation'.

Molly stood on the steps of The Hall and knew exactly how Marie Antoinette must have felt that night at Versailles when the peasant women had stormed the palace. Towards her, shoulder to shoulder, filling the whole width of the drive, marched an army of people.

At the little bridge over the River Lyn the crowd became wedged. A bottleneck of humanity built up. Those behind, unaware of the hold-up, pushed impatiently forward. Molly feared for the bridge. The good-natured hum of the crowd began to change its note, like a swarm of contented bees who are suddenly disturbed and deprived of their pollen. Poor PC Lay was jigging up and down and gesticulating wildly in an attempt to stop the crowd from pushing. Then two young men on the bridge, scrabbling as if for their lives, hauled themselves up on to the parapet and jumped into the river. Like a bottle being uncorked the crowd was released and began to run for the fête ground with the intense and pre-occupied gaze of those who frequent the January sales. It did not bode well for the rest of the afternoon, thought Molly, anxiously scanning the sky and praying for thunder. Anything to make at least half of them go away. But the morning's clouds had disappeared, the sky was so blue it looked as if it intended to stay that way and the sun shone down with a vengeance.

'It will end in tears,' she muttered to herself as she sped along the top of the terrace and bumped into Sebastian's minders carrying large black boxes out of the drawing-room.

'What are those?' she called in passing.

'Sebastian's surprise for the fête,' replied the Old Etonian minder.

'Ah, I see,' she said, though she didn't and wondered why she had said it when she didn't but then, she realised, she often did.

Quick though she had been in racing around the house, the 'mob', as she now thought of them, had got there before her. She could see Hector in their midst, puce with rage, and shouting – which was pointless since no one was listening to him, and even if they were they could not have heard a word he was saying. She could see the problem: already stall holders were doing brisk business and the fête not even opened. To Hector this was the equivalent of starting tea before the Queen had arrived.

PC Lay bounded up. Well, bounded wasn't quite accurate – he struggled through the mass and almost crawled up the bank to the top terrace. He looked a wreck, having lost his hat and tie, and was clutching what remained of his buttons.

'Mrs Parminter, can I use your phone? Some kids nicked my radio.'

'Of course, Peter. It's madness down there, isn't it?'

'You can say that again. Ten PCs and an inspector are supposed to be here from Lynchester to help me.'

'I imagine they're held up in the traffic, don't you?' Molly said sympathetically, but also injecting a hint of encouragement into her voice since the young police constable had cause to be worried.

'I know the church needs the money, Mrs Parminter, but I could wish we weren't raising it quite so quickly. I really don't see how I'm to be expected to cope alone,' PC Lay said with feeling and with what, Molly feared, sounded suspiciously like defeatism.

'We'll manage, PC Lay, never you fear. We can't let a few yobbos defeat us, can we?' Molly said briskly, in what Hector called her Battle of Britain voice.

There was a noise from the policeman but it was difficult to interpret. It certainly did not sound like a rallying cry, more the death rattle of a vole, Molly thought as she led him into the house and to the telephone.

'Don't you think you should lock up, Mrs Parminter – you've got a lot of valuable stuff here you know,' PC Lay said knowledgeably as he waited for his call to connect.

'Really? You don't think . . . ? Oh surely not . . . ? We never have . . .'

But Peter Lay merely nodded his head with the sad and lugubrious expression of one who has seen it all and cannot be surprised by anything any more. In the six months he had been at Sarson the highlight of his career had been the apprehending of Chips and his gang caught red-handed scrumping Farmer

Feather's apples. He had failed to catch Simon Larkin, the resident poacher, who was invariably so drunk he rarely managed to poach anything and had come to rely on being arrested so as to get a square meal at the police station. Given this knowledge, Molly felt such a depth of weary resignation somewhat overdone.

Nevertheless, crime had increased dramatically in Lynchester and was inching its way insidiously towards Sarson Magna. So she went quickly round the house locking doors and windows. In the kitchen she found even more people than the last time she had popped in. But before she could find out who they were her sensitive nose detected a strange smell.

'Is there something burning?' she asked.

Tabby and her friends began to giggle in a particularly inane and irritating way.

'I can smell a most peculiar smell. Have you been burning joss sticks?'

'Nothing's — burning — Mummy,' Tabby said, spluttering between each word.

Reassured, she turned back through the door only to hear a great burst of laughter from those in the kitchen. The young could behave most peculiarly at times, she was thinking as she cannoned into Hector in the hallway.

'This was not a good idea,' he said looking at her sternly. 'I could have told you it would end like this.'

'But . . .' she started.

'I'm getting the boy now, get it over with before further damage is done. You'll live to regret all this, Molly . . .'

'Yes . . . but . . .' she found herself saying to his back as he stalked to the rear of the house. 'It was your flaming idea . . . Why don't you wear jackboots while you're about it . . . ?' she shouted with futile rage, knowing he didn't hear.

The stalls were practically empty. Cuckoo was as pink with excitement as her chiffon dress and picture hat. For the first time ever she and Hope had sold every raffle ticket. There had only been one untoward incident when Cuckoo had noticed a young scruff at the next stall pinching a pot of jam.

'You unspeakable townie, put that jam back,' she had ordered shrilly as she had leapt up and, with amazing alacrity for one who claimed she couldn't walk more than a few feet, raced across and hit him with her pink parasol. When his mother intervened, using language which luckily Cuckoo didn't understand, Cuckoo had hit her too.

'I've had a wonderful time, Molly dear,' she beamed. 'And darling Trenchard has, haven't you?'

'Dearest Cuckoo was so brave, Molly,' Hope twittered proudly.

Molly made the necessary complimentary noises, knowing that her face betrayed her astonishment at seeing the two women such bosom friends. The fête was usually the occasion for one of Cuckoo's louder rows with Hope, since then she had an audience.

Molly could see few of the locals in the main area of the fête but she wasn't surprised – since they had supplied everything on the stalls their interest in them was fairly limited. But she knew she would find them at the 'Cow Pat' enclosure.

The Cow Pat competition was the highlight of the fête. The same area of parkland was always fenced off and the rules of the game, laid down in the mists of time, were never varied.

The concept of the game was quite simple. Approximately a quarter of an acre was marked off in 2-foot-square sections, nearly six hundred in total. Each square was numbered and for sale at 50p. When the sale was complete – either when all the squares had been sold or none had been sold for a quarter of an hour – the cow was brought in. The winner was the owner of the square in which the cow unloaded its pat. The lucky winner could be in receipt of as much as £150, the other £150 going to the fête committee. It was a sort of bovine roulette. The legality of this arrangement, and where the fête committee stood in relation to the Gaming Act, was something that Hector preferred not to dwell on. But it had been played for hundreds of years and, as yet, no authority had been brave enough to step in and deprive the inhabitants of Sarson Magna of their annual gamble.

With so much money at stake the rules were important. Should the pat land in several squares the winner was the one who had the widest section. Should the cow perform several times, in different squares, again the largest, and widest, was the winner. The measuring of the pats was a serious and time-consuming affair performed by Hector with his metal ruler. By the rules, he was the only person in the village not allowed to buy a ticket and therefore guaranteed impartial. Should the pat end up in an unpurchased square or, unthinkably, the cow did not perform – this had never happened in living memory – then the money was the cow's, or rather the farmer's.

The local farmers took it in turn to supply the cow and this year it was Farmer Feather's with his long-lashed, dewy-eyed Jersey, Wendy.

In the past there had been unscrupulous farmers who had tried to interfere with nature, dosing their poor animals with noxious potions to constipate them. So fifty years ago it was decided that, for two weeks before the competition, the squire should take care of the cow and her diet.

The selling of the squares had been brisk and had even continued during the speeches.

First the vicar droned on, with no one listening. Then it was Hector's turn, and he spoke so close to the microphone that his speech was turned into a sort of manic screech. Not that it mattered, for no one wanted to listen to him either. Finally it was Sebastian's turn and the roar that greeted him must have been heard in Lynchester.

'Wotcha, mates,' he shouted cheekily, and the crowd yelled back in unison 'Wotcha, Seb!' His planned speech was two minutes long but it took over five to deliver since whatever he said produced a cheer accompanied by more shouts of 'Wotcha Seb . . . .'

Molly was totally perplexed. For a start, why? and secondly, she could not understand why Sebastian's beautiful accent should have disintegrated, in her opinion, into virtually incomprehensible cockney.

She thought that Sebastian seemed to be promising them a big surprise but only if every item on every stall was sold. Judging by the stampede to the stalls, Molly had been right in her interpretation.

The last of the cow pat squares were sold. Wendy was led in, to much excitement. All round the enclosure the crowd of punters were calling to the cow, trying to persuade her to move nearer their square. The noise was deafening. Wendy studied the crowd seriously from beneath her long lashes. The expression on her face was of such hauteur as she looked around, as if she had decided they weren't worth bothering with. Instead she began to munch at the particularly fine grass.

For ten minutes the crowd had been calling her name, coaxing, cursing, urging her. At last she stood stock still, raised her fine head and surveyed them seriously. The crowd held its breath . . . Her tail gracefully arched . . . Still no one dared breathe.

'*Gotcha! pretty lady, Gotcha, Gotcha, Gotcha . . .*' Sebastian sang lustily into the public address system accompanied noisily by his whole group – his surprise present to the crowd.

The rooks in the vicarage elms rose in one terrified flock. PC Lay fell off his bicycle in surprise. All the babies in the village began to cry as the cacophony of sound assaulted eardrums by the dozen.

Wendy's tail gracefully arched back down. She lifted her head, ears pricked back, huge eyes rolling – and bolted.

Over at the donkey ride, Cyril, the replacement donkey, had been tied up to a fence while Pat Jenkins slipped away to watch the opening.

At the sound of Sebastian and the Drones in full concert, Cyril's ears also went back, his eyes rolled and he bolted too with half the fence clattering along behind him. Across the Green he careered. The fence became entangled with the guy ropes of the tents that housed the temporary lavatories. Filled with terror the donkey heaved, the fencing budged, the tent collapsed, revealing Mrs Potter-Smythe enthroned on the portaloo.

Back at the cow pat field things had begun to turn nasty. Farmer Feather was volubly claiming his £150. The crowd, equally volubly, disagreed. There was nothing in the rules to cover a bolting cow.

Who pushed whom first it would be impossible to say and, within seconds, was academic as the inhabitants of Sarson Magna were, not to put too fine a point on it, bashing the living daylights out of each other.

Sebastian and the Drones played on.

Chapter 7

The Morning After

To say that Hector was angry upon his return from the village would have been a gross understatement. He was volcanic with rage.

'Have you seen this!' He stormed into the kitchen where Tabby, Sebastian, his manager and the four other members of the Drones were having a late breakfast. Molly was at the Aga finally understanding what being a short-order cook meant and, as yet, there was no sign of Mrs Hodgson. Hector slammed a copy of the *Sun* on to the table. 'I'm getting on to the editor, the Press Council, my MP. They're not getting away with this,' he ranted.

'What's the problem?' Tabby, using her most bored-sounding voice, asked, from behind a large wedge of toast.

'This.' Hector pointed dramatically to the headline.

'LAGER LOUTS SMASH SARSON – DOCTORS FIGHT FOR PC'S LIFE .'

'No one's fighting for Peter Lay's life, he twisted his ankle falling off his bicycle. The district nurse bandaged him up,' Molly said, pausing in her cooking. That particular expression by journalists had always struck her as remarkably silly, conjuring up as it did the vision of masked doctors fighting each other with épées or even fisticuffs over the prostrate form of their patient. 'Don't the newspapers exaggerate?'

'Exactly. Lies, all lies,' Hector rumbled.

'Oh that's funny,' Tabby giggled.

'Don't be silly, Tabitha. There's nothing funny at all. I've been quoted.'

'Oh no, Hector. What did you say?' Molly advanced anxiously on the table, fish slice rampant.

'I didn't, and that's why I'm angry.'

Tabby picked up the newspaper. She began to read aloud. *'Squire Hector Parminter, 58 . . .'*

'Bloody liars', Hector snorted. Not, however, prepared to reveal his true age of 52 to the assembled company.

Tabby glared at him and continued, '. . . *spoke exclusively . . .'*

'See, see what I mean? All lies. I never said nothing to no one,' and then he coughed with embarrassment at his ungrammatical inelegance.

'. . . *that five hundred lager louts had wrecked his village fête . . .* I didn't see any "lager louts", Daddy.'

'Exactly.'

'So who did all the fighting, Sir?' Sebastian asked politely.

'Those were villagers to a man – not a "lager lout" in sight,' Hector said proudly.

'They were behaving as if they were,' Molly said, turning back to the Aga.

'That's not very loyal!' Hector barked. 'Whatever next, Molly.'

'I'm just telling the truth.'

'Yee . . . !' Tabby shrilled. 'Look, I'm in too.' Listen,' she started, jumping up and down with excitement. *'Shapely, beautiful Tabitha Parminter (19) Squire's daughter describing herself as Sebastian's bit of stuff . . .'* She shrieked with laughter, while Hector and Molly both shuddered. *'Said . . .'* and then Tabby began to blush, and as quickly, went white. She closed the paper, folded it neatly and laid it on the table. 'I didn't say that,' she said in a very quiet voice, not at all the way Tabby normally spoke. 'Honestly . . .' she looked frightened now.

'What does it say?' Molly again advanced on the paper.

'Mummy don't, don't look, please.'

'Don't be silly, Tabby. I've got to read it.' She then picked up the paper, began to read and wished she hadn't. It stated that Tabby thought 'lager louts' were fun, only young people letting their hair down who got a bad press from fuddy-duddys like her father. That yes, she and Sebastian were going steady and, she confided, they intended to marry later in the year.

'Oh, dear,' Molly laid the paper back on the table where it was

64

scooped up by Sebastian's manager. 'Which bit in particular is upsetting you?'

'All of it. I never said that to her. I never did.'

'Who were you talking to, Tabby?' Sebastian asked gently.

'Emma Thomas, I've known her for years. We were in the Pony Club together. She works on the *Lynchester Gazette* – I don't understand!' Tabby wailed, and Molly put her arm about her. 'We were just chatting and she said wasn't Sebastian gorgeous and I agreed.'

'Just that?' Molly stroked her daughter's hair then wished she hadn't when she found her hand sticky with gel.

'Well,' Tabby twisted her cumbersomely clad feet. 'Well . . . I did boast a little bit. I did say he's my boyfriend.'

'This is bad, Seb. Bad for your reputation I can tell you.' His manager sighed wearily.

'What do you mean, *his* reputation. My daughter is a highly respectable young woman . . .' Hector blustered.

'Mr P. I'm sorry. I put that badly. Of course Tabby's a sweety – none better. What I meant was Sebastian's image – the fans can't accept a married pop star.'

'Married? Who's married?' Sebastian looked up from his cornflakes.

'Oh no . . .' Tabby covered her face with her hands and rushed noisily from the room, sending a chair crashing, frightening the cat, and slamming the door.

'Poor kid.' The manager began to pick his teeth. 'She obviously didn't understand about reporters.'

'But if Emma's on the *Gazette* why is this in the *Sun*?' Molly asked, puzzled.

'Freelancing – it's done all the time. There isn't a reporter alive you can talk to with confidence that you will be reported correctly. I'd appreciate it in future, Mr P., if you and your family channelled all such enquiries through our office. We've the experience to deal with the piranhas, you see, Mr P.'

'Mr O'Connor, I don't know why you insist on calling me Mr P. My name isn't P-E-E or P-E-A, as far as I can recollect.' Hector spelt out the words.

'Why thank you very much, Hector. That's very good of you. Mateyer, isn't it – you call me Thin, if you want, that's what my mates call me.'

Molly could see that Hector, while speechless for the moment, was unlikely to remain so for long. She quickly slipped a plate of scrambled eggs in front of him, poured him coffee – in a cup rather than a mug – and kissed him on the top of his head. 'There, there, darling,' she said in the most placatory voice of her repertoire.

'Have you seen this?' The door flew open and Cuckoo, a flutter of pink frills, swished into the room with Hope, looking even more anxious than usual, trailing along behind her. 'No one tells me anything,' she shrieked in her high-pitched voice and swung round accusingly to face Molly. 'I blame you for all this, Molly. You've made the child secretive. Imagine!' she said and pausing, dug deep into her pocket, produced a small scrap of pink handkerchief and delicately blew her nose. She sat down abruptly beside the largest of the minders. 'Imagine, young man, how hurt I felt reading of my only granddaughter's engagement in the newspaper. 'She began to cry so prettily that the minder had to swallow hard as he put his large hand over hers, giving it a comforting squeeze and tutting consolingly.

'Now just a minute, Cuckoo . . .'

'I might just as well be dead for all that anyone cares.'

'But Cuckoo . . .' The phone rang. Just as well, Molly thought, as she crossed the kitchen to answer it, for she was rapidly beginning to feel an almost uncontrollable longing to throttle the old woman.

'Molly? Molly, darling I've just seen the paper, how exciting . . .' It was Lulu.

'Good God, it's not in other papers is it?' Molly asked anxiously. 'Which one?'

'Well . . . it was . . . The newsagent must have made a mistake . . . I wouldn't like you to think . . .' There was an even longer pause. 'The *Sun*,' Lulu said, her voice strained with embarrassment.

No sooner had Molly replaced the receiver than Hyacinth called, and then Pat Jenkins, and then Bat Rogers' wife Jolly.

It was an extraordinary thing, Molly thought, she'd never heard any of those people have one good word to say about that particular newspaper and yet, it would appear, they all read it. That, or the newsagent had gone mad and right now the inhabitants of the council estate were burrowing their way through *The Times*, *Telegraph* or *Independent*. Not, of course, the *Guardian*, she couldn't recall ever seeing anyone reading that in Sarson Magna. But maybe she was out of touch; it would seem the ideal daily for that aggressive woman at The Larches. Molly laughed, and then laughed louder. Everyone looked round but she just couldn't stop; in truth she was relieved to find she could find something to laugh about. Cuckoo returned to her damp complaining, but no one was listening. Thin O'Connor was deep in conversation with Hector. The minders had taken up the cooking where Molly had left off. Sebastian had left the room and the other four Drones were busily playing drums on the lids of the marmalade and jam jars on the breakfast table.

'So, what do we do?' Molly, having finally regained control of herself, asked.

'We'll have to publish a denial,' Thin said.

'Will they?'

'The *Sun* probably won't, but every other paper will report it just to poke their tongue out and behave all holier than thou. That's what usually happens.'

'Poor Tabby, she must be feeling mortified.'

'To say the least . . .' Hector added.

But before he could finish the door opened and a smiling Tabby noisily clumped into the room, holding Sebastian by the hand.

'That's settled then,' Sebastian said grinning broadly. 'I thought I'd come to open a fête, not get engaged.'

'Oh Seb, what you gone and done now?' Thin leapt up.

'Asked Tabby properly. I'd intended to anyway – I suppose this just made me ask a little sooner.'

'Oh Tabby,' Molly felt a quite ridiculous desire to cry.

'Seb you can't do that, it's a bad career move,' Thin wailed as the other Drones noisily congratulated Sebastian.

'No one asked me,' Hector said ominously.

'I think it's Tabby he wants, Sir, not you,' the Old Etonian minder joked.

'Champagne, Daddy, have you any left in the cellar?'

Hector stood, his thumbs in the small pockets of his waistcoat – a particularly nice checked one that Molly had bought him in a Simpson's sale – always an ominous sign.

'What a lovely idea,' Molly said, far too brightly. 'But perhaps we should celebrate in the drawing-room.'

'I repeat. No one has said anything to me,' and Hector glowered in the direction of Sebastian who was staring at Tabby with an idiotic expression on his face. Molly felt sorry for Hector; she knew exactly how he felt. As she had spent many a happy hour planning Tabby's eventual wedding, no doubt Hector had also rehearsed his own interview with the prospective bridegroom, probably when taking his bath, for the acoustics in their bathroom were perfect for speeches. Now here the future bridegroom was, across the room, and not a word had been said. Poor Hector was to be left with a well rehearsed speech, in which elder statesmanship, advice, and a little judicious financial probing were blended with paternal benevolence, all unused. A redundant scenario.

Molly slipped around the table and whispered urgently to Sebastian, who blushed most charmingly and quickly turned and requested, 'a quiet moment alone, Sir'.

The expression on Hector's face was one of such undiluted happiness that Molly knew she would treasure its memory for ever. Hector with shoulders squared, back ramrod straight, ushered Sebastian away to his study.

Upon their return, Hector placated and glowing with self-satisfaction, Sebastian still smiling inanely, Cuckoo still in tears – but tears of joy, she insisted to anyone who would listen – Thin O'Connor finally calmed down. Undoubtedly even he could not continue to complain in the face of such happiness. The champagne flutes were collected and wiped; since they were so rarely used they were covered in dust. Hector coughed, preparing to make a speech, when the back door flew open.

'Have you heard?' It was Mrs Hodgson, all a fluff and flutter, as she would say.

'We've read it,' they replied in chorus, Thin waving the *Sun* at Mrs Hodgson.

'Oh not *that*,' said Mrs Hodgson, dismissing such old news. 'It's Mrs Potter-Smythe, she can't face the shame of being caught on the lav. Her cottage is on the market. Well, she didn't last long did she?'

A week later Molly was walking purposefully down the drive about to kill two birds with one stone. The issue of Colin Mann's old Harrovian tie had not yet been resolved and she had invitations to Tabby's engagement party to deliver.

Molly never approached the Dower House without a sense of wishful thinking. The house had, originally, been the Manor to Sarson Magna – until one of Hector's ancestors with delusions of grandeur had built The Hall. Had he had less money and more sense the Dower House would have been her home instead of the over-large, starkly austere, rather intimidating house which was the cause of constant struggles, both physical and monetary.

She paused in her step to admire it, as she always did, as most people did when they passed by – many were the car crashes that almost occurred when strangers, suddenly seeing the house, slammed on their brakes for a better view.

The Dower House was Elizabethan – warm red mellow brick, brown beams, chimneys in barley-stem twists and curves, latticed windows, flagged floors, linenfold panelling, oak doors – the lot, a gem. The only addition ever made was a Victorian conservatory, but that was at the back and therefore not visible from the road. The Clements, the previous owners, had installed central heating – so sympathetically it could not, at first glance, be detected – and had updated the plumbing and the kitchen, but that was all.

It had only six main bedrooms and five reception rooms including the great hall – which to Molly made it a most desirable, manageable house. If only they lived here she might have been able to change her car every other year as Lulu did instead of buying a banger every five years or so and driving it until she finally had to pay someone to take it away for scrap. She might have been able to take holidays, they might have been able to afford a small flat in London and they might not even have had to sell her jewellery. And, most certainly, the flashings would have been repaired. Molly made herself stand up straight, and berated herself for such idiotic thoughts. She didn't live here and that was that, she told herself, as she did umpteen times a year.

She pulled the bell-pull – that must be Victorian too. Did Elizabethans have bell-pulls? Surely not. Surely they hammered on doors which were swung open by serfs who existed solely for that purpose. Ah happy days . . . !

'Molly.'

'Sue.'

They kissed the air above each other's shoulders and Molly wondered why, when it was a habit she regarded as quite ridiculous at the best of times let alone with a virtual stranger such as this. 'That's what the Common Market has done for us,' was Hector's opinion, 'made us all pansy like the rest of the Europeans.'

'What a pleasant surprise, come in, do.' Sue held the door open welcomingly.

'I haven't called,' Molly said hurriedly, aware how often she said how she disliked such informality. 'I was just bringing you this, saves on the postage . . .' She held out the envelope with the party invitation and wished she hadn't said that, it made them sound like paupers.

'How kind. But please come in, the kettle's on.'

'I can't stand people who just drop in. I couldn't, really,' Molly said.

'Can't you? I love it – so informal. So, well, countrified. I insist,' Sue smiled in her winning way and Molly stepped over the threshold just as she had hoped to all along.

'Let me show you what we've done, while the kettle boils,' Sue disarmingly invited.

With the business of the old school ties Molly had not known what to expect and had steeled herself to the eventuality that anything was possible. Instead she found admirable chintz sofas and chairs, delightful modestly restrained curtains, not at all like the dreadful dust traps she had seen in the dentist's magazines. A good collection of early English oak furniture and a plethora of portraits. She had doubts about the authenticity of the suit of armour she noticed on the turn of the stairs; it would need closer inspection. And the bindings of the books in the library were a little too uniform and blazoned with such untarnished gold leaf as to raise a question or two.

Everything looked wonderful yet there was something lacking and Molly was not sure what it was. The latest editions of *Interiors*, *Country Life*, *Horse and Hound* and *Harpers & Queen* were laid out on the coffee table as if they had been lined up with a ruler. Vivaldi's *Four Seasons* pounded out from concealed speakers wherever they walked. Molly looked about hopefully for a sign of *Woman* or maybe a Tom Jones record but neither, nor anything similar, was to be seen.

Molly congratulated Sue on how lovely everything looked and was a little taken aback when Sue quite blithely told her how much it had all cost. In Molly's circles, although money was an abiding interest, it was never discussed. Molly should have been shocked, but instead found Sue's openness rather refreshing.

'Kitchen or drawing-room?' asked Sue.

'Oh kitchen please, don't go to any fuss for me.' Molly beamed, since the kitchen had not been included in the hurried inspection of the ground floor.

Here Molly was in for a surprise. The Clements, she knew, had had a kitchen built in, at enormous expense, the units of which Molly had often dreamt about – literally. But the whole of the Clements' kitchen, except for the Aga, had been torn out and in its place was a large oak dresser, table and several chests and cupboards. The stainless-steel sink had been replaced with a stone one above which was a wooden plate rack of great antiquity. It was an almost exact replica of her own kitchen, the one she loathed, the one she felt sorry for herself for having to work in.

'You've changed everything,' she said, aware of the horror in her voice.

'Oh yes, I can't abide a built-in kitchen, so *passé*. No one has them any more. China or Indian?'

'China please. Don't they? Have built-in kitchens, I mean. Lulu's got one . . .'

'Oh dear, how rude of me, don't tell her what I said *ever*, will you?'

'My kitchen's like this and I long for a nice plastic one.'

'Molly, don't even think of it. Yours will be worth a small fortune, it really will.'

'Good gracious,' said Molly, sipping her tea and resolving never to tell Hector.

It was the basket of vegetables and fruit on the table that alerted Molly to what ailed the house. The contents of the trug were arranged by colour, some tumbling out and on to the table, and with the jug of marigolds beside it, it looked as if someone was about to start a still life painting. Of course, she was sitting in a *designer interior*. It was only a matter of time before this house would be featured in one of those glossy magazines that Molly could never afford to buy. Why did people do it, she wondered. Was it simply to show how rich they were or was it because they were so unsure of themselves and their own taste that they were stuck with the conformity of someones else's?

'I loved the fête. What a riot! Sorry about the poor donkey.'

'We're still not mentioning it – donkey or fête it's bad for Hector's blood pressure. But we made over £2,000 for the church. The vicar nearly died of shock, it's usually nearer £300.'

'Then you've made £4,000. Colin told the vicar he'd double whatever you took.'

'How kind. But we could never keep him to it. He wouldn't have known about Sebastian and the Drones when he offered.'

'But he did. He offered on the morning of the fête. Don't worry, he can well afford it and Colin never lays out money unless he wants to, he's usually got a reason.'

Molly registered this comment and was so worried by the implications that she had to take another cucumber sandwich to cover up her discomfort.

'When you've had enough tea perhaps you would like to see the upstairs?'

There was nothing Molly wanted more even if she did despise

her own nosiness, so she refused a second cup and the two women were soon climbing the stairs past the suit of armour which, close to, Molly was certain was genuine. But it was in such good order that it looked artificial – it must have cost a mint. But then, as Sue had told her, furnishing the house had cost a small fortune. She wondered what it must be like to be able to order everything from scratch. She had never had that pleasure, not just because of lack of money, but because she had inherited the tastes of the other Parminter women over the centuries. There had been nothing left to buy. Molly often thought that perhaps, if she and Hector had lived in a small house, it might have been fun to collect furniture and things bit by bit. Molly had a sneaky idea that that way everything was appreciated far more.

They inspected the children's rooms – Charlotte's was a dream, with a four-poster, and a bathroom attached, which Molly would have mortgaged her soul for. Come to think of it, she thought, the list of things she would do that for was becoming alarming large: she just had to hope the Devil would never materialise and put her to the test. But when she saw Colin and Sue's room another was added. Not one bathroom but two, not one dressing-room but one each! Molly thought of her treks along cold corridors to her own bathroom, one of only two for such a large house. Molly did not count the bathroom in the old servants' quarters – so bleak and dark one needed a miner's lamp before entering it. But looking about this perfect bathroom she found yet another situation where she could be taken hostage by Lucifer.

'You've done so much in such a short time,' she said with genuine admiration. What little work the Parminters ever had done seemed to take months of negotiation even to get Mr White the local builder to come and look. After much pencil-sucking and scratching of head a price might be agreed but he would only disappear not to be seen again for another six months. That was one of her worries over the flashings. If the miracle happened and they ever got the money to have them mended it would undoubtedly be years before Mr White and his henchmen would condescend to come. By then the flashings would have deteriorated further and the money would have disappeared again.

'I don't usually like built-in cupboards but they are more convenient, and who but our closest friends ever see our dressing-rooms?' said Sue as she opened one of the mahogany doors with a flourish.

Molly was trying to work out how to say something about mahogany and rain forests without being too offensive when she stopped dead in her tracks. Row upon row of ties met her gaze. Eton, Rugby, Winchester, the Guards, the Garrick – they were only a few, the ones Molly recognised.

'What an extraordinary collection of ties!' she exclaimed, she hoped innocently.

'Colin loves stripes. I buy them for him. There's a lovely shop in London, you can get any combination of colours there.'

'Undoubtedly you can,' Molly said weakly. Surely the woman realised? She wasn't, or at least did not appear, stupid. But then as Molly's theory about people proved, those who seemed thick invariably had Ph.D.s or their last book was put up for the Booker, whereas those who were relentlessly bright had usually done nothing of any note and lacked even one original thought. 'Which one is your husband's school tie?' she asked, in as nonchalant a voice as she could muster.

Sue riffled through the ranks of ties like an efficient filing clerk and emerged with a particularly virulent purple and emerald green job. 'This one. Not that he likes it much. He just wears it to old boys' days, governors' meetings, things like that.'

'And where would that be?' Molly asked, averting her eyes from the vertiginous stripes.

'Lynchester Comprehensive. That's where we met. He was in the fifth form and I was in the third.'

'You're from Lynchester too?'

'Oh yes, didn't you know? I was a hairdresser. I eventually had my own salon, lovely little place on Porter's Green.'

Molly's hand leapt involuntarily to her hair, as it always did when she met a hairdresser. Molly's hair was not her crowning glory. She had the type of fine, wispy hair that hairdressers regarded as a challenge, and many were the promises of curls, bounce and added thickness she'd been given, to no avail – the hair

74

always won. Perms never lasted. Sets disappeared within hours and as for blow drys they were a memory by the time she had reached the car park.

'You've got lovely hair,' Sue said, as if reading her thoughts.

'Me?' Molly found herself giggling.

'It's such a pretty blonde, so fine.'

'I hate it. I can only wear it straight, it won't hold a curl.'

'But it's perfect as it is in that short style. If I was your hairdresser I wouldn't change a thing.'

Molly touched her hair again and knew she was grinning inanely. 'I wish you were my hairdresser, too.'

'Colin won't let me do it any more. When he became so successful he didn't like me working, you know how men are?' she said with so much regret in her voice that Molly found herself putting her hand out and taking her arm in sympathy.

'I'm sorry. How silly of him. I'd love a job if only there was something I was good at. I'm sure it would help my mind wake up a bit, I sometimes think I'm becoming a vegetable as a housewife.'

'That's what I think. I'm sure I was much more interesting when I had my salon. But Colin's so insecure, you see. He thinks people would think less of him if I worked. He's so afraid he won't be accepted by the right people, that they will think he's unsuccessful. It means so much to him. That's why he insisted we both take elocution lessons. I can understand, but I still think it's all so silly. I mean, what's wrong when you're from Lynchester to sound as if you are?'

Molly agreed but at the same time thought it was a strange conversation to be having. If they had gone to all this trouble to cover their tracks what was the point in telling her all this and wasting the money they had spent in the first place? Molly was normally suspicious of people who opened up too early in an acquaintance, it usually meant they were after something. Confidences were for old friends and then only imparted with a great degree of caution, not for people one barely knew.

'Gracious, if there was anything I could work at Hector would push me out of the door as fast as twinkling and live off the proceeds. I've often told him he would have made a good pimp.'

Molly laughed a short embarrassed laugh which she always did when her thoughts were in conflict. She did not like to think she was two-faced but the way her mind sometimes worked she often felt quite schizophrenic.

'You're a real treat to talk to, Molly. Not like some of the stuck-up cows around here. I tell you, you're lucky with your husband – provided he doesn't turn you out on the streets,' and Sue was laughing too, but Molly detected that it wasn't a truly happy laugh. And Molly decided, there and then, that she liked the woman. Sue seemed different, almost like a child, and Molly found in her case that she set suspicion aside. In any case, anyone who was nice about her hair was special in Molly's eyes.

Sue looked at her watch. 'It's very early, only a quarter to five but you wouldn't fancy a little G & T or something, would you?'

Molly agreed with alacrity. She often wondered, if Hector were a multimillionaire, whether in fact she wouldn't become an alcoholic – she loved a drink at this time of day but finances as they were there was usually only British sherry available, the amontillado and the gin being reserved for guests. Not that Hector's whisky was treated in the same way as the gin. She had complained about that frequently, finding it very unfair. But Hector most reasonably had said she was welcome to his whisky; he could be reasonable for he knew full well that she hated the stuff.

In the drawing-room Molly stood at the window. At the far end of the garden, in the large paddock, were two men with a long measuring tape.

'What are those men doing?' Molly asked idly.

'Those are Colin's blokes. They're measuring up for the stands and shops and the loos I expect.'

'The stands? The loos?' Molly repeated like an imbecile.

'Yes, didn't you know? Colin wants to build a theme park – jousting and a village with stocks, that sort of thing. As Colin says, so many tourists come here and there's nothing for the poor souls to do – just antique shops. It'll be fun, don't you think?'

'Fun?' Molly's voice was growing weaker by the minute.

'That's Colin for you – everything has to make money, you see. I put my foot down about the house though.'

'The house?' Molly was fully aware how idiotic she must be sounding.

'Yes he wanted us to hold medieval banquets with serving wenches and so on but I said no, some things have to be sacrosanct I said. It's not as if it's Woburn, is it?'

'No.' The word was barely audible.

Chapter 8

The Council of War, and Colin Fights Back

'IT'LL BE NEON signs before we know where we are.' Porky Naughton was in the chair.

'And charabancs,' Bat added.

'And God knows what,' Jib nodded his head sagely.

It was odd how often these three spoke, one after the other, as if on parade, Molly thought. She was making notes, or supposed to be but instead found herself doodling odd birdlike creatures with beaks and yet with paws — she wondered what a psychiatrist would make of them — and she was finding it increasingly difficult either to concentrate or to take these proceedings seriously. She even wished she hadn't said anything at all to Hector thus forewarning him and leading to the formation of this self-proposed village preservation committee.

The whole meeting was her fault but she had not thought about the problem deeply enough on the way home from Sue's. She had bumped into Dr Linklater's wife and had had a natter about the fête, about Tabby's engagement, and about the breast-scanning fund that Lily Linklater was setting up. All these matters quite put the Manns' scheme to the back of her mind so she had not had time to think about the possible consequences before, at dinner that evening, she had mentioned it to Hector, in passing.

The effect was electrifying. Hector's soup spoon clattered, his glass of wine disappeared in one draught and he banged the table and said 'He's building *what*? What on earth are you talking about?' and glared at Molly belligerently as if everything were her responsibility. She could believe messengers were once killed for bringing bad news.

'There's no point in looking at me like that, it's not my fault,' she said, affronted. 'I didn't ask him to build the damn thing.'

'I knew that fellow would be up to no good. Sensed it the moment I met him. Too sharp by half. Why on earth the Clements sold to his sort in the first place I'll never know.'

'You thought he was wonderful a month or two ago.'

'I never did. You women were fawning all over that man, but I knew . . .' he tapped the side of his nose with his forefinger.

'You knew nothing of the sort. It was only when Sebastian mentioned the old Harrovian tie that anyone had the least suspicion about him.'

'There you are, what did I say? Says it all, doesn't it?' Hector looked smugly at her, having decided he had won the argument, although in fact, if one thought about it, he had said nothing of significance at all – it was an ability which, while irritating Molly, she had to admire. When caught in a tight corner Hector always managed to sound as if he was still in control.

'I think they are very nice people, especially Sue. They can't be acceptable one week and *persona non grata* the next. They're still the same people.'

'But the tie is a deception.'

'But it isn't. Sue's quite open about their background and if you go there no doubt you'll be shown the ties too, he's got hundreds of them. He just likes stripes – I think it's rather endearing . . .'

'Endearing! Really, Molly, you are capable of saying the most stupid things at times. What about this damn mock village then – that's devious, that can't be described as endearing.'

'No it isn't. Sue told me all about it and undoubtedly Colin will apply for all the relevant permissions.'

'And why should Sue choose you for all her confidences? Answer me that.'

'Perhaps she likes me, some people do, you know,' she said with spirit, while at the same time wishing that Hector did not always hit the nail on the head quite so accurately.

'She's using you to get at me.'

'Oh really, Hector. Why on earth should they do that?'

'They need a friend in our camp, that's why.'

'You talk as if you were head of M.I.5 for goodness sake.'

'I'm on the planning committee and Colin Mann knows I am. You should be more discreet in your choice of friends, Molly.'

'Sometimes you talk such twaddle, Hector,' she said with exasperation in the face of such cynicism.

'Well, I can scotch his plans. That I *can* see to.' Hector leapt from his chair – something she hadn't seen him do in years – and was away on the telephone for ages while the toad-in-the-hole collapsed and cooled.

Luncheon engagements had been cancelled so that this meeting with Porky, Bat, Jib, Lulu and the vicar could be convened the following morning.

'Until we see the plans I don't really see what we can do,' the vicar said in his professionally reasonable voice.

'It enables us to muster the ranks. Forewarned is forearmed,' Porky intoned, as if lecturing a military academy.

'What if it's all right? I mean what if the council passes his plans?' Lulu enquired.

'Well they won't will they? That's why we're here.' Lulu was rewarded with a withering glance from Hector.

'But you don't know that,' she bravely persisted.

'It might be advantageous to the village.' It was the vicar being reasonable again.

'Advantageous! Advantageous! What's advantageous about a vulgar scheme like this?' Porky bellowed. A reasonable voice disagreeing with him always over-excited him. He took it as a personal affront.

'But we don't know it's vulgar.' The vicar, for once, was not to be deterred, which surprised Molly. As his wife was a bundle of worries and anxieties so was her husband, as though they had infected each other with nervousness.

'Of course it will be . . . people like that are sure to make it so.'

'People like what, Porky?'

'You know exactly what I mean, Molly.'

'No, I don't. Do you mean if Hector wanted to do this in our park it would be all right?'

'Of course it wouldn't.'

'Fine then, let's get that straight right from the start, can we? That it's the principle you're against and not the people behind it.'

'What on earth's got into you, Molly?' Hector looked at her with a deep and ominous frown. 'Sorry about that, Porky, I'm afraid my wife is enamoured with the Manns.' He smirked at the General and poured him another large scotch.

'I beg your pardon?' Molly, rapidly going pink with indignation, jumped to her feet. 'You will not apologise for me, Hector. How dare you! I meant what I said. I stand by it,' and she sat down again unsure how to continue.

'I think Molly's right. I don't think we should let the silly tie business get in the way of our judgement.' Lulu stepped in quickly before the men could hijack the meeting completely, which was what usually happened.

'There's nothing silly about wearing a tie you're not entitled to wear. It shows a highly suspect, I'd go as far as to say a dishonest, mind at work.' Porky was at his most pompous.

'Oh poppycock,' Molly snapped. 'He likes striped ties, there's nothing sinister about it at all.'

Everyone except the vicar and Lulu looked at Molly with the sympathetic expression reserved by some for mental defectives.

'Ties or not we are not getting very far.' Hector's look at Molly was a private semaphore of 'shut up' signals. Molly resentfully went back to her doodling.

An hour later the meeting broke up with, as far as she could make out, little resolved. All they could do was to warn the various relevant organisations – English Heritage, the Daughters of England Society. She felt really sorry for the Manns now. The Daughters of England Society was run by large-breasted bossy women who would have made excellent dictators, and who would move in on the Manns, making their life virtually intolerable, organising petitions, objecting to everything. Molly had seen it happen before. She wondered if the cities too were infected by gangs of the same breed of middle-class, middle-aged women so convinced of their own rightness in all matters as to bully and boss as they roamed across the shires. She and Lulu were instructed to remain friends with the Manns and to report back to the committee – to be moles, no more no less. Despicable, they both concluded. Everyone was turning into unpleasant busybodies, they muttered to each other in the hall. What was the point in having a council and masses of officials if they couldn't leave it to them to sort out? Molly whispered. It was an aspect of the society she moved in that she found the most unpleasant – the theory, just like the Daughters gang, that they knew better than anyone else what was best for others.

And was this scheme such a bad thing? It was well to the back of the Manns' property, surrounded by trees. Certainly, as their closest neighbours, the Parminters wouldn't even be able to see it, nor would it be visible from the village. It would create jobs. And it would give the tourists something to do, for apart from the pub and the church and the antique shops there was nothing for them in Sarson Magna.

As the cars of the committee swept down the drive they overtook Mrs Hodgson, whose legs were pumping up and down on her bicycle as she raced home to tell the neighbours in Churchill Drive what she had overheard. In fact she hadn't overheard, she'd eavesdropped, an easy thing to do with the meeting being held in the dining-room. She'd merely listened through the serving hatch from the butler's pantry and had heard every word.

By that evening another meeting was being held at No. 2 Churchill Drive. Convened, his parlance, by Fred Hodgson.

'Them bastards are at it again,' Fred was addressing the assembled company. 'As soon as there's a scheme voiced in this village to better our lives, them stuck-up nobs put the kibosh on it. It's not good enough.'

There was a rumbling of agreement.

'What they're doing is no jobs – for us.' He stabbed his chest dramatically with his large index finger. 'No extra money – for us,' stab. 'No entertainment for the likes of us,' stab. 'We'll fight, brothers and sisters, we'll fight them till there's no breath in our bodies – it's our village as well as theirs.' He ended dramatically and stood back as if waiting to be applauded. Much to Fred's disappointment, no one clapped or cheered. There were times he felt he was wasted in Sarson Magna. Ever since last year, when he had been voted area union representative for the NUR, it was the TUC where he felt he should be, where he knew he would be fully appreciated.

'You can't say that about the Squire,' Jean Hodgson added defensively. 'The Parminters have been here long as anyone has.'

'True. But then who's leading them bastards? Hector Parminter – that's who,' Reg Whistler said with feeling.

'You can hand in your notice tomorrow, Jean,' Fred ordered.

'But I like it there. Why should I give up my job? Mrs Parminter's very kind to me and we need the money.'

'Hang on, Fred. Don't act too fast, we need Jean up at the Hall – she can be our mole. The best thing we can do, I reckon, is to go and see this Mr Mann ourselves and tell him what's what.'

In the time-honoured way of the 'gentry' – a word which, these days, only themselves used – there was no sense of urgency in warning the various organisations they had listed. None of them would have dreamt of telephoning the regional organisers or any of the paid officials. No, they waited until they could arrange to speak to the chairman or chairwoman in a social capacity. Then, gin and tonic in hand, and during normal chit-chat they would feed the relevant information as if it were just another snippet of gossip. That's how they had always done things in these parts and none could see any reason for change.

By acting in this way, they fell into Colin Mann's hands.

As soon as the Churchill Drive 'committee' had called *en masse* to speak to him, Colin had swept into action. Late as it was, he had telephoned his architect, surveyor, accountant, the head of a graphic design firm with whom he'd been at school, and the head of a public relations firm in London which he had often used in the past. A meeting with them all was arranged for early the following morning.

The so-called preservation committee had the wind taken out of its sails when, within the week, through every letter box in Sarson Magna and a radius of five miles, dropped an invitation to a meeting to be held at the community centre where Colin would explain his plans and where 'refreshments will be available'.

No general election meeting in Sarson Magna was ever so well attended – only the very young and the infirm were absent. Naturally there was much interest in what was to happen but the invitation to 'refreshments' ensured a good turn-out. Colin was no fool.

Inside the community centre – a bleak building of pebbledashed breeze-blocks and chronically leaking cisterns, decorated inside in that cream and green so favoured by municipal functionaries – the inhabitants began to settle. On each seat they found a glossy brochure which included a potted history of the village; tourist statistics in easily understood graphs; an artist's impression of Colin's plans. From the murmurings of those studying the booklet, 'pretty' was the word which Hector heard the most frequently, much to his annoyance. Behind the long table on the stage was a large television – the largest any of them had ever seen.

The positions in which they chose to seat themselves showed the already existing divisions in the village. It was as if they were at a wedding. All in favour of Colin sat noisily to the right of the hall for all the world as if they were friends of the bridegroom.

On the left-hand side, stiffly upright, noisily shrill, sat his opponents. At their head, in the front row sat Hector, Bat and Porky. Jib Walters, because of a severe attack of gout brought on by over-indulgence, was laid up in bed.

Hector craned round to see who was where and with whom, while pretending to be looking for something or someone specific. He could quite understand Bill Blunt, the pub landlord, taking Colin's side and also the council estate contingent sitting in solid support – obviously they would be affected by the prospect of jobs and extra money. However, he was pleased to see that there appeared to be one dissenting voice, his own Mrs Hodgson sitting ostentatiously isolated at the back of the room but on 'his' side. There was a woman who knew about loyalty, not, he frowned, like his gardener Flint who sat with the opposition. But Hector noted, with satisfaction, that all the inhabitants of the executive estate were behind him to a man and a woman.

84

He was not altogether surprised to note Annie English's large form, in one of her habitual brightly coloured kaftans, sitting beside Flint. Hector had never been sure about Annie – not only did she serve foreign food, enough in his eyes to make anyone suspect, but on top of that she was a writer. Anyone who made a living from any artistic pursuit was suspect in Hector's eyes, and 'scribbling' was most suspect of all – 'pinkoes', was how he referred to them. Annie was as rich as Croesus from her writing; a totally wrong state of affairs, since 'scribbling' could never be regarded as a proper job – not that he'd ever read anything she'd written. Apart from his newspapers, Hector read only *The Field* and *Farmers Weekly* and had never felt the need to expand his literary pursuits. This was something of a family trait since his own father had read only two books – *Pig Sticking and Hog Hunting in India* by Baden-Powell and *Mein Kampf.* And when one thought what a bad lot was the writer of the latter, it only proved how dangerous reading and writing could be. As to poetry – Hector frequently worried about Molly's fascination with the stuff, she'd even been known to write some of the rubbish herself, not that Hector had seen it. He'd been quite hurt when she said she didn't want to show him, he really couldn't understand why. Rich as she was, Annie should have been one of *them* but somehow she never was, and there were times when Hector had the uncomfortable feeling that she was laughing at them all.

The vicar and his wife arrived. Hector waved, indicating spare seats in the front. The couple seemed to hover, twisting this way and that, biting their lips, anxiety oozing from every pore. The vicar whispered to his wife, she nodded and they stood, still twitching, at the back of the hall but safely in the middle. Hector grumbled to Porky that it was what one would expect from a cleric.

But Hector was in for a greater shock. Hovering at the doorway of the hall was Molly. She looked around anxiously registering who was where and with whom. Her face was drawn and anxious, the face of someone who had not been sleeping well – as she hadn't. For nights now she had tossed and turned knowing what she was going to have to do and knowing how difficult it would be.

She gave Hector a weak almost apologetic little smile and then did a strange little bob as if in front of the high altar and, with the shifty expression of one who is caught doing wrong, sidled awkwardly on to a seat behind the Churchill Drive inhabitants. There she sat studying her hands intently, as if she had noticed them for the first time, but still she could feel Hector's glowering look burrowing into her.

At eight-fifteen on the dot Colin called the meeting to order. Colin should have been a politician: he had craftily arranged the time on purpose to ensure that *EastEnders* was over and the gathering would be well attended. At the sight of Colin's Guards' tie Hector had to physically restrain an empurpled Porky.

Within minutes of Colin beginning Hector's heart was sinking rapidly as he realised that here was a highly professional adversary. He was explaining the reasons behind his Elizabethan Village Tourist Attraction, the EVTA as he referred to it.

Behind him was a large plan of the projected village which he explained at length, using a snooker cue as a pointer. He talked about tourism, and Hector, Bat and Porky yawned ostentatiously in unison. Then he moved to job creation – they yawned again. Added prosperity for the village drew a loud snort from Porky. And then, and then Colin did something very clever. He stated he was doing it to make himself even richer. The left side of the hall shuddered at such blatant vulgarity, the right side exploded into laughter, cheers and shouts of 'Good on yer, mate,' and 'Good luck'. In this one sentence Colin totally exploded what they had fondly hoped was one of Porky's most potent arguments – the ruination of the village for greed.

Then the need for the large television was revealed as the lights were switched off – there were no dimmer switches, the village could not afford them – and a video of similar ventures was shown. The film was worthy of the English Tourist Board at its best. Everything was in lovely colour, Morris dancers danced, knights jousted, town criers cried, and all the people were happy – no litter, no excessive noise, not a coach or a lager lout in sight.

The lights were switched on. Flanked by his experts and advisers, Colin smiled and asked if there were any questions?

Porky lumbered to his feet.

'Mr Mann. These jobs you're creating. Once the building work's been done what jobs will be available for our people? Tell me that.' He jutted his jaw forward aggressively in the bulldog manner that had frightened many a subordinate over the years.

'I shall need shop assistants, waitresses, cooks, guides, maintenance men, gardeners, car park attendants.'

'Seasonal work, then?' Porky smiled smugly. 'You'll be using students, those sort of people. Not really work for the villagers.'

'Good gracious no, General. I'm relying on the project running for twelve months of the year. Hence the covered video experience hall and the swimming pool. No, these will be permanent posts and, what is more, our company policy will be to employ only local people.'

Porky sat down and harrumphed his annoyance.

'What have swimming pools got to do with Elizabethan villages?' Nan Carter from Myrtle Cottage asked with indignation since not only was she their resident botanist, she was also highly regarded as the local historian.

'Not a lot, Mrs Carter, I admit. But then the English weather being as it is you've got to offer indoor alternatives. And we shall be issuing "passports" to all locals, who will have free use of all the amenities.'

The cheer nearly raised the roof.

'You do realise you risk destroying one of England's most beautiful villages?' It was Mrs Martin from The Larches on the new estate.

'I don't think so, Madam. Far less damage, in fact, than the new estate has caused. I shall be building to blend in with the old village, which can hardly be said of the houses on your estate, can it?' He smiled his beautiful smile, which immediately removed any sting from his remarks.

'I suppose so.' Mrs Martin sat down quietly. Molly was most impressed with Colin's skill in dealing with someone she had found so belligerent, and whom she had been avoiding ever since.

This was dreadful, thought Hector, they were getting nowhere. He stood up; Molly looked anxiously at the floor. She always did when he was about to speak, anxious that he might make a fool of himself.

'I do feel, Mr Mann, that the relevant authorities such as English Heritage, the National Trust, the Department of the Environment might not be too happy when we inform them of your plans. As we shall, Mr Mann, as we shall,' Hector said in his best barrister-at-law manner.

'No need, Mr Parminter,' Colin said, breezily. 'I've already informed them and sent the draft plans. I have also asked for any advice they can give me and assured them that we shall liaise throughout.'

Hector felt dreadfully foolish as he sat down and vowed to say no more. There were others willing, however, and as the meeting progressed it began to get more heated. Hector did wish people would not fall into the use of clichés quite so promptly. It was only a few minutes before one old buffer was saying 'I didn't fight Hitler for this . . .' Why was Adolf always brought into these arguments, wondered Hector, what did he have to do with it? Someone quoted 'this sceptred isle . . .'. One woman feared an upsurge in rape and pillage and another felt it would be dangerous for dogs. All in all it was a pretty limp fight. And then Cuckoo leapt up, pink frills all aflutter, as if even the fabric of her dress was agitated.

'Young man, you're a mountebank,' she shrilled, to hisses from the right side. 'You come here unasked and inflict your vulgar commercialism on us innocent citizens, giving nothing in return. I won't have it, do you hear?' She waved her umbrella menacingly.

'Sit down you potty old crow,' an anonymous voice called out. 'It's all right for the likes of you,' shouted another.

Hector leapt up, duty bound to defend his mother, whom he had tried to dissuade from coming but, unsure what to do or say, he just whirled round impotently.

'Please, please, everyone,' Colin was quickly on his feet, arms raised, like the Pope when he blessed people. 'I don't want any hard feelings or people falling out over my little plans. And whoever shouted like that should apologise to dear Mrs Parminter. Now,' he nodded in the direction of an aide. 'I hadn't planned to mention this tonight since I didn't want to be thought unfair to the opposition. But . . .' The aide unrolled a large plan which he pinned up on the wall. Colin picked up his snooker cue again. 'You see these fields of Farmer Feather's – the ones at the back of the church – I've purchased them, and shall be applying for planning permission to build fifty houses . . .' he could not finish, there was such uproar. Those on the left were indignant with rage and those on the right furious at what they saw as his betrayal. Colin patiently waited for the uproar to clear and finally held his hand up. 'To build fifty houses, of which twenty will be low-cost houses for purchase by local first-time buyers . . . whose mortgages I will be pleased to subsidise.'

'That's done it, Porky. We've lost. They'll march on Number 10 for that,' Hector said despondently. 'The MP will have to support that.'

'Why did you have to sell the bloody land in the first place?' Porky growled.

'Hang on, I didn't. It was my old man.'

'Whoever it was it's your family's fault.' And Porky angrily stormed out of the hall.

Hector followed. As he drew level with Molly he stopped. He drew himself to his full six feet, squared his shoulders, and glowered so ferociously that Molly, who had stood up, sat down again quickly.

'Traitor,' he hissed.

'That's not fair, Hector. I just think it may be good for the village.'

'Too much poetry, that's your problem,' he rumbled, before disappearing into the night leaving a perplexed Molly to join the others who had enthusiastically descended upon the refreshments.

Colin had obviously hoped that, over the pasties and beer he had supplied so generously, the debate would continue amicably and constructively. He was wrong. Quickly tempers flared again. Voices were raised, fingers stabbed the air, fists were shaken. The culmination came when Reg Whistler looked as if he were about to throw his pint of beer over Sean Martin from Wood Close. But, thinking better of it, he downed the drink in one and decided to give Sean a piece of his mind instead.

'You incomers have no right to interfere in our village. You don't belong.'

'It's my village too,' incensed, Sean raised his voice. 'At least I own my own house which is more than can be said of you lot in your subsidised housing paid for by the likes of us.'

There was a buzz of smug agreement from the Wood Close residents who lined up behind Sean and faced the opposition as one. Reg was now flanked by the rest of the tenants and a very ruffled group who had long since purchased their council houses.

'Think you're something special 'cause you live in Wood Close, don't you?' Reg sneered. 'Know what the dustmen call you lot? Go on, ask me. Cornflakes Close, that's what they call you – that's all you've got in your dustbins. Poor quality of dustbins they've told us.'

'I beg your pardon,' Sean blustered.

'Snooty lot. And you ain't got two coppers to scratch your arse, you lot.'

'Well, really.' Jill Martin clutched at her husband's arm.

'Poor as church mice with your mortgages and HP payments. Don't you tell me what's what, we know.' Reg was beside himself with excitement now.

'And who's not paid their Poll Tax, then?' Sean trumpeted triumphantly. Sean worked in the local Poll Tax office and knew these things. There was a gasp of shock from the Wood Close residents at such unprofessional conduct on his part.

But at the words 'Poll Tax' it was as if a red blanket had been waved at a crowd of bulls. A roar went up from Churchill Drive and that was when Reg hit Sean smack in the face and the fight that followed was swift and bloody before Colin could restore sanity.

Molly made her way up the main street alone. Her hands were deep in her pockets as she thought of the consequences of the meeting. Ahead of her were some of the Wood Close people who paused as if making up their mind whether to go into the Parminter Arms.

'But *they* might be there,' she heard Jill Martin say.

'Who, that horrible Whistler fellow?'

'No, those dreadful old boiled shirts. I can't stand them, I can feel the hairs on my arms when they're about. They think they own the bloody place and everyone in it.'

'What, old Hector and Co?' A man laughed unpleasantly.

'You don't want to let those old fossils worry you, Jill. Pompous old farts the lot of them . . .'

'Good night, everyone,' Molly had the satisfaction of saying sweetly as she drew abreast of them. She continued up the High Street with dignity. But inside she was seething with anger; she and Hector might be in disagreement, but how dare those people call him names like that? She wanted to hit them, hit them really hard.

She turned into the drive. What on earth was happening to her world and to her? No one in the past would have talked about Hector like that. He'd always been a respected squire, almost a paterfamilias to the whole village. Someone to whom people brought their problems. And here was she, normally a placid soul, who in a war would automatically be a conscientious objector, longing to hit someone with her handbag.

Everyone seemed to be fighting. First at the fête and then tonight. In the past there might have been the odd scrap outside the pub on a Saturday night with no hard feelings the next day. Now the fighting was aggressive, it occurred without people being drunk and was far more frightening.

Mrs Hodgson's theory was that this new aggression in today's society was due to 'something in the water'. What it was or who had put it there Mrs Hodgson was splendidly vague about, while still managing to imply that it was some dastardly plot. Molly had laughed at her but now she wondered: maybe Mrs Hodgson was right after all. Perhaps there was a pollutant turning everybody nasty.

What was happening was a tragedy and Molly knew she wasn't exaggerating.

Chapter 9

'Civil War'

AFTER THE MEETING it was as if the whole village were ruffling its feathers in indignation.

The Churchill Drive contingent and their assorted followers were still full of fury that 'they' should have the temerity, the cheek, to stand in the way of the progress of 'us'. The executive wives on the executive housing estate were rueing the day they had sided with Hector and Co. for the following day not one cleaning lady turned up for work – there were some things more important than money they declared, laying down their ozone-friendly polish and feather dusters. While strike action persisted many a nail was broken, much dust settled at Wood Close and many a coffee morning was cancelled.

Those in the village who were against Colin seethed with voluble indignation – 'the history of centuries is at risk'; 'the heritage, of which we are only the custodians, must be defended'; 'we are witnessing the destruction of rural England'; – blah, blah! The group might have been short on ideas but was far from short of clichés. What they did not say, except to their nearest and dearest, was that they resented the likely inconvenience and, probably of most importance, it would lead to a devaluation of their houses.

In those families where there was disagreement the atmosphere was most unpleasant. Cuckoo was making Hope's life hell, ranting against her traitorous daughter-in-law as if Hope had personally orchestrated Molly's defection. Cuckoo refused to have Molly anywhere near her, an action which could not have made Molly happier.

Hector was a different matter, and his reaction made her sad for he had barely spoken to her since the meeting. They were like Roundheads and Cavaliers, thought Molly. She was certain she was a Cavalier, for she could not imagine herself as a Roundhead. But in that case Hector would have to be the Roundhead and she couldn't, for one moment, imagine that – he liked his whisky too much, and weren't Roundheads an abstemious crew? In any case he had had a stained-glass window put in the church to the memory of his parents so he couldn't possibly be. The only other comparable situation she could think of was, she supposed, the American civil war. But Molly's knowledge of American history was sketchy to say the least, gleaned mostly from the cinema. She had, in the past when she still went to the cinema, seen *Gone with the Wind* at least ten times, a habit which annoyed Hector out of all proportion. He'd accused her of fantasising over Clark Gable and of being stupidly romantic, as well as wasting money. She'd never told him why she had kept going, she realised no man would ever understand. She had gone because she hoped each time to find that the end had changed. But at least, as a result, she knew a little more about that particular war than Hector did. She rather fancied herself as a Confederate – such a pretty grey uniform – but since they had lost the war she felt it wasn't too good a choice and opted to be a *Unionist* instead. For several days, as a joke and with the hope of thawing the freeze between them, she had worn only dark blue. As a gesture it was completely lost on Hector, for when she explained she was a Unionist he had thought she'd gone mad and joined a trade union.

Hector's attitude was bad enough but matters were made worse when she realised that Mrs Hodgson had given up speaking to her; these days she only sniffed. It was a most unpleasant sniff and had nothing to do with a cold in the head. Molly was well aware of the judicious use of the sniff. In the far distant days when they could still afford a cook – an autocratic woman who had terrified her witless – Molly had first been introduced to the domestic worker's sniff. She had for ages thought it was just her bad luck until Lulu had confided that her cook did the same. The one thing the sniff indicated was that things were far from well below stairs. The atmosphere in the kitchen was becoming so intolerable that it could not be allowed to continue.

'Mrs Hodgson, I don't see why we should fall out over this whole silly business.'

A momentous snort was the only reply from the region of the sink where Mrs Hodgson was allegedly scouring the pots.

'Please, Mrs Hodgson.' Molly pleaded to her cleaning lady's back which was rigid with hurt, and goodness knows what other emotions. Until recent events Molly had not been aware just how fond of the woman she had become, how much she missed their natters, how she looked forward to Mrs Hodgson's mornings. And if she never spoke to her again then Molly would never find out her particular little problem. All this antagonism was wearing her down rapidly.

Sniff.

'Stop that stupid sniffing. This minute,' Molly said so sharply it took her by surprise as she slammed the apple she had been peeling down on the table. 'I can't stand it a moment longer, do you understand? If you won't speak to me then get out, that's all I've got to say.'

'Pardon?'

'You heard me.'

'I'm angry.'

'So am I.'

The protagonists glared at each other across the table. Molly with apple corer in her hand, Mrs Hodgson with a Brillo pad in hers.

What Molly did not know was that Jean Hodgson was not really cross with her but with the whole impossible situation, and most of all with her husband and her neighbours. It was they who had asked her to be their mole. It was hardly her fault if, in the process of her 'moleing', she had changed loyalties and sides.

They should never have asked her in the first place. Had they known her other secret they never would have — her first secret being her little problem with Mr Hodgson. Unknown to anyone who knew her, so well had she disguised her feelings, Jean Hodgson was a sham, for she was a roaring snob. She had stayed

94

with the Parminters rather than move to Wood Close with all the other cleaning women because she felt strongly that there was more kudos in working for the Squire's wife. Although, at times of elections, she always had a Labour poster prominently displayed in her front-room window, in the secrecy of the polling booth she always voted Tory. Her husband, a trade unionist and staunch, card-carrying, member of the Labour party, would have murdered her had he known. But her biggest secret of all was that she thought Hector the most wonderful man in the world and those nights after her hubby had had his way with her she would settle down to sleep thinking of Hector in the certainty that such a gentleman would never do to her what her husband did. If she was very lucky she would dream of him. So, given all this, it was inevitable that she would cross the floor, so to speak.

She knew exactly what Mrs Parminter was going through – her Fred hadn't spoken to her either all that week. With him, of course, there was a plus side. Since he wasn't speaking to her he seemed to have lost the 'urge' to do it. That, at least, was a blessing.

'I'm sorry, Mrs Parminter,' she suddenly blurted out.

'So am I. I wish Colin Mann had never come here.'

'Me too.'

'Let's have a coffee, shall we?'

'What a good idea, just like old times,' said Mrs Hodgson, hauling the kettle on to the Aga. And when she sniffed this time it was a genuine sniff, as tears welled up in her eyes.

Molly and Mrs Hodgson might be friends again but it did not solve the problem with Hector and the others. She was certain that Hyacinth had cut her dead the other day. Certainly she had popped into the post office rather sharply. Pat Jenkins had phoned up to cancel a dinner party with such a lame excuse that Molly nearly laughed. And the telephone seemed very silent these days. Lulu had told her she was being stupid. Molly had resented this hugely. Lulu might be her best friend but Molly felt that did not give her the right to call her stupid or any other rude names. She had often thought Lulu was behaving like an idiot with some of the more unsuitable men in her life, but she had always had the courtesy not to tell her friend what she thought. Molly certainly did not subscribe to the idea that friendship gave one the right to blunt speaking – as bad as being honest about a friend's new hat, and as dangerous. On the contrary, Molly felt it was critically important, where friends were concerned, *never* to speak one's mind.

The one good thing to come out of the whole catastrophe was that she saw much more of Annie English. Quite often now she crossed the village to the other side where Annie had a fine Georgian house on the road to Lynchester. She had always liked Annie and, unlike Hector, adored her cooking. But she had never been able to see much of her because of Hector's innate suspicion of anyone artistic, and thus of anyone he did not fully understand. In fact Molly was certain he was afraid of Annie.

It amazed Molly how the woman ever found time to write the huge books which were the source of her fortune. Whenever she visited, the house was teeming with people. It was as if Annie had once held a party which somehow had tipped over into the next one and so the party never appeared to end and never would.

Molly admired and envied Annie's independence. There had once been a Mr English but Annie was admirably vague about him. Instead she had a succession of somewhat exotic live-in lovers rather younger than herself. In normal circumstances the local community would have been sufficiently shocked to ostracise her but Annie was not normal – Annie was a celebrity, and the village was proud that someone so famous should choose to live amongst them. And so, disapproval and censure in her case were set aside.

But Molly realised even if Annie had been cut dead by the whole village she still would not care. And here was Molly fretting and worrying about the effect her defection had caused, while Annie could not give a damn. She did not care a tinker's cuss what people thought of her. She was how she was and they had to take her or leave her. Annie had no intention of changing for anyone.

It was on one of her visits to Annie's, fairly frequent in the past couple of weeks as if visiting a co-conspirator, that she first saw a dim dawning of hope in the intolerable situation with Hector and the village. She sat in Annie's drawing-room amazed as she always was by the eclectic style of the room: a huge jumble of colours, fabrics, periods, and yet it worked.

'You're getting your knickers in a twist over nothing, you know,' Annie said, as she mixed Molly a ferocious gin and tonic, which from past experience Molly knew would rapidly make her legless.

'But I hate to see the village divided in this way.'

'This village is always divided over something or other. It thrives on feuds. If the villagers could not find something to divide them they would invent a problem. Look at the fuss every time someone wants to organise a bypass petition – I hear bossy Potter-Smythe and her husband have been banned from the pub.'

'Really? I hadn't heard about that, it will make life very difficult for them.'

'It's her own fault. Never organise anything, never join a committee – that's been my motto all my life and one I stick to religiously, it's safer.'

'The poor woman only thought she was acting for the good of all.'

'Her sort usually do, that's their problem. It's also why I find them so insufferable.'

'Oh, I don't know . . .' Molly said rather limply.

'Look at the drama over the community centre when it was first built – half wanting it and half loathing it. And remember the row when Hector sold Upper Cottages to that developer? You and he suffered agonies for months.'

'That's true, I'd quite forgotten.' Molly sipped the drink, so strong she could feel it rushing to her brain and knocking cells senseless in its wake. 'I know you're right but it still makes me sad.'

'It won't happen, you realise – Colin's mock village, I mean. More's the pity, this place needs something to liven it up, give employment. Have you seen those poor kids from Churchill Drive of an evening, standing about the Green, loitering with nothing to do?'

'But Colin's village wouldn't help them, it would close in the evenings, they still wouldn't have anywhere to go to amuse themselves.'

'It would give them jobs and money and then they could afford to go to Lynchester to the cinema, the discos. They might be able to afford little cars, motor bikes.'

'Then they would all kill themselves.'

'You are in a doom, aren't you, Molly? What a pessimistic idea. But it won't happen because it won't come to anything.'

'It won't?'

'No one seems to have worked it out. He's using this mock village as a cover. He wants people to get hysterically worked up about it so the village is divided and there's less chance of a united front to object to his beastly housing estate. That will really ruin the village – fifty houses be blowed, there's room for several hundred horrible ticky-tacky boxes and undoubtedly he'll apply for the lot. I'm sure he's no intention of building his mock village on his own doorstep – it's the last thing he wants. All that rubbish about making him richer – oh yes, he'll be richer but not by spoiling his view from his own front door.'

'You think so? Do you really think he could be that Machiavellian? I don't think I like that at all.' Molly was quite affronted at such an idea but not enough to refuse another gin, which was an error.

'But whose cottage is right plonk in the middle of the proposed site? Whose driveway cuts right across the land?' Annie asked forcefully.

'Gussie Ford at Dump End Cottage.'

'Exactly. He can offer her a million and Gussie won't budge an inch. She wouldn't leave her dogs for all the money in the world.'

'She could take her dogs with her,' Molly reasoned.

'Not the dead ones. Not the ones in her pets' cemetery. She'll never leave them – ever. Have another gin?'

And so excited was Molly that she did, which was stupid in the extreme as she found out when she had to weave her way home right across the centre of the village, hoping no one would notice her.

Outside Mrs Potter-Smythe's a 'For Sale' sign was up. Without thinking too deeply about what she was going to do, Molly stalked up the path, knocked on the door and was invited in by a very surprised Mrs Potter-Smythe. Inside the cottage there was no sign of Mr Potter-Smythe and Molly realised she had never met him and wondered if he was a figment of Mrs P-S's imagination. But it was hardly the sort of thing one could ask. Over a totally super-fluous sherry Molly begged Mrs Potter-Smythe to reconsider her decision to sell, pointing out that there were not nearly enough people with her fine-tuned community spirit. She was moved almost to tears as she explained how much she personally had come to depend on her over the party subscriptions. She had to blow her nose as she declared what a great loss it would be to one and all if the Potter-Smythes decamped.

Mrs Potter-Smythe twittered, and blushed – which was so out of character and looked so peculiar on such a large, big-boned woman that it made Molly hiccup – or was it the excess of alcohol? Molly was past caring.

She had to promise to call Mrs Potter-Smythe Sybil, and having done so, she suddenly found it necessary to kiss Sybil on the cheek which seemed to surprise the recipient as much as it did her. This prompted Sybil to launch into a long speech of how happy she'd been here, how much she was dreading having to start anew. Arm in arm they marched outside and ceremoniously knocked the 'For Sale' sign down. Then they went back inside for a celebration drink.

'You're drunk,' Hector said accusingly upon her unsteady return to The Hall.

'Yes, I am,' Molly replied, she thought, with a marked degree of dignity.

'Disgusting! If there's one thing I can't stand it's a woman the worse for drink.'

Molly snorted with derision. 'You really have a lot of nerve Hector. You're the last person with the right to criticise me. How many times have I seen you dead drunk, not just tipsy as I am?'

'That's different,' Hector said huffily.

'There's no difference at all. If you can get drunk so can I.'

'But Molly . . .'

'The problem with you, Hector, is you were born in the wrong age – you would have been far happier as a Victorian.' She said it with great seriousness as if she had given the subject a lot of thought, which was surprising. She had only just this minute thought of Hector as a Victorian. But, having thought it, she could not imagine why it had not occurred to her long ago. 'You're like a paterfamilias telling me what, and what not, I can do.' She was warming to her theme now. 'Well you can't. I'm a liberated woman and you're pompous – so there.'

'Molly!'

'Oh shut up Mollying me. I'm fed up, I really am.'

'There seems little point in continuing this conversation in your present condition,' Hector said with such an air of pained disapproval that Molly had an almost uncontrollable urge to hit him. 'Where's my supper?'

'Get your own . . .' Molly swayed out of the sitting-room, enjoying the satisfaction of rendering Hector speechless.

The next morning she apologised, which was a mistake. It gave Hector the excuse to lecture her which she resented enormously. The silliest thing she had said last night was that she was a liberated woman – nothing, she realised in the cold light of morning, was further from the truth. Hector had her firmly squashed under his little finger. As he discoursed on her behaviour she resolved that things must change; she refused to spend the rest of her life as such a wimp. She waited patiently for a pause in Hector's lecture and then, without a by-your-leave, she interrupted.

'I said I was sorry, Hector, I'm beginning to regret I did. Last night I said you were pompous – I retract any apology I made in relation to that statement. It's true. Without doubt you can be one of the most pompous people I know and I suggest you do something about it.' She turned on her heel and left, with the heady satisfaction of rendering Hector speechless twice in twenty-four hours.

The day before the party to celebrate her engagement Tabby returned from London to announce she had given Sebastian his ring back.

'But why? Sebastian seemed such a nice and charming boy,'

Molly asked with concern, though she wondered why, when she saw how cheerful her daughter looked.

'He is, that's the problem.'

'Oh, Tabby, I just don't understand.'

'It's so drab being with someone so relentlessly nice – it's so uncool.'

Uncool – that was a word Molly had used in the sixties when proving how trendy she was. It was strange how slang seemed to wait twenty years before repeating itself.

'But even your father liked him.'

'Exactly.' Tabby rolled her eyes heavenward exaggeratedly.

'I don't see it at all, in my day any girl would have given anything for a fellow like Sebastian.'

'But it's not your day any more is it, Mummy?' Tabby gave Molly her clenched-teeth smile, always a danger sign.

'I give up,' Molly sighed.

'That's what I did, or rather I did to Seb,' Tabby said brightly. 'Bless you, Mummy, I just knew you would understand. Did you get any Potnoodles in for me?'

At this point Molly felt a good mother would have given Tabby a sage and helpful lecture upon love and Sebastian's qualities. She didn't. It was not out of cowardice but because she could still remember her own resentment when her mother had lectured her for giving up a man she thought more suitable for Molly than Hector. It was Tabby's life after all to lead as she wanted, even if it was hard to stand back and let her make mistakes. Molly felt that if, prior to conception, prospective parents were told that the first sixteen years were the easiest and that after that the worry got worse, it would ensure the end of civilisation.

It was too late to cancel the party. Molly had been cooking non-stop for the past three weeks. The freezer was full to bursting. There was nothing for it but to go ahead.

Hector was none too pleased when she explained what had happened. It was a difficult interview given that Hector was still smarting, not only from her defection but from her views of his personality.

'What do you mean, it's OFF?' he barked at her.

'He's too nice, it appears.'

'But that's what made him so right for her,' Hector sounded as puzzled as he looked.

'Maybe we should have disapproved a bit more, then they might have stayed engaged,' Molly said sadly.

'You mean because we liked him . . . that made her go off him?'

'Probably.'

'I don't understand the young.' He shook his head.

'If it's any consolation, neither do I,' Molly put her hand out tentatively towards him. Hector grabbed it as if with relief. 'Pax?' She smiled at him.

'Oh, please. It's been dreadfully lonely the past few weeks.'

'For me too,' she laughed, relieved their feud was over. Hector gave her a small kiss which she realised was all she was going to get for the time being – Hector was not an over-demonstrative person.

'I ordered all that champagne,' he said, aggrieved.

'Can't you unorder it and get something else?'

'I doubt it. I didn't get it from Brentwoods – it was much cheaper from Tesco. I'm not sure if I can take it back.'

'Then I should save it for the next time. I've an idea that Tabby is going to be one of those young women who make quite a habit of getting engaged.'

'Oh Lor' . . .'

Molly spent most of the afternoon telephoning, explaining to everyone that everything had changed and it was no longer an engagement party but just an ordinary one instead. It would have been too embarrassing if people arrived with presents for the happy couple.

The following day Molly was nervous. This would be the first time that the village had been together for a function since the dreadful general meeting.

The start of the party was sticky. Molly and Annie stood on one side of the room with the others lined up, somewhat belligerently, they thought, on the other side. Lulu flitted back and forth between the two groups pretending nothing was untoward. Molly minded, Annie found it funny.

But it was Annie who suggested that perhaps the solution was to spike Hector's champagne cocktail with another bottle of brandy. He had decided that having got the champagne they might as well drink it, it wasn't as if it were vintage. He had also worked out that it would probably be cheaper in the long run as everyone would get drunk faster. Molly wondered why men so often evaluated alcohol by its potency and ability to get one drunk as quickly as possible – it was extremely juvenile, she thought.

With scant regard to cost Molly tipped a whole bottle of Courvoisier into the cocktail and prayed Hector did not find out until she could replace it. The result was almost instantaneous, judging by the increase in noise which rose to a satisfying crescendo. Soon people were crossing the invisible line to talk to Annie and Molly once again.

This effect had happened just in time – the Manns were the last guests to arrive and as a result received a tumultuous welcome which took both of them by surprise. They had a crate of vintage champagne. Hector, through the haze of alcohol attempted to be a little distant, but not so distant Molly noted, to refuse the gift which, instead of being served, was hastily secreted for another day.

Molly could not get out of her mind Annie's theory on Colin. She looked at the man and could not believe it to be true. He had such an honest, open face, no doubt it was Annie's over-active writer's imagination at work. When she saw the Manns moving about the room in an almost apologetic way Molly felt angry for, and almost protective towards, him. She wished some sort of solution could be found so that everybody was happy. She was fully aware that in the morning, when the cocktails had worn off, things were likely to return to antagonism. Everyone now was so drunk that Ken Livingstone would have been welcomed with open arms.

Chapter 10

Hector Discovers a Solution

OCTOBER STALKED IN, making a great fuss, and was wet. During the unusually long hot summer Molly had been able to forget about the flashings for a while. But now the old worry returned. Apparently they were in for yet another winter without the problem being solved, for each time she raised the subject with Hector he always seemed to have far more pressing business elsewhere.

Admittedly he was very busy. He had his council work, the Conservative Association that seemed to take up more and more of his time, and now there was the Colin Mann affair. Molly was no longer *au fait* with what was going on. This was not Hector being spiteful. Rather, Molly had decided if they were to live in harmony it was better if she knew as little as possible and did not become involved. Judging by the phone calls and the number of meetings called with Porky and Co. they were very active in their campaign.

She was busily cleaning the silver for she had had a mysterious telephone call from her son James announcing he was coming home for the weekend with a friend, and could things be 'decent'. Molly, although consumed with curiosity, did not like to ask whom he was bringing for she felt strongly that parents should never pry – hence the mystery was of her own creation.

Molly was in a fair tizzy. It could only mean one thing, she explained to Hector: he was bringing a young woman home to meet them and, if he was doing that, then it was serious. It was important for James' sake that they should make a good impression and Molly insisted on the main part of the house being opened up. Hector was all for the girl meeting them as they really were and that they should entertain in their normal quarters. This argument kept them going for several days but Molly emerged victorious and Hector grumbled magnificently as he opened up the rest of the house. There was so much to do that Molly had to persuade Mrs Hodgson to get her sister, Jilly, to give a hand, which she would, on occasion, if bribed sufficiently and provided she did not have to lift anything since, as she was fond of saying, she had a back. Molly always wanted to congratulate her whenever she said this but it was too obvious a comment even to be funny.

It always saddened Molly when she went into these rooms – it struck her as a house which had been deserted and had been left to moulder alone. There was always the musty smell of insufficiently aired rooms which required vast applications of Shake-and-Vac by Mrs Hodgson and Jilly. Molly felt sorry for the rooms' contents, which were so rarely admired by anyone. She thought how dreadful it must be to be a Chippendale mirror and then never have anyone look at themselves in you, or be a chair and not be sat on – as though your existence were of no importance. She kept such thoughts to herself, knowing that Hector would have looked at her most askance if she had confided in him.

Molly made a special trip to Lynchester to buy enough food for the weekend. It was ages since they had had anyone to stay – Sebastian had been the last and as he had spent all his time in the kitchen that didn't really count. Normally careful and watchful of every penny she spent, she felt that the usual restrictions did not apply to a special occasion like this. So she bought smoked salmon, a huge piece of sirloin, and a brace of pheasants. They could have had a brace from the park, or wild duck, but she could no longer persuade Hector to shoot them. He had given up about five years ago, announcing one day that it upset him too much and made him think of Jemima Puddleduck all the time. While sympathising with such finer feelings, it was of enormous inconvenience to Molly since game had always played such an important part in her careful budgeting.

The food hall of Marks and Spencer was Molly's downfall and she had to steel herself to write the cheque, imagining her bank manager's pained expression when he saw it.

'You've gone potty, woman,' was Hector's greeting as he helped her unload the car. This was proving difficult, for whenever he went to pick up a bag Molly, fearful that he might see the contents, swooped on it like a demented shoplifter. She knew that Hector would not understand the necessity of bagged and washed salad, nor ready-made quiches – best for him that he saw none of it.

As it was, he had a good old rumble about the flowers which, Molly admitted, did look excessive but then she knew from past experience that at The Hall one either had to have banks of flowers or none at all. One pot of chrysanthemums ended up looking like a bunch of daisies, the rooms were so vast.

The silver shone, fires glowed, the flowers looked wonderful. Hector and Molly sat in the formal drawing-room having a courage-boosting drink while they waited for their son and his friend to arrive. Or rather Molly was in need of fortification whereas Hector, she noted admiringly, was completely calm.

'Doesn't it all look so lovely,' Molly said proudly.

'Wonderful,' Hector too looked around the elegant, polished room with pride. He raised his glass to Molly. 'Wish we could do this more often.'

'It would be nice. The rooms seem to be calling out to be lived in.'

'I haven't given you much of a life, Molly. I am truly sorry, you know.'

'What on earth do you mean?' Molly looked up, startled.

'I'm sorry I'm such a failure. You should always live like this, you deserve it. I've let you down . . .'

'Don't be silly, Hector, it's not your fault.'

'But it is. If only I was clever like that Mann chappie, or like Lulu's son, and able to make masses of money, then I could give you the life you should be leading – using these rooms, with maids, cooks, that sort of thing. Then you wouldn't have to work so hard.' He looked dolefully into his drink.

'Darling, please don't talk this way. I'm perfectly happy.'

'If I hadn't been so insistent you might have married John Wellborough.'

'Who?' she feigned ignorance, for normally if John's name ever came up, Hector was likely to disintegrate into a huge jealous sulk.

'You knew him before you knew me. I spoiled it for you, turning up when I did. If you had married him you'd have everything you could possibly want in the world.'

'And probably be divorced, to boot. He's on his fifth wife you know.'

'Ah, but if he'd married you he would never have needed the other four, would he?' There was a distinct tremor in Hector's voice.

'Oh, my darling, what a sweet thing to say. I married the only man I wanted. I've never regretted my decision. I love you, Hector,' she said, aware that a tear was tumbling down her cheek and into her gin.

'You mean that?'

'Of course I do,' she said, crossing the room to sit beside him, taking his hand in hers.

'Even if I'm pompous.' He looked at her slyly.

'Ah, even more so because of that,' she laughed and he leant forward and kissed her gently full on her mouth. She put up her hand to touch his face and felt the suspicion of a tear on his too. 'Oh, Hector, I love you, so much' she sighed, just as a car squealed to a halt outside.

The food was perfect and Hector had excelled himself in his rootling amongst the few bottles left in his cellar. Mrs Hodgson had volunteered to come in and do the washing up, so everything should have been perfect. But it wasn't. Molly did not like her guest and as the evening wore on she was not too sure about her son either.

Shar, the girlfriend, who was really called Charlotte Shawton-Smythe, did not impress Molly from the moment she confidently swept into the front hall, had imperiously held out her hand as if bestowing a favour, and proceeded to talk non-stop. While Molly was fully aware that some people talked too much from shyness she was sure this was not one of those cases. She had always felt that a degree of backwardness in coming forward was not to be sniffed at in the young.

In her bathtime daydreams Molly had a fantasy that one day a sweet, eager for love, young woman would enter her life on James' arm. The girl in the dream was always blonde with china-blue eyes, and wearing a pretty frilled dress – not black-haired, dark-eyed, white-skinned, with a scarlet slash of a mouth which matched exactly the red of her dress. A dress which even Molly, ignorant of fashion as she was, could recognise as having cost the earth.

'I've a friend called Sybil Potter-Smythe, I wonder if you're related,' Molly said, since she couldn't think of anything else.

'I doubt it.' Whatever Shar said it seemed as if she were sneering; an awful impediment, Molly thought.

'Smythe is only a tarted-up spelling of Smith,' Hector volunteered helpfully, to be rewarded with a look of such loathing from Shar that Molly was amazed he survived it.

'Really, Dad,' James frowned.

Hector, mistaking James' 'really' for a question rather than an admonishment, launched into one of his lectures; unfortunately this one was about the sort of people who disguised the fact they were Smiths. Then he confided what he thought about hyphens which, he was at pains to let everyone know, wasn't much. It wasn't until much later when they went to bed that the whole dreadful muddle was sorted out. Molly, gently pointing out that perhaps Hector had been a little rude, learnt, to her horror and his, that he hadn't heard Shar's full name – only the Shawton bit and not the hyphen or the Smythe.

'Oh, Lor' now what do I do? Apologise?'

'I fear that might make matters worse. Say nothing, it's usually best in such circumstances. Let's hope she just thinks you're an eccentric or something.'

'You don't seriously think that James is thinking of marrying her, do you?'

'I do hope not. She seems so hard, not at all what I'd imagined. But don't you think that James has changed too? All he seemed to want to talk about was money.'

'People do discuss money these days. It's all to do with the whizz kids in the City.'

'But I thought they were all poor now after that large explosion.'

'Big Bang? No, that's what made them rich; Black Monday made them poor.'

'It must be most uncomfortable being rich one day and poor the next, hardly worth being rich if that's what happens. But James seems to be so grown up, for some time I've felt he was older than me, quite silly.'

'Pomposity, all bankers catch it, haven't you noticed? In any case I thought you were the expert on that particular characteristic,' and he gave her his look that was not exactly sly but more as if was telling her he was winning a point and saying 'Got yer.'

'I hope he recovers or grows out of it then,' she said, preferring to ignore the 'pompous' comment. That was the trouble with Scorpios like Hector: she had long ago learnt that they never forgot a slight. No doubt Hector would go to his grave still making digs at her for every imagined insult.

'Did you notice the way she was looking at the furniture and paintings? Like an antique dealer,' Hector shuddered with distaste. He spent his life refusing to see dealers let alone sell to them. To him they were all vultures circling over his beloved house and contents as if it were a rotting corpse.

'She actually mentioned one or two pieces of furniture to James, I heard her.'

'Good God,' he said, amazed that there were people other than antique dealers and the insurance blokes who discussed one's furniture.

'And did you notice how many people she knows? Amazing. She even seems to know Prince Charles.'

'Then she doesn't. Those who do never mention him. I'm coming to the unpleasant conclusion, Molly, that this young woman is vulgar . . .' was Hector's last word as he turned over to go to sleep.

They were awoken by the banging of a gun. Hector was out of bed in one leap.

'Who's shooting at my Jemimas?' He rushed to the window muttering about poachers and Botany Bay and peered out. 'It's that Shar woman, what a cheek . . .' He raised the sash. 'Stop killing my birds,' he yelled, waving his fist vehemently. Pausing only to put on a dressing gown he raced from the room. Molly's instinct was to put her head under the pillow until the disturbance blew over but instead she felt duty bound to go downstairs and try to calm everyone down.

She missed the row between James and his father. By the time she arrived neither appeared to be speaking to the other.

James cornered Molly later in the kitchen as she was preparing lunch, getting as much of dinner ready in advance as she could, and doing her dips and things for the small drinks party she had arranged for early in the evening. He took this opportunity since Shar was lying down, feeling tired.

'What's got into Dad? Yelling at poor Shar like that.'

'He hasn't shot any of the game for five years. He just stopped one day and he doesn't like other people doing it on his land.'

'That's ridiculous, he hasn't gone vegetarian has he?'

'No, he's just gone off killing things. He doesn't mind eating the game provided someone else has killed it and on their land. I can understand it. The older one gets the more one is aware of the preciousness of life. Could you just hand me that knife over? The little one with the crooked blade . . .'

'How are the flashings?'

'Don't even talk about them,' Molly laughed as she chopped the parsley.

'Why doesn't Dad sell something, get things fixed.'

'He couldn't do that!' Molly looked at her son with horror. 'He feels that he's only a custodian of everything, that he's duty bound to hand on the house with its contents intact to you and your son.'

'That's plain stupid. I shall sell off masses when it's all mine.' James poked his finger into the jar of cocktail onions and Molly noticed for the first time what a fat finger he had. She laid the knife down quite calmly, and turned to face him.

'Don't ever let me hear you saying anything like that again. And, if you ever say that to your father I shall take it upon myself to make certain you don't inherit a damn penny.'

James laughed loudly, the pickled onion rolling about in his mouth. 'You wouldn't.'

'Yes, I would. I'm warning you. Now, if you don't mind moving, I've a lot to do. Why don't you go and see Cuckoo.'

'Do I have to?' James pulled a face.

'Yes,' she replied shortly.

Molly was so angry that she decided to do what she always did when upset – make bread. Never, even in her worst nightmares, had she imagined that she would ever hear James talk in that way. All the sacrifices they made, all the things they went without were all for him and this flaming house. What if they were wasting their time? That could kill Hector.

She kneaded the dough with great enthusiasm, imagining it was Shar she was mangling. In the way of all mothers it was the girl she decided to blame for the change in her son. She would have to watch the situation and to act as necessary. No one was going to hurt Hector, that was for sure.

The weekend creaked on. The drinks party was riveted by Shar, and Lulu commiserated fulsomely with Molly as she left.

And the dinner party she gave was monopolised by Shar. The other guests were astonished that someone could have so many emphatic opinions on so many diverse subjects. By the end of the evening Phillip Jenkins had been graced with a lecture on modern farming and where he was going wrong. Bat had learnt how the RAF should be reorganised and Jib was rewarded with a run-down on what was wrong with the modern navy. Annie English was told in no uncertain terms that the publication of her kind of literature was a prostitution of publishing. Molly had quite expected fireworks from Annie, she did not know whether to be relieved or disappointed when Annie just smiled what she called her 'My bank account's full, what about yours?' smile.

Molly could feel relief in every one of her pores when she finally stood on the steps and waved her guests away.

Shar had left a huge pile of glossy magazines in her room. She had obviously come armed with her favourite reading matter just in case the family bored her – judging by how well thumbed they were they had obviously filled her with ennui. Good, thought Molly, as she collected them together and took them down to the sitting-room to read later, for such magazines were a treat.

That evening, before supper – the cold remains of Sunday's joint – she found Hector engrossed in one of Shar's magazines. She spoke to him several times but he was so engrossed there was no response. Finally she rattled the back of the magazine.

'Aren't you talking to me?'

'I've got the solution to all our problems, Molly. It's all here in this article. It's about an agency. We're going to take affluent guests, that's what we're going to do. We can live like lords and they'll be paying for it. We're going to be as rich as Annie English and you can't get richer than that. Let's have one of Colin Mann's bottles of champagne. This calls for a celebration.'

Chapter 11

Hector Organises

ONCE HECTOR HAD made his mind up, he wanted immediate action. Such enthusiasm, while commendable, did have its disadvantages, mainly that he rapidly became ratty when things did not happen as quickly as he wanted.

The following morning, he telephoned the agency he'd read about – Aristocratic Homes Inc. – and was told that their representative, Mrs Carruthers, could not possibly call until the following week.

'It won't be necessary for me to meet your Mrs Carruthers, I'm sure you're a highly respectable firm, the article in *Harpers* did you proud. I know most of the people mentioned – that's recommendation enough for me. I'm just phoning to let you know that I'm happy to take as many guests as you want.'

'It's not as simple as that, Mr Parminter. It's our policy for Mrs Carruthers to inspect all new properties and owners.' The female voice purred diplomatically down the telephone wires.

'Inspection! Did I hear you correctly, young woman?'

'You did, Sir. We inspect everyone, dukes, barons. If the Queen wished to take part in our scheme Mrs Carruthers would undoubtedly inspect her. Our standards are very high, our clients discerning.' The voice continued, soothingly, as if the speaker were used to dealing with the sensitivities of the Hectors of this world.

Luckily Molly was in the room and was able to put out a restraining hand as she saw Hector's colour rising rather alarmingly.

'Perhaps you would like me to send you our brochure, Mr Parminter, and our requirements? Then you could study them prior to Mrs Carruthers' visit.'

'Very well . . .' Hector was torn between telling them to go to hell, his innate good manners, and the thought of making money. 'Yes, send them, then I can see if your set-up is suitable for *me*.' He put the phone down before the voice could come back with a reply. He was immeasurably cheered by his last remark, feeling the call had ended with him having the upper hand. 'Really! Imagine! What's the world coming to . . . ?' he muttered as he went off to make lists.

Hector had been very impressed by the brochures, Molly less so. Certainly they were very well produced and highly professional. Hector had tended to look only at the pictures but, as she read about what would be expected of them, it appeared to Molly that she would be hosting an endless stream of house parties and she knew what that would mean – work.

Molly felt ridiculously nervous when the day dawned on Mrs Carruthers' appointment. She could not sit still and although she, Mrs Hodgson and Jilly had gone through the house with a fine toothcomb she was still, as the car drew up, flitting about with a feather duster which she had to stuff quickly into a large Wedgwood pot in the hall.

Neither Molly nor Hector had ever met anyone like Mrs Carruthers before and thus were unsure how to handle her. Hector's offer of sherry was briskly rejected with the information that Mrs Carruthers never drank when working and Molly willed Hector not to make daft jokes about policemen. Mrs Carruthers was a short, stout woman in a very riskily patterned checked suit and, given her size, Molly thought the risk had not worked. She had a large commodious handbag, so big that when she delved into it neither would have been surprised if she had disappeared. She rootled noisily about in the contents, apologising as she did so. Finally her hand emerged with a pad and pen which she waved in an almost triumphant gesture, as if the handbag usually won. She sat without having been invited, slipped on a pair of extra-ordinarily bright red spectacles and said 'Well?'

Hector looked at Molly and she at him. 'Well, what?' Hector replied.

'Tell me all about yourselves. I have to sell you. There's a lot of competition.' She spoke in short sharp sentences in a strange voice which sounded as if she was suffering dreadfully. She wasn't, but the words were as they emerged tortured almost out of recognition. 'Why should my clients come and stay with you? There are far grander and far more aristocratic homes available. Persuade me they should come here,' she smiled, at least Molly presumed that's what it was.

'I beg your pardon . . .' Hector began with a marked degree of huff, glaring belligerently at Mrs Carruthers.

Molly quickly took the initiative. 'This house is a famous Palladian gem. There is not one article of furniture which is not English. Our paintings are renowned, we have a Gainsborough, a Millais and best of all a fine Turner.' Molly crossed her fingers behind her back at the lie. 'We are situated in one of the most perfectly preserved English villages, with easy access to London by train and road. Lynchester with its fine cathedral, merchants' houses and excellent shopping is close by. Shooting on our land might be available – at extra cost of course. My cook is a master of his craft.' At that enormous fib, Molly crossed her ankles for good measure. 'While, of course, we would be privileged to welcome your clients, I feel certain they would feel equally privileged to stay with us.' Molly felt quite giddy at the end of this speech – undoubtedly the longest she had ever made. 'I think I would like that drink now, Hector,' she said with feeling. Hector, while not standing with his mouth open, looked as if he would feel more comfortable if it were.

'Excellent.' Mrs Carruthers scribbled rapidly in her notepad. 'Now, if I could inspect the rest of the house. This room of course, is almost perfect,' she said, encompassing their drawing-room with an imperious sweep of her hand. Molly could have bit her tongue out for thanking the woman, and then wondered what the 'almost' might mean.

The three of them trooped off to the dining-room which appeared to meet with her approval, the library likewise. They passed the ballroom door, Hector saying the decorators were in. This was only a small untruth. The builders weren't there yet, but they soon would be. A nasty rash of black mould had suddenly appeared, making the Adam-green walls look as if a mad pointillist had been at work. As if this wasn't bad enough, the room, as if out of spite, had hurled down a large piece of moulding in the night which, because of its weight, was still *in situ*. It was not too fanciful to say the room had shed the plaster on purpose. Large parts of The Hall had a distressing tendency to choose such moments to fall, usually when guests were due.

They climbed the staircase which excited Mrs Carruthers into making an impassioned speech about how much her lady clients would enjoy sweeping down such stairs, making a grand entrance. She looked severely at Hector when he joked lamely that that was news to him, he had always thought the stairs were for climbing to go to bed.

The bedrooms were subjected to the most intense scrutiny. Beds were jumped on – Mrs Carruthers bouncing up and down on their beds, her check suiting making an optical whirr as she did so, was a sight neither of them would forget in a long time. Molly could have wished the curtains weren't so worn, even more so when she saw Mrs Carruthers purse her lips at them. Wardrobes were flung open.

'Never forget the clothes hangers. You'd be surprised how many of my naughty owners do. It causes many complaints. Whatever you do, don't have your house name or crest put on them – the whole lot will get nic . . . ,' Mrs Carruthers coughed, 'stolen,' she added quickly. 'Avoid bathrobes, especially if monogrammed – they walk out of the place.'

'Good gracious, what about the silver?' Hector asked, worried about his lack of insurance.

'Oh they don't bother with that. They invariably have far superior stuff at home.'

The antiquated state of the bathrooms had been worrying Molly the most. And she knew that her whole appearance was one of cringing apology as she opened the door of the first.

'Ah, wonderful!' Mrs Carruthers brimmed with pleasure. 'They'll love this, adore it. The mahogany, the taps. Marvellous. The best I've ever seen.'

'Really?' Molly asked, a wobble in her voice as she endeavoured to jump from apology to surprise and pleasure in one word.

'You should build more however.' Mrs Carruthers looked sternly at them as if regretting her prior enthusiasm.

'I've already consulted my architect,' lied Hector heroically, for he was an honest man and to have lied twice in one day was an unheard-of thing.

'Good. There are those who expect *en suite* facilities. Not all understand the true concept of the English country home as we do.'

Molly nodded but was unsure what concept she was in agreement with. And if she did not know, she had serious doubts whether Mrs Carruthers knew either.

'There's a couple of things, Mrs Parminter. The bedrooms are a little spartan, wouldn't you say? A few more ornaments. Pictures. That should do the trick. And, I fear the curtains and bedspreads . . .' she tutted, shaking her head mournfully.

'I know, I'm sorry, they haven't been changed in years.' Molly was furious with herself for sounding so apologetic but Mrs Carruthers was one of those people who made one slip into the mode effortlessly.

'Nothing wrong with them, not changed since my grandmother's time.' Hector blustered an explanation.

'Evidently.' The tone of Mrs Carruthers' voice was not lost on either of them.

Downstairs in the drawing-room Mrs Carruthers finally accepted the drink Hector had offered her. While Hector and Molly waited for her decision she scribbled quickly in her book, appearing to be doing complicated calculations. She sucked her pencil, gazed out of the window, took the whisky she preferred to sherry and downed it in one.

'Given the state of the soft furnishings, the rather worn aspect of the chairs and sofas, I think we should be talking in the region of £200.'

'Two hundred pounds?' Molly and Hector said in unison, both battling not to sound too excited.

'Including food and drink of course.' Mrs Carruthers packed her book away and folded her hands over the bag.

'Of course.'

'This money – that's for the week?'

'Good gracious, no, Mrs Parminter, per night per couple.' And they jumped as Mrs Carruthers rewarded them with a sample of her raucous laugh.

'Of course,' they both said, laughing as well, but to cover up what might be construed as ignorance or, in Hector's view far worse, stupidity.

'And you? What's your commission?'

'Nothing to worry you, Mr Parminter. The clients book direct with me. I shall pay you. It's much nicer, you see. It makes the clients feel as though they are your friends if no money changes hands.'

'Ah, I see.' They were beginning to sound like a close harmony duet.

After they had signed their agreement, had accepted Mrs Carruthers' advice book, which was £7.95 – deductible, she explained, from their first booking – and Mrs Carruthers had finally left, they collapsed into each other's arms and Hector gave Molly a huge bear hug.

'It's going to be money for old rope.' Hector twirled her in the air.

Once Hector had read Mrs Carruthers' book, *Entertaining our Foreign Friends*, he was less sure how easy it was going to be.

'It will be hard work, Molly, but I'm game if you are.'

She was fully aware, from past experience, that it would not matter how 'game' Hector was. His idea of what constituted work never coincided with her interpretation. But what could she do but agree? At last she could see light at the end of the tunnel as far as her flashings were concerned.

It *was* hard work. China was sorted, matched, washed and stored away in readiness. Linen was inspected and mended, blankets washed and dried. Going around the house with Mrs

Carruthers had been, Hector explained, what showing a prospective buyer around your house must be like – ghastly. Suddenly they had been forced to see it with fresh eyes, and what they saw was depressing. The bedrooms were so rarely used they were the mustiest of all. Some beds needed new mattresses and even Hector could see that the carpets in two rooms were far too threadbare; all needed redecorating. The builder was summoned and after much head-scratching offered to do them at £700 per room, plus materials. Hector went white. His cheque book was saved by the builder doubting if he could start this side of Easter.

'We'll have to do them ourselves,' Hector announced.

Molly went to Lynchester to discover that all the papers she wanted would take three weeks to order. She went to Marks and Spencer and bought everything there.

'Marks and Spencer? I thought they sold socks and knickers.'

'Don't pretend to be a blundering old buffer, Hector. You know full well they sell all sorts of things.'

'I didn't know they did wallpaper,' he said, sheepish at getting caught out. Molly had noticed in the past couple of years a tendency in Hector to play at being a doddering old man, she couldn't imagine why. Ideally, she thought, he should have been a judge so that he could make asinine queries in court about the meaning of colloquial English words.

'I hope you're not going to mess everything up?' he said fretfully.

'Why should I do that?'

'Homes should look lived in, I don't want to end up with it looking like some beastly hotel. That flaming woman didn't know what she was talking about.'

Molly had to agree, an English gentleman's home should have a degree of shabbiness about it; one didn't want the glistening perfection of the *nouveau riche*. But, on the other hand, the shabbiness should not be quite so drastic as it was at The Hall. It was going to be quite a task both to make the house acceptable without destroying this particular flavour, and also to keep Hector happy.

They decided they could only decorate one room at a time. Hector and Flint moved all the furniture out on to the landing, rolled the carpet up and Flint lent them his longest stepladder and pasting table. They erected the table and left. Molly sat waiting. They did not return. She looked out the window to see Hector on the front drive supervising some village lads who were pulling weeds for pocket money. Molly opened the window.

'When are we starting?' she called down.

'Starting what?' Hector said with such a patent air of innocence that Molly slammed the window shut with a bang.

'I knew it! I knew it would have to be me. It's too bad,' she complained out loud as she angrily unrolled the paper. She climbed the ladder and found if she stood on tiptoe she could just reach the picture rail. She measured out and matched the paper.

An hour later she was hanging the third strip. It was tiring, but it was satisfying. Already she could see how the room was going to be.

The door opened. Hector appeared. He crossed the room, studied her handiwork, leaned against the wall, and then lifted his thumb, squinting along it like an artist.

'What's the matter?' she asked from the top of the ladder, teetering dangerously as she smoothed the first bit of the paper down.

'I think you're a couple of degrees off vertical.'

'It can't be. I used a plumbline.'

'I don't care what you used, it's out. I've a very good eye, you know.'

Molly chose to ignore him and, pretending he wasn't even in the room, continued smoothing down the latest strip of paper.

'You've got an air bubble there . . .' Hector pointed to just below the picture rail.

With exaggerated slowness Molly smoothed the paper, chasing the bubble with her clean cloth.

'And another there . . . and another . . . and over here . . .'

'Get out!' Molly screamed.

'I was only trying to help.'

'Well, you're not!'

'That roll's definitely off centre you know . . .'

'Go!' Molly hurled her brush at him, the ladder rocked and she came crashing down into the bucket of wallpaper paste.

'I say, are you all right?' Hector looked anxiously at her. 'You haven't broken anything, have you?'

'No, Hector, you're quite safe, I'm all in one piece and can continue to wallpaper. Now,' she was speaking slowly, through her teeth, 'get out . . .' And even Hector realised she meant business.

Chapter 12

Molly's Inheritance

IN THE EVENT Hector himself had to finish the wallpapering. But Molly also enlisted Flint to help him – she did not trust Hector entirely, no matter how keen his eye.

On the second day, with only two more rolls to go to complete the first bedroom, Molly received a telephone call that her great Uncle Basil Pigeon had died; the funeral was to be the day after next, in Kent.

'We can't both go, there's too much to do. What if Carruthers telephones with our first booking? Do you think your Aunt Fifi will be hurt?'

'I'll say you've got gout. Uncle Basil was a martyr to it, she'll understand that.'

'You shouldn't lie about health, it's wicked, that's what my old nanny used to say. I'll get gout now, you'll see.'

'Of course you won't. I can hardly say you're too busy here, can I? That sounds too uncaring.'

'Do you think he's left you anything?'

'Really, Hector, what a thing to say. Even if he has don't get too excited, it'll be worthless whatever it is, the poor dears had nothing.'

'I can't say I remember him. Did he come to our wedding?'

'Of course he did. Aunt Fifi is the one you and your cousin thought was an old whore, and you both vocalised your theory rather loudly,' Molly said, in the tone of voice that indicated the insult still rankled even after all these years – as most family insults do.

'I didn't, I'd never be so rude.'

'You did, accompanied by much juvenile mirth. Unfortunately

my mother overheard and told her mother who then told her brother – Uncle Basil.'

'I remember putting my foot in it over an Aunt Bertha.'

'Aunt Bertha *is* Aunt Fifi.'

'Then why's she got two names?' Hector was using his usual ploy when in the wrong – going immediately on the attack.

'Because she was an actress; Fifi was her stage name.'

'Good Lor' – your family never fail to amaze me.'

Molly chose to ignore this slight and instead testily asked him to move off the bed so that she could get on with her packing.

'Well, if I was that rude, then it's best I'm not going. She wouldn't want to see me, would she?' He had the grace to look rather shamefaced. Molly had not been fooled for one moment; she knew that Hector remembered the incident clearly and was still ashamed of his behaviour. It had always puzzled her that he should have been so unkind about the over-rouged old lady. She had always put it down to too much alcohol and showing off.

'At least you'll be able to finish that bedroom. I should be back in two days – you and Flint together will have done another by then, won't you?' she smiled sweetly as she snapped her case shut.

The journey to Uncle Basil's was tedious. She went first to London. She had intended staying overnight with James in his very comfortable and spacious flat. But the thought of meeting his girlfriend again quite decided her against the idea. She telephoned Tabby instead.

When she arrived at the basement flat in Camden Town which Tabby shared with three other students, she wished she hadn't invited herself there either. If Tabby's bedroom at The Hall worried Molly the state of the flat could have made her terminally ill had the years not given her a certain resilience. After seeing the fly-blown state of the kitchen her only consolation was that Tabby must have the immune system of an ox. It would seem that the flat-mates, another girl, Jonquil, and two boys, Josh and Cliff, believed so strongly in democracy, and the equality of the sexes, that no one did any housework, washing up or, judging by the cartons, cooking.

There was much that Molly would have liked to say to her daughter but decided that perhaps it would be better, at least less fraught, if she didn't. It was not a pleasant evening. At first, though everyone was reasonably polite, Molly could not rid herself of the notion that she was in the way and that they were entertaining her on sufferance. For herself she could not understand how anyone could choose to live in such discomfort. Molly was aware that the expression on her face was one of distaste and disapproval but could not seem to remove it. And she could not have a bath – someone was tie-dyeing in the bathroom. There was no food, and when the lack of it was mentioned, everyone looked at her so expectantly that she ended up paying for a Tandoori take-away and beer and wine from the off-licence for all of them. Since she had paid for the alcohol it struck her as rather unjust when a somewhat inebriated Cliff, without warning, launched a diatribe delivered in a loud hectoring voice, that all land should be nationalized forthwith.

Molly endeavoured to change the subject by asking Tabby if she could see some of her paintings. Tabby glared. Molly was at a total loss to understand why, with Tabby, if one showed interest it was interfering but if one didn't one didn't care about her work, her future, her life. One could never win. Finally, with the maximum of sulky flounce, Tabby produced a lump of what looked like plaster of paris with a couple of tin openers embedded in it. Molly would have been the first to admit that she knew little about modern art, but upon seeing this object she was glad she didn't. When it was produced at least she was saved from any more accusations of being a parasite on the backs of the workers – Cliff's latest topic – for everyone switched to an excited discussion of Tabby's 'art'.

'You don't like it, Mother.' At the accusing tone in Tabby's voice Molly's heart sank.

'I don't exactly understand it, Tabby,' Molly said, flustered, not wishing to discourage talent at such a tender age.

'I knew you wouldn't. You never like anything I do.'

'It was so much easier when you used to do those nice still lifes and landscapes,' Molly said, wistfully remembering the pretty pictures the girl could paint and of which she, as her mother, had been so proud.

'God, isn't life hell! Why am I so misunderstood?' Tabby said dramatically, and stormed from the room. Molly wondered if Mrs Klee or Mrs Picasso had had her difficulties.

'Oh, dear, I appear to have upset her.'

'She has been working on that for over a month now. It's a pity you asked to see it in the first place.' Her tormentor of earlier glared at her, obviously thinking her a philistine.

'Yes, well, modern art isn't everyone's cup of tea,' she said briskly, picking up her handbag and making for the room where she had been told she was to sleep, before she lost her temper, which she thought might be imminent.

Her bed was what Tabby had called a futon; she said that *everyone* had them, they were good for posture and the Japanese wouldn't sleep on anything else. As she tossed and turned, attempting to find a little comfort, she thought the futon explained a lot. Any race which could willingly inflict such discomfort upon itself, wouldn't, she supposed, think twice about killing whales and dolphins.

She remembered dear Sebastian with affection and wondered if Tabby ever saw him. She certainly hoped that neither of those young men was her present inamorato – they looked so dirty for a start, and were so angry and took themselves so seriously that she could not imagine them ever enjoying anything. It seemed to her a tragic waste of youth, which should be a time for happiness and irresponsibility. She would have to have a long talk with Hector about Tabby when she got home. Molly would have mortgaged everything to ensure her daughter had a chance in life. They could ill afford to send her to art college but the least they could hope for, she thought, was to see some *art* come out the other end, not lumps of plaster which any infant in Sarson Magna primary school could do – and better. She thought perhaps she understood Tabby's sulk and anger. The girl was no fool, probably she knew herself that what she was doing was not good enough. She sensed the child was doing what others expected of her, and not what she wanted to do herself. It wouldn't last, of course, nothing with Tabby ever did.

She wondered if, when her daughter announced art was no longer for her, she dare suggest a nice safe secretarial course.

Molly was stiff in the morning and with no one else awake, she could only leave a note for Tabby. She felt such a hypocrite as she scribbled her 'thanks' for having her – why did one do it? Why didn't she have the courage to write the truth – that futons were for the young and fit, that her friend was the rudest she had ever met, that Molly was tired of Tabby's continual tantrums, that her art wasn't art, and that the flat was a pigsty, and it was about time Tabby got her act together. It was a nice thought.

She crossed to Victoria. As she looked out of the taxi window at the clutter in the streets she felt as she had at the flat. She didn't belong here, either. This was no longer her London. She had spent two very happy years of her youth here working first in a hat shop and then as a receptionist for a doctor friend of her father, who understood about social life interfering with work.

Then, London had been a jolly place not the frightening city she found it now. In those days she would have taken the tube without a thought but this time she had had to promise Hector faithfully that she would lash out on taxis, and had been silently grateful that he had insisted on the extravagance. Or was she showing her age? Had the city of her youth been anathema to her own parents? The buildings had been dirtier then and there had been the last smogs – but much less traffic and one could breathe. Whereas nowadays she felt choked and quite dizzy from the lack of oxygen in the air. To take her mind off it, and the worry that Tabby was living here, she began to read her newspaper. She flicked through it idly. On page three, in a column a bare inch high, was the report of a murder the previous day in the very borough she had been staying in. Less than an inch of newspaper space to report on the brutal snuffing out of a life; yet in her time such a murder would have been front-page news. It was as if the city and its inhabitants did not care any more. She shuddered and wished she could go safely home. Instead she caught the train for Faversham. There she took a bus to the small hamlet on the Thames estuary.

As the bus moved along the road that ran beside the estuary, past the rows of wooden summer houses, she remembered the child she once had been on this bus travelling with her brother to stay with her favourite great-uncle and aunt. She had richer relations, and ones who lived in grander houses than Basil and Fifi, but none that were such fun. It was as if neither of these adults had ever grown up. They had had the capacity to find the joy of a child in the simplest things – a tiny shell so small one needed pincers to pick it up; finding a jellyfish still alive and gently replacing it in the sea; searching diligently for cuttlefish bone for their neighbour's budgerigar; or studying for hours a furry caterpillar in their garden, which had never known insecticide. The high spot of each day of the holidays had been following the tide out across the mud, ribbed hard by the sea so that one could feel the tiny ridges with one's feet as if one were walking on a giant pulsating Ordnance Survey map, searching for cockles. As the bubbles rose in the dark brown mud they leapt, digging frantically to get the delicacy beneath, before it burrowed even further away from them. And then, some days, as a special treat, Basil would walk them right out to the water's edge and let them play on the wrecked Messerschmitt – telling them a giant octopus, but one that liked children, lurked there. And the tide would turn and they would leave the plane to drown again with its ghost crew and they would race the water two miles back to the land. Once home, the cockles would be thrown into pans of boiling water, hissing bloodcurdlingly – they never realised then that they were hearing the death agony of the poor little crustaceans. And then, in the house on the bluff which looked more like a boat than a house with its look-out tower and round windows, would follow the most wonderful suppers of the fresh cockles with Fifi's own bread.

And Molly had let Basil die without seeing him for nearly five years, not having stayed here once in the twenty-seven years she had been married. Never having told him what those summers had meant to her, and now it was all too late. That was the problem with death, the nasty way it had of creeping up and catching you with things left undone and things left unsaid.

Now she had to face Fifi, and what would she think of her and her neglect? She need not have feared. Her welcome from Aunt Fifi was as gushingly warm as it had always been, as if her neglect of them had never happened.

Fifi had always been the wrong name for her aunt. Fifi belonged to a young slip of a girl, not the large fat woman Fifi had been ever since Molly could remember. Molly was glad Hector had not come, for Fifi, in her late seventies, wore even more make-up than she had on the day of that unfortunate remark.

She had been sad at the news of Uncle Basil's death, but upon seeing her aunt the true grief came out and she burst into tears. Fifi hugged her tight. 'I'm sorry I haven't been to see you both. I should have come.'

'Tush. You had your own life to lead, Molly, your own family. Basil and I did not expect to see you, not once you were married, whatever next? We had the privilege of sharing some of your childhood with you, didn't we?' Fifi smiled kindly at her. 'But time goes so quickly, and the years slide by. Don't worry, my dear.' Aunt Fifi led her into the drawing-room, a large room which ran across the front of the house and from which only the path and the sea were visible. Here the other mourners were gathered, already well into the gin and whisky – no messing about with tea where Fifi was concerned.

She watched her aunt busily fussing over people, cheering up the miserable, chivvying everyone. She thought of Cuckoo with her endless carping and moaning. She remembered her own mother who, for the last fifteen years of her life, had been spiteful and miserable. Yet she had money, wanted for nothing, not like poor Fifi who had never had enough. Molly wondered now if the cockle suppers had been because they couldn't afford anything else. She wondered why the old always fell into one of two camps – kind and uncomplaining, or bitter and twisted, hurling insults at the drop of a hat. There never seemed to be a middle way.

Basil was to be cremated, which surprised Molly until Fifi explained to her that he had ordered it years ago thinking it a rakishly modern thing to go up in smoke. The problem was he had lived so long – to ninety-five – that he had not realised that nearly everyone was cremated these days.

'Just as well, or the old horror would have arranged to be sent off in a spacecraft – imagine the trouble and expense.'

Molly hated the service. She had been to cremations before and the places always gave her the creeps, far more than any churchyard ever did. The buildings themselves were soulless like factories of death, and she hated the gardens, too immaculate for her taste, with the flowers in regimented rows. Everything was so plastic, and impersonal. From the way he spoke about Basil the priest had obviously never known him. Even the flowers looked artificial, and the clanking of the curtain as it closed on the coffin sent goose bumps all over Molly. It seemed unbelievably tactless and in rather dubious taste for the song, 'Smoke gets in your eyes' to be played as the coffin disappeared. She later discovered that this had been at Uncle Basil's request. Hector would have enjoyed that, she feared. She resolved that when she got home she would talk to Hector about what they were to do when their time came. He so loathed talking about death – especially his own – to the extent that Molly suspected he had decided he was certain he need not go at all. But Molly didn't want to depart this way; she wanted to be curled up snug in a grave with Hector.

After the funeral and tea, and just before she was to leave for her long journey home, Fifi took her out into the hall and pointed to a large wooden crate.

'I've arranged for the carrier to pick this up for you, Molly, it's far too heavy for you to take.'

'What is it?'

'Do you remember those pictures of children playing that you loved as a little girl? Twelve of them there were.'

'The Huxtable Rivers copies?'

'Yes, those. Basil always promised you should have them.'

'How very kind of him. But I don't want to deprive you of them, Aunt Fifi.'

'No it's better this way, then I know that you've got them. I shan't be long myself now . . .'

'Oh you mustn't talk that way.'

'Without Basil – there isn't much point, Molly. And funny things happen to your possessions when you die. They get into the wrong hands, if you know what I mean. Things disappear. I'd rather sort everything out while I still have my marbles.'

'So long as you don't mind . . . I should love to have them.' She kissed her aunt.

'How's your flashings, Molly?'

'Don't even ask, Aunt Fifi,' Molly laughed as she followed the distant cousin who was giving her a lift back to Chatham.

She was glad to be going home. Uncle Basil's death had saddened her but it wasn't just that – it was London, Tabby.

She rarely went anywhere these days except Lynchester. There were times when she felt quite sorry for herself that she didn't; now she was not so sure. She felt she never wanted to go anywhere ever again, that she belonged in Sarson Magna – a place and people she understood despite the recent problems. But one thing she was sure of. As soon as she got back she was going to arrange to have Aunt Fifi to stay, no matter what Hector thought of her.

Chapter 13

Molly Is Put in the Picture

I NVOLVED WITH HER wallpapering as she had been, and then with her visit to Aunt Fifi, Molly found, a week later, that she was out of touch with events in the village. She needed Mrs Hodgson to put her straight. So her first morning back, instead of doing any work, Mrs Hodgson and she settled at the kitchen table with a coffee and prepared for a cosy natter. Not that Molly had baldly asked for the latest gossip, nothing so vulgar. She had suggested that Mrs Hodgson looked a little peaky and perhaps a coffee would put her right. Mrs Hodgson accepted this charade graciously, at the same time knowing full well what was expected of her. She did not leap in with the choicest items of gossip, nothing so crass, but instead a full ten minutes was spent on the subjects of the weather, Uncle Basil's funeral, the need for a new bucket and mop and the prices at Tesco compared with the village stores. These niceties dispensed with, they could get down to the business in hand.

None of the cleaning women had gone back to Wood Close – Maggie Smith was now working in the pub, Sylvia Spender had gone to work for Annie English and the others had all been taken on by Sue Mann. Mrs Hodgson had never had much time for the Wood Close inhabitants, regarding them as a jumped-up lot – especially the Martins both of whom, she confided, had started life in Dockland, the least salubrious part of Lynchester.

'There's nothing wrong in bettering yourself, Mrs Hodgson. Good luck to them.'

'I agree, Mrs Parminter. Nothing wrong in it at all. But it's not nice when you don't invite your old Mum round to tea because you're ashamed of her, like that Jill Martin, is it?'

'Well, put like that, no.'

'And they're all so stuck up and everything's on H.P.'

'But you don't know that.'

'Yes I do,' Mrs Hodgson said, affronted. 'My nephew works in Dixons and Fred's brother works at Clover's garage and his sister works in that Leather Land shop – oh I know who hasn't paid for what, I can assure you.'

'Of course, Mrs Hodgson, I should have known better,' Molly said without a trace of irony.

'And Reg can't move an inch. That Sean Martin put his back out at the community centre attacking him like that. Reg reckons he's going to sue.'

'Good gracious. But I thought Reg started the fight.'

'I can't think where you got that idea from, Mrs Parminter.' The look she received indicated to Molly that who the protagonist was had been decided otherwise and perhaps it would be better if she did not let on what she had witnessed. 'Sal Blunt is to have all her teeth out.'

'Poor woman, hardly her image is it?' Molly said, thinking of Sal the highly made-up landlady of the Parminter Arms who had a penchant for short and very tight black leather clothes. 'She's rather young for that, isn't she?'

'Young?' Mrs Hodgson laughed. 'She's fifty-five if she's a day.'

'She's worn well then.'

'Not if you see her first thing in the morning she hasn't,' Mrs Hodgson said darkly. 'That Colin Mann is going ahead with his plans,' she continued.

'I thought he might.'

'But Gussie Ford won't see him.'

'I'm not surprised.'

'They do say if he gets that estate we'll have a proper medical centre like they've got at Lynchester.'

'Really?'

'And the school would never have to close.'

'That would be a good thing.'

'And everyone reckons that Miss Truro's gone funny.'

'In what way?'

'She's had her hair permed and highlighted. She's plucked her eyebrows and she's had electrolysis on her moustache and she was seen in Lynchester going into Top Shop.'

'So?'

'Well it's not right at her age and in her position. Not setting an example is it? You don't expect the village schoolteacher to doll herself up like a tart do you?'

'Aren't you being a little bit hard on her? Tart is a strong word to use,' Molly lamely admonished, while wondering how long it could possibly be before Mrs Hodgson was sued for slander by someone or other.

'You wait until you see her,' Mrs Hodgson said even more darkly. She sucked her cheeks in looking at the ceiling. 'And the offertory box has been stolen . . .'

'Oh, no! The poor vicar.'

'Bakery Antiques is now a café.'

'What a lovely surprise, I was convinced it would be yet another antique shop.'

'Oh yes, and Mr Potter-Smythe lost a packet on the gee gees.'

'Good gracious, you don't mean to say someone has seen him? How on earth do you know that?'

'My Uncle Cyril's wife's cousin works . . .'

'I know, I know, in the betting shop,' Molly laughed. 'And all this has happened in just that short time I've been away? What a village!'

'I don't know. I think it's been quite quiet myself after the recent excitement.'

Molly had been right. Hostilities were not yet over. She was on her way to Mr Lambert's hardware store with a long list of DIY requirements when she saw Sue speak to Sybil Potter-Smythe and Sybil flounce past without replying.

Molly hurried to catch up with Sue and suggested they walk to the shops together. Again she found herself with that strange need to protect her and thought she had better not mention this to Hector – he had very reactionary ideas about women and their friendships.

'It's not as if it's my fault is it, Molly?'

'Don't worry Sue. I'm not exactly flavour of the month either.'

'I am sorry . . .'

In the General Stores Molly was more than pleased, however, by the treatment afforded Sue. Betty Trotter, who was gossiping to Twink, immediately excused herself and virtually hurtled across the small shop to Sue.

'Anything I can do for you, Mrs Mann?' Betty's smile glowed.

'I've made my usual list, Mrs Trotter. And Colin's added this booze order if it wouldn't be too much trouble.'

'Trouble? It's a pleasure, Mrs Mann.' Betty's eyes greedily scanned the long order. 'I'll have to order the malts, Mrs Mann. There's not much call for them round here,' she said loudly, no doubt for Twink and Sybil who had joined her, to hear. 'I'll get this done immediately and up to the house by noon.'

Twink and Sybil's annoyance was plain to see in their ostentatiously turned backs and the rigid set of their shoulders as they studiously examined a display of Campbells soup cans as if it were a Warhol exhibit. Their fury was understandable since the Trotters had long ago given up delivering to anyone. But money spoke, even if these two were not prepared to admit the fact. Bribery, they were heard to call it later. Betty by now was running round the shop filling the wire basket with the Manns' order.

'I know I can get everything cheaper in Lynchester but I think we should patronise the local traders as much as possible don't you?' Sue said, rather loudly for her. Usually she tended to talk with her chin down, something which at first had annoyed Molly but which later she decided she understood, presuming it due to Sue's insecurity about her accent.

'Undoubtedly,' Molly said, but having the grace to colour slightly. She would have liked to help the Trotters as much as Sue but long gone were the days when she could afford to; Tesco had her main patronage now. The village store was for when she ran out of something; she was fully aware that this was not fair if she wanted the village shops to survive but, in her defence, when she did pop in it was always with a marked sense of guilt.

134

'Hello Twink, Sybil,' Molly said to the upright cashmere-covered backs.

'Molly,' they both said, springing round, as if noticing her for the first time – totally ridiculous since Trotters' shop was full when it had more than three customers.

'Lovely day, isn't it?'

'For the time of year.'

'I was about to suggest to Sue that we tried the new café at the Old Bakery. Why don't you two join us?' Molly was smiling, determined that all this feuding had gone far enough.

'Not this morning thank you, Molly,' said Twink, looking pointedly at Sue.

'Nor me,' Sybil added, almost regally.

'What a shame. Another morning perhaps?' Sue smiled brightly.

'I shouldn't think so, thank you, Mrs Mann,' Twink said politely. Yet in the time-honoured way of the English middle classes, Twink conveyed her anger, loathing and total conviction in her own superiority to such as Sue by the set of her shoulder, the arch of her eyebrows, the narrowing of her eyes, the set of her mouth in a thin line. None of these tribal indicators was lost on the others but Molly couldn't help but wonder if a good old fishwife screaming match might not be a more satisfying way to behave.

They were almost out of the door, and almost out of earshot, when both heard Sybil Potter-Smythe confide maliciously to Twink, 'The new café should knock any profits that Mann creature hopes to make from doing teas in his unspeakable venture. It's truly excellent, wonderful cakes . . .'

Sue paused in the doorway and turned back into the shop.

'How kind of you to say so, Mrs Potter-Smythe,' she smiled broadly. 'My husband will be pleased to hear you so strongly recommend the cakes. You see, he bought the Old Bakery. It's *our* café. Good morning ladies,' and Sue virtually skipped back out of the shop. 'That shut them up. Come on Molly, my treat.'

Molly followed Sue, but not without a backward glance and a sheepish smile at Twink and Sybil who were both peering angrily over Betty Trotter's window display of breakfast cereals. She felt intolerably guilty. It wasn't as if Twink and Sybil were great friends. She had often found both women irksome and a shade ridiculous. But on the other hand they were neighbours and fellow villagers and no community could survive with this perpetual sniping going on.

She compounded all this guilt later when she didn't even tell Hector it was Sue with whom she had enjoyed coffee and cakes in the new café.

The following morning Hector was the colour of a petunia as he studied his mail and reports over breakfast.

Colin Mann had applied for planning permission for his Elizabethan Village Tourist Attraction. And, even worse, some elements on the planning committee, it appeared, were not averse to the scheme.

'Well there's no point in asking you, of course,' his thick eyebrows met in the middle as he frowned vexatiously.

'Ask me what?'

'We're going to have to organise a petition. Alert people to object. That sort of thing. But with your views . . .'

'I should ask Twink and Sybil, they'd undoubtedly be thrilled to bits to help you,' Molly said as equably as possible as she loaded the tray with the breakfast plates. Rowing with Hector again was out of the question.

Chapter 14

Colin Shows His Hand

A FEW DAYS later Sue Mann telephoned to invite Molly for lunch, just the two of them, on any day that would suit Molly. Molly plumped for Thursday, her one free day. With Cuckoo at her friend's house and Hector in Lynchester no one need know she was out for the day. She need not lie to Hector or, worse, tell him the truth and then face his wrath. She had never, in all the years of their marriage found herself in such an intolerable position. It made her wonder how women ever embarked on affairs — the guilt, the subterfuge required must be totally exhausting. But Colin's Elizabethan Village project, his new housing estate plans, Molly felt should be regarded as business and that civilised socialising should be allowed to continue. Good gracious, she thought as she changed for her luncheon appointment, if the world behaved like Hector and his cohorts, where would the United Nations stand? She was sure that before *glasnost* the Americans had enjoyed the odd 'knees up' with the Russians and vice versa. Why should Sarson Magna be different?

Fortified by such reasoning, Molly set off for the Dower House with a clearer conscience than she could have hoped for. Why, she thought, when Hector got back she might just throw into the conversation, casually, where she had been.

Sue had said it was to be just the two of them so she was a bit disconcerted when Colin opened the door. With the outline planning application to be heard the following week, she immediately feared she had been asked as a person sympathetic to their plans who also happened to be Hector's wife to . . . what was the word? Molly frowned into the sherry she had been given. What were those people called who badgered politicians at Westminster into seeing things their way? 'Lobbyists', that was it — though self-seekers, she thought, might be more apt. She placed her feet squarely on the carpet and braced herself, ready to point out that Colin was wasting his time lobbying her since Hector had already declared an interest and would not be part of this particular planning committee. But her fears were groundless. Not once during a delightful and delicious meal was the venture discussed.

It was only over coffee that Molly got the first inkling of why she had been invited. Colin asked her casually how well she knew Gussie Ford.

'Very well, I've known her for years,' she stated airily and immediately wondered why, when asked if one knew someone, one always took pride in saying one did, even when they were mere acquaintances. Molly knew a man who dined out frequently on the boast that he had known a mass murderer – that was going too far, she felt. The truth was that Gussie, although a resident of Sarson Magna for ten years, could never be counted a great friend of Molly's. This was not a criticism of Molly, for Gussie had chosen to keep herself very much to herself and had never really been part of the village. None the less here she was, claiming a friendship she didn't have. She was about to qualify her initial statement but didn't have time before Colin, smiling his wonderful smile – a young Dirk Bogarde sort of quizzical smile, she thought – was asking if she would accompany him to call on Gussie.

'I think it's only right that the old girl should have a friend of standing with her when I speak to her,' he said.

'But, Colin, she's not . . .'

'I don't wish to be accused of harassment, you understand. And you are such a respected member of the community. You would make the ideal, how shall I put it, chaperone? Adviser to the old lady? You see, Molly, I don't want to be accused of intimidating her, now do I?'

'But Colin . . .'

'I've had a recce around the place and it's desperately run down – weeds everywhere. She's obviously in need of financial help.'

'But, Gussie likes . . .'

'So what do you say, Molly. Will you help us?'

Molly knew that, in fairness to Hector and to herself, she should refuse to get involved. She was being used, there was no doubt of that. This was not a particularly pleasant thought and she felt a shade disappointed in Sue for having deceived her over the lunch. For all that, she found herself agreeing. She was not pleased with herself for accepting, nor with her motivation; she was going out of sheer nosiness, no more, no less.

'That won't be necessary. It's no distance, we can walk,' she said as Colin held open the door of the Rolls-Royce for her.

'I'd rather drive, if you don't mind.' He smiled again – was it a young Bogarde or maybe a James Mason sort of smile, she wondered as he handed her into the car. Since he was as fit as a fiddle she could only presume he was insisting on the car to impress Gussie with his wealth.

It was only minutes before they were bumping over Gussie's long, pot-holed driveway, a large pack of barking dogs in attendance. It was a multi-breed pack – two St Bernards daintily stepped over three miniature dachshunds, while several alsatians, a rottweiler and any number of Heinz 57s lolloped around the car in enthusiastic greeting.

'Good God, how many dogs has she got?'

'It varies. She rescues them, you see. If she can't find new homes she keeps them. She's never been known to turn a needy dog away. She's dedicated her whole life to them.'

'Poor old thing – it must be a great financial drain when you think . . .' Colin began, but stopped in mid-sentence as out of the door of the cottage a woman of stunning beauty appeared. She was tall and, while slim, moved in a voluptuous and rather provocative way. Her hair was a tawny mane, her face totally devoid of make-up. In torn jeans, T-shirt and bare feet she looked a million dollars, Molly, not for the first time, thought with envy.

'That's . . . God, what's her name . . .' Colin flicked his fingers in exasperation.

'That's Gussie. I always think she looks like one of Annie English's romantic heroines, don't you?'

'But I could have sworn she was that actress . . . you know the one, starred in that film about elephants . . . got an Oscar . . .'

'Kate O'Moyne. Yes, that's her. But Gussie is her real name.

She gave up acting years ago for her dogs. Lovely isn't she?'

The Rolls sighed to a halt and a most impressed Colin checked himself in the driving mirror and eased himself out of the car, his hand already outstretched in greeting. Molly made the introductions.

'I did write, Mrs Ford, you didn't reply.'

'I never open letters if I don't know who they're from. Even when I do I don't necessarily read them. Ask my bank manager.' She flung her head back and laughed a low rich laugh that would have been more in place in a darkly lit bedroom than in an English garden in the afternoon. 'Gin? Brandy? Tea?' she asked as she ushered them in, much to Molly's surprise. She had only twice been in this cottage and that was when she had been invited. She had never heard of anyone turning up uninvited and getting in.

The first thing one noticed upon entering Gussie's cottage was the smell – if one liked dogs, the smell was delightful; if not, then it stank. The second thing was the furniture. After the rather ramshackle exterior with a thatch in need of renewal the beautiful, highly polished and valuable antique furniture came as something of a surprise.

Molly watched Colin's expression as he took in the scene. She could almost hear his brain clicking like a calculator as he amended the figures.

Soon they were settled in comfortable chairs with large drinks in their hands, surrounded by inquisitive dogs and a bevy of cats. Molly talked to Gussie about the dogs; for the time being Colin was silent as he marshalled his thoughts.

'I thought your interest was dogs, Mrs Ford,' he suddenly said smiling the most charming of his megawatt smiles, as he surreptitiously tried to divest himself of two long-haired white cats which had decided they liked him.

'Gussie, please,' Gussie returned his smile with one of her own, of mega-megawattage. 'I love all animals – dogs, cats, donkeys, goats, chickens. I'd have an elephant if I had the room. It's men I can't stand.'

Colin choked on his brandy and a flicker of regret passed across his handsome features. 'Not all men, I do hope.' His lips parted, perfect white teeth flashed, and Molly felt terribly in the way.

'All men.' Gussie chuckled and, topping up their drinks, did not expand further. Molly found this disappointing, she would love to know the reason why. Probably because she was so beautiful; Lulu had once told her that the more beautiful one was the more one attracted bastards, though Molly could not understand this. 'So, Mr Mann. I presume you've come to offer me a ludicrously inflated price for my cottage and land. How much?' Gussie asked, dispensing with any social niceties. Molly was impressed.

She watched Colin, certain she saw him change mental gear again.

'£175,000.' Now he was wasting no time on small talk.

'Oh come, Mr Mann. I could get in excess of £200,000 with no trouble. Weekenders would die for a thatched cottage of this age, isolated, with such a large garden, two hours by train from London. More brandy, Molly?'

Molly accepted even though she knew she shouldn't, but with luck she would sober up before Hector returned from Lynchester. She was more than surprised by Gussie's reaction – it looked as if she was willing to sell after all. Annie English had been wrong.

'A quarter of a million,' Colin said calmly, and Molly wondered how rich one had to be to mention such sums without moving a whisker.

'I think you can do better than that, Colin. May I call you Colin?' The husky actress' voice almost purred like one of her cats.

'£300,000.'

Molly *was* impressed. Hearing such unbelievable sums being bandied about was not a common experience for her. But it was the calmness of them both that impressed her the most. She found herself wishing Hector was here, he could never believe this when she told him – *if* she told him, she hurriedly corrected herself.

Gussie sat tapping the side of her glass with her finger. Her nails were bitten down to the quick yet, with her looks, they should have been long and painted. If Molly had nails like that she would have sat on them, she thought, but then Gussie was like Annie and did not care what anyone thought of her.

'£350,000 . . .'

Molly was aware of a clock ticking and a cat purring.

'£375 . . .'

Even the dogs had stopped panting and sat in a silent semicircle.

'£400,000 . . . I can't go higher than that. No higher.' Colin leant back in his chair. Molly wondered if his face was shiny, or was that a thin film of sweat she could see on his skin? Still Gussie did not reply and the silence was becoming oppressive. Molly looked from one to the other wondering which one would crack first. Back and forth her head twisted but neither of the others, she realised, was aware of her presence. Colin coughed and looked up at the ceiling as if taking an inordinate interest in the oak-beamed ceiling. 'Half a million and that's way over the odds. Take it or leave it.'

Molly looked at him with concern. He was mad, stark staring mad. She had sat here with a brandy totally unaware that, sitting opposite her, the poor man was quietly going off his rocker. It was what happened in Gothic novels, not in Sarson Magna on an autumn day.

'Colin, my dear . . .' Gussie finally spoke and smiled her actress' smile. Molly watched, fascinated. She had noticed actresses smile in this particular way before. Their lips, like roller blinds rolling back, parted as if they were part of a puppet's mouth, controlled by strings. Such lips never creased or puckered or smudged their lipstick. Pink gums were exposed, improbably white teeth gleamed. Molly had tried to emulate this smile, alone, in front of her dressing-table mirror, but had only succeeded in frightening herself with the resultant grimace. Actresses must be born with square mouths she had concluded; no one could learn to smile that way. 'Colin my dear, such a price!' Again the smile – like an alligator, Molly thought and shuddered. 'At that sum you're going to be cutting it fine aren't you? On only fifty houses? After you've paid me, plus what you paid Farmer Feather, the building costs . . . ? Why you'll hardly have any profit left at all, will you, my dear? What with the first-time homes, and little me? Why, this is bordering on philanthropy.' Colin shifted uncomfortably in his chair. 'Come clean, Colin,' Gussie leant forward, the T-shirt straining across her fine breasts, a waft of her perfume in the air.

'It's more like three hundred houses you're planning, isn't it?' Gussie pounced.

Molly was so shocked at this that she found herself pouring another brandy without it being offered, and blushed at her appalling lack of manners.

'Yes.' Colin said abruptly.

'I thought so. Then we're talking of massive profits, aren't we? Half a million for poor little me seems a trifle mean, don't you think?'

Colin now helped himself to the brandy. Molly was shocked. She had been shocked at Gussie's apparent keenness to sell when fifty houses were involved, now it was for three hundred. Fifty or three hundred it should have been the same, but it wasn't, Molly found – anyone who could allow that number of dwellings to be built was beyond the pale. This was greed she was witnessing. She was deeply disappointed. She had always respected Gussie giving up fame and wealth for her animals; now it looked as though even she had a price. The village would be ruined, never the same again, the indigenous population finally swamped. She would have to join the others now, tell Hector. Mrs Hodgson must be told to warn the Churchill Drive people, she herself would have to brave Wood Close and warn them. There was one good thing: at least the village would once again be united. Colin and Gussie must be stopped.

'I think my offer is more than generous, Gussie.'

'So do I, Colin.' Gussie laughed gaily and Colin was beaming from ear to ear.

'We have a deal then?' He was already holding out his hand to seal it.

'Oh, I didn't say that. Good gracious me, no,' she smiled, and Molly found herself thinking that if piranha fish smiled it was undoubtedly like Gussie – and she had thought her smile such a beautiful thing. 'Come with me . . .' Gussie held out her hand to Colin and like a man mesmerised he got up and followed her, Molly trailing along behind.

Gussie led them into the garden, along a weedy path, weeds which she pointed out with pride. Through a gate they went into an old walled garden. There stood rows of small granite blocks, on each a single name.

'This is why I can't sell to you, Colin. This is where my old friends lie. I can't let their bones be disturbed. I would never be able to live with myself.'

'Dogs?' he said, a deep frown on his face.

'And cats, and a goat – my friends.'

'You're mad.' Colin swung round to look at her and Molly was shocked to see how his eyes were blazing with fury. 'What was that charade in there then?'

'I was curious, that's all,' Gussie said calmly.

'You'll turn down a fortune for a pile of mouldering bones? You need to be certified!' Colin was shouting quite menacingly now.

'Maybe I am mad. But then maybe I'm sane and it is you who are mad,' Gussie said very calmly and Molly found herself thinking how utterly wonderful her smile was after all, and all thoughts of alligators and piranhas were wiped from her memory. Molly was back to looking from one to the other like a Wimbledon spectator. Colin, she realised, could never understand. For a man whose whole life had been dedicated to the pursuit of money to comprehend a woman who had turned her back on its pursuit was completely outside his ken.

'I intend to have this land. I shan't give up. You'll live to regret this afternoon,' he said very spitefully, Molly thought, turned on his heel, and stomped out of the garden. A minute later they could hear the wheelspin as he accelerated like a maniac down the drive.

'I did enjoy that,' Gussie said, linking her arm with Molly's. 'But poor you, he's forgotten you.'

'He only wanted me here as a witness that you hadn't been harassed.' She laughed.

'Conceited fool. Just like a man.' She stopped and pointed. 'Look at that view, Molly,' she waved her arm to encompass Farmer Feather's fields, hedgerows unchanged in a thousand years, the copse a cover for generations of partridge, home to so many badgers. 'This must never be destroyed, Molly. We owe it to future generations to see it stays this way.'

'You're right, Gussie. I feel such a fool. I've been used and I fear I've been taken in by Mr and Mrs Mann.'

Chapter 15

The Hall Is Opened for Business

MOLLY THOUGHT SHE was prepared for Hector's reaction to her news about Colin and Gussie and her own change of heart. But nothing could have prepared her for the degree of insufferable smugness that he exhibited. Molly, with the fate of the village uppermost in her mind, restrained her initial impulse to throw an egg at him across the kitchen table. Instead, with an expression of apparent placidness, she beat the eggs with such ferocity that her omelette turned out more like a pancake. Hector droned on about his ability to read character, and inevitably wittered on about her stupidity.

'We'll hear no more of his stupid ventures,' he finally said, flicking open his copy of the *Lynchester Gazette*. Molly kept silent. She was not so sure.

As far as Hector's hotel project was concerned, in the days that followed, Molly had to admit that Hector's talent for making lists was formidable. She was a great list-maker herself, she always had been, but these days, in her forties, lists were becoming essential if she was to remember anything and not to create impossible muddles. But Hector's lists were a work of art compared with her own untidy scribbles. His were meticulously typed on A4 paper with underlined headings, while hers tended to be in pencil on any old scrap of paper which came to hand.

His obsession with these lists could have been wearisome but Molly realised that while so involved with them he had ceased to make snide remarks about the Mann incident. She knew it could not last, but for the time being she welcomed them.

Hector had issued everyone, from Molly to Flint, with a sheet of paper indicating their own sphere of responsibility. At the end of each day's work these, with tasks duly ticked, were handed back to Hector. He then cross-checked everything against the large master plan he had pinned to the wall of his study: at a glance he could see how work in the house was progressing, where reinforcements might be needed, where people weren't pulling their weight – or rather where Molly, Flint, Mrs Hodgson and Jilly weren't, for there was no one else. He had quickly decided that for complete efficiency what was needed was a time-and-motion study, which had taken him hours to evolve. With this he drove everybody mad, following them around with his stopwatch, a souvenir from his short athletics career at Cambridge.

So excited was he by the discovery of his new talents, that it did not take long before he decided that more sophisticated aids were required. After much thought about the initial outlay and an interview with his bank manager, masterly in its optimism, Hector ordered a personal computer.

His elation was so great that he couldn't eat his breakfast on the day it was to be delivered. The young man who arrived with the machine explained the workings of it which, Hector declared confidently, appeared simplicity itself.

There were certain areas about which he was a little vague but it was unlikely that Hector could ever have found it in himself to confide his uncertainties. Certainly not to the callow youth with an advanced case of acne who was giving the instructions, in a voice heavy with catarrh, while his fingers flew about the keyboard. Hector reasoned with himself that if the likes of this fellow had mastered the technique of using the personal computer then it would be child's play to him.

He was wrong. Within two hours of being left alone with the machine Hector was in a great sulk and the instruction manual had been hurled out of the window to be retrieved by Molly. The next day the computer stood unloved and unused in the corner of the room and Hector went back to his old manual typewriter, telling anyone who cared to listen, and even those who didn't, that the computer was a useless instrument which had broken down on the first day.

The main problem with the lists was that Hector had made the system so complex that he alone in the house, probably the whole world, understood it. As most of his time was spent organising it, he was unable to help with the work to be done. What little free time he had was spent in Lynchester purchasing ledgers, work-books, finding out about PAYE, and having long discussions with the manager of the Black Bull about the best way of running The Hall profitably with paying guests.

In the way of all hoteliers, Sheridan Clerke liked to shroud the whole subject of catering in an air of mystery which implied it was the most difficult business in the world. One that could only be mastered after long years of apprenticeship. A career in which there was no place for amateurs. Hector was a willing pupil sitting at the feet of the master – or rather sitting on a bar stool in the Bishop's cocktail bar of the Bull – absorbing the intricacies of inputs and outputs, cellarage, stock control, quantity control, all the controls. Each lesson tended to be accompanied by a bottle of wine, occasionally two, so that while Sheridan imparted the knowledge acquired from years in the catering trade, he was at the same time increasing his takings agreeably.

Hector's other task, and one into which he flung himself with dedicated enthusiasm, was the purchasing of wine for his clients. Many a long hour – tedious, he would have Molly believe – was spent in the cellars of Brentwoods, the wine merchants, choosing which wines to buy. What little wine Hector had left in his own cellars he had no intention of frittering away on his guests. To ensure that he purchased quality combined with economy necessitated much debate and tasting with old Cyril Brentwood – sessions of such complexity they frequently took a whole afternoon in the cold dark cellars. Often he returned home somewhat muddle-headed to explain to Molly the personal sacrifices he was obliged to make and just how complex the whole hotel business was.

'Nonsense,' she said matter-of-factly. 'This is not the Bull, for goodness sake, with fifty bedrooms. Ours will be a glorified house party. Let's face it, we can only take six guests – it's hardly likely to be that complicated.'

But Hector could not share her nonchalance, so he doubled his sessions with Sheridan – to be on the safe side.

When Mrs Carruthers finally rang with a booking, Molly had expected to get into a real dither but was pleasantly surprised to find that she felt very calm. Hector, however, was running around like a headless chicken.

Molly had also been making lists, if not as detailed or beautifully presented as her husband's. She had menus worked out, shopping requirements made. So all she had to do was pick up the telephone and order from the suppliers she had chosen – well, not chosen exactly, they were the same she always went to. But because she was now in business she had been sufficiently emboldened to request a discount – and to her astonishment everyone gave it. This led her to insist on everything being delivered to which, with equal surprise, she heard them agree, for deliveries to Sarson were a thing of the past. All that remained was the question of staff, so she called Thistle and Updike – suppliers of staff to the gentry, established 1894 – to enquire about hiring a butler, a chef and a maid. It was as easy as ordering her groceries. But the idea of putting in an order for people in the same way as for meat reduced Molly to a fit of the giggles.

The staff arrived. This had been Molly's greatest worry but in fact they appeared punctually at the time she had stipulated, they were smart, settled in cheerfully and told her she was not to worry about a thing. They called themselves the Three Musketeers and told her they always worked together – not surprising since the butler was husband to the maid, and the chef was her brother. The chef promptly organised the kitchen, the butler his pantry and the maid redid the rooms that Mrs Hodgson had already done that morning, going as far as to remake the guests' bed to her own satisfaction. Molly hoped Mrs Hodgson never found out; it would certainly bring on an attack of her 'legs'.

At lunchtime the carrier arrived with Molly's pictures from Aunt Fifi. She had time to unpack only three, and hang them in the guest bedroom. She stepped back and looked at them, and felt as if she were welcoming old friends into her house. She supposed the studies, in oils, of children playing in gardens bursting with flowers and butterflies, were rather idealised for many tastes. They might, she supposed, be damned as too chocolate-boxy. But she was glad to find she still liked them as much as she had as a child.

'They're pretty.' Hector had come into the room without her hearing.

'Gracious, you made me jump. I was miles away thinking of when I'd last seen these.'

'Pity they're not the originals. Why were they copied?'

'I think it was because of Uncle Basil's father. He'd got into serious trouble gambling and was forced to sell the originals but first he had them copied so his wife would never find out what he'd been up to. He confessed to Uncle Basil on his deathbed. Or that's the family story.'

'They're good copies. I know old Huxtable Rivers' stuff.'

'Really?' This was a great surprise to Molly who had never seen Hector look at a painting in all the years she had known him, apart from when yet another expert came to study the questionable Turner.

'In my *Children's Illustrated Bible* – there were several reproductions in there. Pretty,' he said vaguely as he left. As Molly rearranged the flowers in the vase on the dressing table she found herself amazed that after all this time she was still finding out things about Hector.

The Drablers were booked in for three nights. Molly and Hector could not believe their luck. An hour before the guests were due Hector raced up to the flagpole on the top of the house, where his grandfather and father had always flown their personal pennant, a practice Hector thought was out of place these days. He said it would make The Hall look like company offices and he wasn't having that. Such things were fine for the Queen, he reckoned, but not for him. There he raised the Stars and Stripes. Molly thought this was going a bit far and made the place look like an embassy, but she hadn't the heart to stop him, he seemed as excited as a little boy.

The Drablers' limousine rolled up at five. They had such pleasant faces that Molly liked them on sight. They were charming in that particular easy American way which made one feel one had known them for years. Within five minutes they were all on

149

Christian-name terms. It was strange, Molly thought, how she did not mind in the least when an American asked her Christian name.

Molly had been somewhat worried that their first guests were to be American, for Hector was not famed for his approval of that particular race. He had often been heard to say that they were rude, vulgar and ate disgusting food. Since, as far as she knew, he did not know any Americans and had never visited the country she had always been surprised at such dogmatic conclusions. She had comforted herself, after Mrs Carruthers' call, that the guests were not French; Hector had even more emphatic opinions on them.

She need not have feared. The effortless charm of the Drablers worked as easily on him as it had on her and within seconds Hector was beaming at them as if all his best friends were American.

There was only one hitch, a small fuss about the chauffeur. Molly presumed the agency would have booked him into the village pub. But he informed her in the nicest possible way that he was usually put up in the staff quarters.

Once she had settled the Drablers in their room Molly sped off to make up another room for the chauffeur – she didn't like to ask the hired maid to do it, unsure if it might not offend her. After all, she'd been employed to look after guests, not chauffeurs. She seemed a willing woman, but Molly did not want to rock the boat. Molly was relieved that the butler and maid were married; at least one staff bedroom was free. They had only slapped on some emulsion paint in three rooms. The remaining bedrooms Molly would not kennel a dog in. In future they might need more staff accommodation; as soon as the Drablers went their first priority must be these rooms. It seemed there was to be no end to the decorating.

They had arranged to meet the Drablers in the drawing-room for cocktails at seven-thirty. Molly found she had time for a lengthy bath and the added luxury of dressing and making up slowly instead of her usual frantic rush. This was a lifestyle she thought she could get used to very quickly.

The evening went like clockwork. The food was perfect, the butler discreetly efficient, the Drablers delightful company.

At the end of the three days Molly and Hector were genuinely sad to see their guests leave and she could see now the wisdom of Mrs Carruthers' collecting the money – to hand them a bill personally would have spoilt everything.

'Did you hear Chuck invite us to stay with them whenever we're in the States?' Hector asked, waving at the retreating car.

'They're so kind, so hospitable,' Molly said, not wishing to spoil Hector's pleasure by pointing out that the way things were it was unlikely they would ever be able to afford to go.

'I've never liked Americans but Chuck and Sophie have made me see things differently. Charming . . .'

Molly was surprised that Hector had the grace to admit that he might have been wrong about over 170 million people. He normally would never concede he could be wrong about anything. He must be mellowing with age, she decided with pleasure, as they turned back into the house.

'Think, Molly, £600 to bank,' he said excitedly, rubbing his hands with glee.

'How much was the computer?' She did not really like to mention it, but thought perhaps she had better.

'With VAT, £565. But that's a capital cost – nothing to do with running costs.'

'Ah I see,' she said doubtfully.

That morning alone in the kitchen Molly did some sums. Having added everything up she did them again and then again.

To staff	350.00
To food	147.47
To flowers	25.47
Mrs Hodgson	18.00
To alcohol	46.00
	£606.94

Whichever way she looked at the figures she could not reduce them. She could not complain about the amount spent on food. They had eaten like kings: there had been the four of them in the dining-room and another four, including the chauffeur, behind the green baize door. Looked at that way, the chef had worked miracles helped, she realised, by the great batches of baking and stock she herself had done prior to the guests' arrival and which she had not even included in her sums.

The flowers were expensive, but that was the time of year – in November flowers were always expensive, come spring they could pick from the garden – Flint permitting. And you had to have flowers.

Alcohol? Maybe Hector need not serve malt whisky in future but then . . . it wasn't as if the Drablers had been heavy drinkers, they had been very modest. If she was honest, Hector had drunk more of the malt than Chuck had.

It was a very long-faced Molly who went in search of Hector.

'The Drablers' visit cost us £6.97,' she said mournfully. 'And if we add on the £7.95 we owe Mrs Carruthers for her book, that's £14.92.'

'What do you mean?' he looked up from the bills on his desk which he was sorting into piles.

'Just that, and I haven't even included heat and lighting, I don't know how to calculate them. Which has to mean we've made a loss.'

'You've made a mistake.'

'No, Hector, I'm afraid I haven't. It's a disaster. Look. Once you'd added those bills up and put them in your ledger, you'd have come to the same conclusion.'

Hector studied her figures.

'You'll have to cut down, Molly.'

'Cut down what? The food bills were remarkably low.' She knew she sounded defensive.

Hector drummed his fingers, stared out of the window and hummed a diddley dum . . .

'It's the staff, isn't it?' he finally said.

'I fear so.'

'But they expect a butler.'

'Yes, I realise.'

'Would Mrs Hodgson dress up in a black dress with frilly apron and cap?'

152

'No.'

'Diddley . . . dum . . .'

'I'll have to take over the cooking,' she said, after a long pause.

'Won't it be a bit too much for you?' he asked, rather spoiling the effect of concern by the buoyant tone of his voice.

'What other solution is there?' she said with sinking heart.

'I'll go and see Sheridan, he'll know what to do and I promised to let him know how we got on.'

Sheridan was tracked down in the Bishop's bar of the Bull. To give him his due, he did try to look sympathetic and managed to hide the vast amusement he was feeling.

'Heads in beds, that's what you're lacking,' Sheridan said knowledgeably. 'Skulls, we call them in the trade.'

'Skulls?' Hector repeated, as if the single word was a magic mantra. Sheridan went on at some length to explain the necessity of numbers. That the more you packed in the cheaper the running costs.

'But it's the fire regulations, you see. We can only take six.'

'Put some on the ground floor. That rule's only for those on the first.'

'Really?' Hector could hardly contain his excitement, he hurriedly thanked Sheridan and went straight back to Molly with the good news. They must, he announced, forget the staff rooms and begin forthwith to decorate the room overlooking the rose garden, which once had been Cuckoo's private sitting-room. While they were about it they might as well do the one next to it.

Her enthusiasm was not in Hector's league but she managed to put on a brave face. What made it even more difficult was Hector's parting shot as he raced off to phone Mrs Carruthers.

'Minimum of six we'll take – that's £600 a night. Maximum ten – That's £1,000 a night. Surely even you can make a profit out of that.'

But the door had closed before she could get her breath back to make a suitably cutting remark – not that she could have done. The witty and sarcastic rejoinders only occurred to her hours later, and usually in the bath with no one to hear them.

Chapter 16

Hector Is Wrong

C OLIN'S OUTLINE PLANNING permission was rejected on a technicality. This outcome amused Hector who was heard to mutter, darkly, that lots of technicalities could be found should Colin not take the hint and apply again.

For nearly a month the Manns had kept themselves very much to themselves. Molly found this unnerving and even began to dream of Colin supervising the building of a Disneyland-like complex round Gussie and her dogs; of skyscrapers down the main street. Hector regarded the silence as proof that the housing estate plans had been a storm in a teacup and they would be better occupied concentrating on his diabolical Elizabethan Village.

Since they had opened The Hall for business Molly did not get out as much as before. Someone had to stay in in case Mrs Carruthers telephoned with a booking. An answerphone machine might have been a more sensible expenditure than Hector's redundant computer. But, with Christmas approaching at alarming speed, Molly had made arrangements for Mrs Hodgson, Hope and Hector between them to man the telephone so that she could go Christmas shopping.

Once again her car was playing up, refusing to start until a large sum of money was spent on its insides. She had arranged for Lulu to give her a lift into Lynchester, where they would shop together and have lunch. She had decided to walk to Lulu's, not wishing to put her out too much. When she found she had forgotten her cheque book and had to return to the house for it, and when half-way down the drive she found she hadn't her purse and had to retrace her steps again she was glad she had opted to walk. Lulu would never forget anything, she was so incredibly well organised.

As she reached the main road a large lorry loaded with scaffolding slowed down and the driver shouted to her for directions to the Dower House. Now what did Colin need that amount of scaffolding for? The roof was sound – the Clements had seen to that. Upon her return she must tell Hector and perhaps get Mrs Hodgson to find out what Colin was up to from the cleaning ladies who worked for Sue.

The whole village was now a network of spies and counter-intelligence. Action groups were cropping up with the speed of mushrooms. Molly's information that Colin planned an estate of over three hundred houses instead of the announced fifty had rocked the village. Consternation was rampant. Only Bill Blunt, landlord of the Parminter Arms, the Trotters and Fred Hodgson were in favour. Even the antique-shop owners, putting aesthetics before profit, had signed all the petitions. Molly could understand the support for Colin from the Trotters and Bill Blunt but was mystified by Fred Hodgson's stand. As always, Mrs Hodgson explained. With the large estate the number of commuters on the 125 to London would increase dramatically. Not only would this make the bosses at BR shelve any thoughts of axing Sarson Magna's station, but Fred was now dreaming of Sarson Magna being upgraded to a parkway. No one had been aware that there was a serious risk of British Rail closing Sarson Magna: its closure was a rumour which circulated regularly – usually when other gossip was thin on the ground. And because of its frequency, it was a rumour that no one took seriously. There had been a station there since Hector's great-grandfather had allowed the railway to be built across his land in return for a station for his own use. But a parkway? That would mean extra cars, extra people, more noise, said some. Prosperity, more jobs, more spending, trumpeted Fred to anyone who would listen. New divisions in the village loomed.

In consequence two further action groups sprang up. One against the closure and one for a parkway. This latter group enraged the citizens of Lynchester, who already had a parkway and now feared that it would move to Sarson. Now there was a Protect Lynchester Parkway action group with pickets everywhere.

Molly crossed the High Street, thinking, as she did so, how quickly and with what ease she had managed a complete about-face. She had been the Manns' greatest ally; now she was in the forefront of those against Colin's plans.

Hector had been keen for her to remain friendly with them but Molly refused. There were times when she thought Hector totally unprincipled. With regret she had turned down Sue's invitation to another luncheon; despite everything, the food was so good and they were extremely generous with their drinks.

Hector was still smug. It was no good Molly pointing out that she hadn't changed her opinions, it was events that had changed. She still thought the artificial village idea was not such a terrible thing, it could have been good for Sarson Magna. She could even forgive Colin his duplicity over the houses. He was, after all, a businessman and undoubtedly they had to use all manner of means to achieve their aims. Her change had been simply over the number of houses planned, nothing else. One opinion had not altered, and that was that Hector and his cohorts had rejected Colin from the outset because of who he was.

Sybil Potter-Smythe was just coming out of her doorway and waited for Molly to catch up. This was a good sign. Sybil and Twink had been quite cold to her and she had not known if it was over the Mann affair or because she had gone into trade.

The Potter-Smythes had lived in the village for six months and still, apart from Mrs Hodgson's relative in the betting shop, no one had seen Mr Potter-Smythe. There had been rumours – of course with a resident of Sarson Magna involved there would be. These rumours veered from the compassionate to the slanderous. The most innocuous was that he was an invalid, confined to an upper bedroom. The worst, which had swept the village like a forest fire, had begun when Sybil had been seen digging a large hole in her garden. PC Lay had decided he should investigate and arrived in time to see Sybil planting a particularly fine *Robinia pseudoacacia* which he was then forced to discuss with her at interminable length. Molly hoped that the mystery of Mr Potter-Smythe would soon be solved. Mrs Hodgson's particular problem was mystery enough.

Sybil kissed Molly on both cheeks. Since Molly's first inadvertent kiss, when in her cups, Sybil always kissed her in greeting. This confused Molly's long-standing friends, who knew that her feelings about kissing acquaintances were as strong as those on the use of first names.

'Molly, I've been meaning to call. I wanted to ask your advice. I hear Hector is resigning from the Parish Council. Is it true?'

'Good gracious, how do you know that? He's still just thinking about it as far as I know.'

'I was told he felt he had too much on his plate – the County Council and . . .' Sybil coughed a shade too genteelly for it to be a proper cough, it was more of a punctuation sort of cough, '. . . the Council and the business you are running at The Hall.'

Molly could not help but think that 'the business', the way Sybil said it, made the whole thing sound extremely shady and not quite nice. It never failed to fascinate Molly how the English language could be spoken with such a diversity of inflections. She wondered how a poor foreigner could ever be expected to understand the language, let alone the people.

'Really . . .' Molly said with no inflection whatsoever so that the word could be interpreted one way or the other.

'Yes,' said Sybil, choosing to imagine a question mark on the end of Molly's 'really'. 'I was talking to a friend on the Council. It was just that I wanted to check with you since I would hate to offend dear Hector. You see I'd rather like to stand for selection myself.'

'Most commendable,' said Molly with the merest hint of sarcasm, at the same time wondering how Hector would react on hearing that he was dear to Sybil.

'Thank you,' said Sybil, and Molly marvelled at how thick-skinned the woman appeared to be. Well, if she was it was probably the best possible recommendation for a career in politics even at parish level. 'To be a representative of my community has always been my greatest dream. Of course I could never even consider such a thing when my husband was a Headmaster – the parents might not have liked it.'

'Of course,' Molly said, puzzled that parents could exist who might disapprove of the Parish Council. It was hardly a hotbed of radical politics.

Side by side they continued along the High Street while Sybil expounded her plans, once in office, as if already canvassing for Molly's vote. It would appear that single-handed Sybil was to get the village bypassed, a community swimming pool, a new medical centre with X-ray apparatus. Molly was amazed at her blatant ambition – at this rate she would possess an MBE by the end of the year, if not earlier.

They had reached the Bakers Café which initially everyone had boycotted but to whose fold the excellence of the cakes had finally seduced everyone. Hyacinth hurtled out, calling Molly's name and waving her hands dementedly.

'Molly, is it true?'

'Is what true?'

'That Hector's resigning from the Parish Council. Only if he is, Porky is thinking of standing in his stead only he doesn't want to stand on anyone's toes . . .'

'I'm standing,' Sybil replied.

'You're *what*?' Hyacinth stood back and looked at Sybil with dismay. 'But you can't, you're a newcomer.'

'And what is your husband?'

'We've lived here years.'

'But not long enough. Why, you should hear what the milkman has to say about your husband and his fellow servicemen,' Sybil said imperiously. Molly remained silent knowing full well there was nothing she could say.

'Servicemen?' Hyacinth said, outraged. Her face was contorted with anger and she clutched the strap of her handbag as if to control herself. 'I think that would be a mistake, Sybil. You've interfered enough with your unwelcome petition. You should keep your nose out of village affairs. You are already regarded as an interfering busybody.'

'Such rudeness,' Sybil boomed, looking in Molly's direction for support. But Molly found herself backing away from the warring women. 'And who do you think you are?' Sybil spoke so loudly that her voice carried into the café and could be heard over the chatter and the rattling of the crockery. Forks heavily laden with cake stopped half-way from plate to mouth. Coffee cups remained poised in the air. Silence reigned.

'I'm someone who knows this village better than you.' Hyacinth squared up to Sybil.

'Ladies, ladies,' Molly eventually spoke up, but rather ineffectually. For to her shame she found she was rather enjoying the confrontation.

'The problem with you service personnel is that you think that everyone is a private in your own personal army. Well, I'm not. I've every right to stand if I so wish.'

'We'll see about that,' Hyacinth said most unpleasantly.

'And what does that mean? Threatening me are you, Mrs Naughton?'

'Go and suck eggs,' Hyacinth hissed. Such a silly expression, Molly began to think when – WHAM! It happened so quickly that Molly didn't even see Sybil's handbag until it hit Hyacinth, knocking her sideways. Was it Molly's imagination, or did a cheer come from inside the café, where a large group of women and children from Churchill Drive were taking elevenses.

'I shall win. I shall make doubly sure now,' Sybil said haughtily before stalking away, head held high.

'Well, really. Did you ever see such bullying, Molly?' Hyacinth blustered and then, suddenly aware of the crowd of faces gawping at her from the café window, she blushed bright red and scuttled away quickly, probably to report to Porky.

Undoubtedly, with one swing of her handbag, Sybil had won the election. If there was one person more unpopular than Colin Mann in the village it was the imperious Hyacinth. Within the half-hour the Sarson Magna grapevine would have made Sybil into a heroine.

Molly contributed to the flight of the gossip by hurrying on to Lulu's, agog to tell her of the fight – a new one that. But there was more drama awaiting her.

Pacing up and down Lulu's drawing-room, her tawny hair making the description of a caged lion not unapt, was Gussie.

'What's happened?' Molly asked, accepting a coffee from Lulu and resigning herself to the fact that perhaps she would not be able to get all her Christmas shopping done today as she had hoped.

'Weedkiller. That's what's happened. All over the meadows, my garden – it's like a desert.'

'Oh, no. Was it Colin?'

'Obviously not him personally. Some minion he paid. Who else is going to kill my weeds?' Molly looked up with surprise as she realised that Gussie's irritation was directed at her.

'I'm sorry,' Molly said quickly. Sorry about the weeds and for being an irritant even though she was not sure why she was, particularly.

'Gussie's worrying about her dogs,' Lulu said in explanation.

'He wouldn't hurt them, surely?' Molly said, her voice brimming with concern, and sat down, shocked at the very thought. Gussie rolled her eyes heavenward with exasperation.

'That man's capable of anything. And you saw him the other day with my animals, you could hardly mistake him for an animal lover, could you? Not even someone like you, Molly.'

Molly looked down at her cup unsure what someone like her meant, but in view of Gussie's ill humour thinking it better to keep silent.

'And look at these . . .' Gussie burrowed into a large straw basket she was carrying and dug out a handful of mail. 'Insurance companies' brochures . . . pension plans . . . estate agents' details . . .' she slapped them down on the coffee table. 'Kitchens . . . built-in bedrooms . . . bathrooms.' Angrily, glossy brochures of a dozen different firms were added to the others. 'Double glazing; thermal insulation; burglar alarms; car phones; sexy underwear.' At each one on her list the pile of documents on Lulu's coffee table grew more mountainous. 'And at home I've every mail-order catalogue you care to mention, and the phone never stops with people trying to sell me things.' Gussie scowled and did not look beautiful at all.

The pile of papers slipped and Molly leapt to save them though she supposed it didn't matter. She did not know what to say. 'Oh dear,' she found herself saying for lack of anything constructive and knew it was a totally inadequate response. So, 'Isn't it illegal?' she hurriedly added.

'Of course it's illegal,' Gussie snapped most unpleasantly, almost as if Molly had sent them herself. 'You try proving that Mann sent them. Just try.'

Again Molly looked down at her coffee as if searching for the solution in its depths. She felt chastened by Gussie's voice but at the same time knew that she would feel a great deal more sympathetic if Gussie wasn't being so rude and bad-tempered with her.

'A friend of mine used to do this sort of thing – as a joke, you know. He once sent a coffin to one friend . . .' Lulu laughed but, Molly noticed, it was a pretty weak laugh. Maybe Lulu had been at the receiving end of Gussie's wrath long before she had arrived; this made Molly feel much better.

'Ha . . . Ha . . .' said Gussie through clenched teeth just like Tabby did and Molly's heart sank, for she had fondly hoped it was something Tabby would grow out of.

'He has to be stopped,' Molly ventured.

'Of course he's got to be stopped – any suggestions?' Gussie sneered so unpleasantly that Molly would have got up and left there and then had not Lulu been semaphoring desperately to her to stay.

'People have got to be told about this. They won't like it, a woman alone being intimidated. I know Hector's working like a demon on the Council to get everything blocked.'

'Bully for him.' Gussie lit another cigarette which she sucked at hungrily and then puffed the smoke in the air in a particularly antisocial way.

'You could turn the tables on him and send him a lot of rubbish through the post too,' Lulu said logically. 'We could all help filling in the coupons in the magazines and newspapers.'

'I can just see Mann cringing with terror, can't you?'

'He certainly doesn't seem to care what people think of him, does he?' Lulu said, putting the coffee tray to one side and getting glasses out of the corner cupboard instead. Ah well, though Molly, no shopping today.

'Isn't it strange to have spent so much money to appear to be one of us and then to throw it all away so quickly.' Molly voiced her thoughts.

'Money means more to him, obviously.' There it was again, that sharpness and irritation.

'Look, Gussie. I'm sorry about everything. I know you're worried out of your mind. But getting angry with us isn't going to help you or the situation, is it?' Molly said gently.

'I'm sorry. It's my dogs. I don't know how I could survive if he killed my dogs,' and to Lulu and Molly's astonishment, Gussie burst into tears. Both women leapt quickly to comfort her, banging their heads together in the attempt, and spoke in unison as they reassured the poor woman that not even Colin would stoop that low. But even as they said it, neither was convinced.

They then spent the next four hours drinking the rest of the coffee and sherry, then wine, then brandy as they planned a counter-attack. As the time passed the schemes mooted became wilder, more preposterous, and more unlikely. Molly had noticed this phenomenon before, particularly with Hector. People, wanting revenge, and fuelled with alcohol, experienced complete changes of character. By the end of the afternoon any one of the three would have been quite happy to hang, draw and quarter Colin with her own bare hands.

Chapter 17

Molly Prepares for Christmas

I T WAS OVER a week before Molly could finally make the arrangements to do her Christmas shopping with Lulu. The delay was caused by Hector enthusiastically throwing himself once more into the Mann controversy. This entailed so many telephone calls, and meetings both at The Hall and in Lynchester that Molly was completely tied up at the house.

The most worrying aspect of Hector's new-found enthusiasm was that he, stupidly Molly thought, spent hours late at night snooping around the Dower House. Nightly she expected a call to bail him out of jail – not that Sarson Magna had a jail but at least to bail him out of PC Lay's lounge. In a way she was quite disappointed this had not happened. According to Lulu, PC and Mrs Lay's lounge carpet had to be seen to be believed. Lulu knew about the décor at the Lays' since she had once spent an uncomfortable hour there when Peter Lay was adamant that she had had too much to drink to drive and she had disagreed with his assessment equally adamantly. She had refused to blow into his machine. 'Aids', she had used as her excuse. But the vertigo caused by the orange and purple whirls on the carpet had been so furious that she had begun to feel quite ill and had finally agreed to blow – the crystals proclaimed her innocence – miraculously – and she had left triumphantly, telling all and sundry that if the Home Office would only lay such carpeting in all prisons, recidivism would disappear overnight.

Hector himself was devastated to find that the Dower House scaffolding was for the old coach house which seemed about to be reroofed. This still did not stop him; he regarded this as a smokescreen for other activities, hence the endless snooping.

Hector suffered greatly for the sake of the community – a bad back from slipping down a bank, a twisted ankle from an argument with a tree stump, and a cough which would have been at home in a terminal geriatric ward.

The annoyance to Gussie was harder to control. PC Lay had refused to call with a warning to Colin not to continue with the postal assaults, on the ground that they had yet to prove that it was Colin sending them. Hector, Porky and the rest regarded this wimpishness as yet another symptom of the spinelessness of the police, the Home Secretary, and the Government in general.

Molly was pleased to see that despite Sybil's attack on Hyacinth and her own irresponsibility in doing nothing to stop the two women, Porky and Hector were still the best of friends. Men were better at that sort of thing – not taking sides, jumping to conclusions, prolonging rows – whereas Hyacinth had cut herself off from virtually everyone.

Jib, whose nephew was a public analyst, had come up with the idea of sending soil samples off to be analysed in the hopes of finding that Colin had used some prohibited substance. The result was disappointing: he had used a proprietary brand of weedkiller available to any farmer.

To help Gussie sleep at night Hector loaned her Flint, to act as foreman to a heartening group of large, able-bodied men from the village, who were to build a large dog compound. The wire and staves were supplied by Farmer Feather who, while happy to bank Colin's cheque, was not so happy when some of the weedkiller drifted on to his crops.

In two days they had built an enclosure and at night Gussie took all the dogs and cats into the house. There wasn't a bed, chair or settee that wasn't occupied by a snoring canine or feline incumbent.

Molly could only hope that everything would now remain quiet until Christmas was over, she already had far too much to do. Christmas for Molly was the same as for every mother in the land. Busy. But this Christmas was to be different, and far busier. Not only were James and Tabby coming but the previous week Mrs

Carruthers, after a silence of four weeks, had telephoned with a booking for six.

Molly had taken the call. She had been concerned that recently there had been what amounted to a deafening silence from Aristocratic Homes Inc. There was no way that they could regard this as a business if guests were to be so intermittent. But at the same time she did not want to receive a call. Molly did not normally behave with such contrariness but she was still confused over the whole issue of The Hall as a glorified guesthouse. She knew that money had to be made somehow or other; she hadn't one word of criticism about the Drablers as guests. But logic told her that not all guests could be as considerate and easy as they had been. It was only a matter of time before someone difficult turned up. Even their friends could be divided into those she and Hector longed to have stay and those who, after the initial euphoria of greeting, they hoped would not prolong their visit beyond the agreed time.

But here were Mrs Carruthers' strangled vowels screeching out of the receiver at her. Playing for time she had said she would have to let her know and would call back within the hour. Mrs Carruthers' response was to tell her quite sharply that she had better make her mind up quickly, that there were plenty on her books *begging* for such a booking.

Molly sat for a while beside the telephone. While she had entered into this business as supportive of Hector as she could possibly be, it had never entered her head that their Christmas as a family could in any way be threatened. Christmases, to Molly, were sacrosanct. Who on earth were these people who wanted to spend it with strangers? Was there something odd about them that their own families did not want them? She had often felt sorry for the people she had seen arriving at the Bull for their special Christmas offer of an 'olde worlde tyme', thinking how sad it must be not to have a warm family celebration. That was until Lulu had pointed out that they probably had to go to hotels because they were so grim that their own families had banned them. Were the people Mrs Carruthers was recommending like that? She dickered with the idea of not even telling Hector about the telephone call but finally decided she was incapable of such blatant dishonesty. So she went in search of him.

She found him putting the finishing touches to one of the new ground-floor bedrooms. Molly had to admit, after his somewhat creaky start, Hector had come up trumps on the decorating stakes. There could be only one explanation – he was enjoying himself. Hector had never been known to do anything he didn't wish to do.

'Mrs Carruthers just phoned with a booking for six for three nights over Christmas.'

'Fantastic!' was Hector's enthusiastic response as he pasted the last strip of a particularly pretty dado in place – large red cherries intermingled with pink cabbage roses.

'But Christmas? Oh no, Hector, we can't.'

'Why ever not? It'll be fun. There would only have been the five of us and Hope, otherwise. You're forever saying this house needs people. This Christmas we shall have them, *and* paying for the privilege.'

'I know . . . but . . . Oh Hector,' she said, concerned. In the past he had never given money a thought, which of course might explain a lot of their problems now, but these days he seemed to be obsessed with the stuff. 'I don't think I want strangers here, not at such a special time.'

'What's special about it? I'll tell you . . .' Hector eased himself down Flint's stepladder. 'You work like a demon every year cooking, cleaning, present buying, wrapping and what happens? Tabby rarely likes what we've bought her and always seems to be on some stupid crash diet so that she refuses to eat. James invariably arrives, unpacks, gives you his dirty washing to do and then clears off to a party the other side of the county, or gets drunk. Neither gets up till long past noon and when there's washing up to do they both mysteriously disappear. That's your normal Christmas. It's always been like that and I can see no reason why they should both suddenly change.'

'But . . .'

'No buts. This year we'll have guests who'll fully appreciate your efforts. You'll have help in the kitchen as you've never had

166

before so that you won't even have to cook. You'll be able to sit back and relax. It'll be the jolliest Christmas of all.'

'Put like that . . .'

'There's no other way to put it. But I think if we agree we should tell Carruthers we want more money to do it, being Christmas and all that malarky.'

'She's already said it will be £225 per couple per night.'

'That settles it then, Molly my love. We can't turn our noses up at, what's 225 × 3 × 3? Good God!' he looked at her with stunned amazement. 'That makes £2,025!'

Steve Ovett could not have got to the telephone faster than Hector to confirm the booking before Mrs Carruthers gave it to one of the other impoverished homes on her list.

Molly telephoned the staff agency to order the Three Musketeers only to be informed that they had already left for their annual holiday in the Bahamas. While digesting this disappointing information Molly, not for the first time, wondered if there would ever be a time when she and Hector could afford a holiday in the sun. Maybe the solution was to shut The Hall and for she and Hector to get a job as a cook and handyman. Instead she had to accept Michael, Florence and Julian who all came as highly recommended as her beloved Musketeers, while all expecting double time since it was Christmas.

She had finally managed to get Hector to sit down while she gave him a lecture on electricity. With so many people in the house what was switched on when would be critical if they were not to have a black-out. He finally acknowledged the seriousness of the situation, asked her to explain it all a second time and then made lists. These lists, with much underlining in red, showed what appliances should not be used in conjunction with others. He pinned them up at critical points and rushed out to buy a gross of candles. While candles would be pretty, Molly did fear the added fire hazard.

Molly was in the kitchen finishing making the last of the mince pies. With such a large household she thought it only fair that she do as much as she could to help Michael, the new chef. Hector's motivating lecture had worked wonders and as she worked she found she was looking forward to this particular holiday. She was not prepared for the trouble, which started the minute James arrived. They had not told him what they were doing, which was stupid of them, she now realised, for when he learnt he was shocked and angry.

'P.G.s? Really, Mother.'

'Really what, James?' Molly said as innocently as she could while continuing to cut out the circles of pastry for the mince pies. She had long ago discovered that when faced with a difficult situation it was always best to have one's hands occupied. She was never sure if she did this to cover up her confusion or as a device to stop her swiping someone.

'I wish you would stop that and listen to me, Mother,' said James, as everyone tended to say.

'I am listening,' came the stock reply.

'You've turned The Hall into a boarding-house.'

'Yes, I suppose we have.'

'Well, I'm disgusted. What on earth will people think? What do your friends think about it all?'

'I haven't actually asked them, I didn't regard their permission as essential,' she said, a shade sharply. The truth was, she preferred not to ask some of them. From Lulu and Mrs Hodgson's reports, Molly knew full well that the village was divided over what she and Hector were about. Several had made references to Colin Mann, and 'one law for the rich and one for the poor' had frequently been heard. This was such arrant nonsense since, compared with Colin, Hector was the poor one. Not that a lot of the villagers would believe that for one moment; to them, if you lived in a big house you were rich. On paper, Hector was wealthy but as the struggle to survive persisted Molly was pretty sure that even the vicar had more spending power than them. 'Lulu says she thinks it's great fun.'

'She would. It's easy for her to say that with all her money.' James prowled about the kitchen like a caged something – she wasn't sure which animal best described her son. But what he said was true. Molly had noticed that the more moneyed of their friends had always had more open minds. Lulu, Annie English, and Porky

– who on top of his General's pension had the income from a huge trust fund set up by his late father, big in meat pies – had all been encouraging. Whereas Jib and Bat, who never stopped complaining about the size of their pensions, the Potter-Smythes and all those who lived in the Upper Cottages had been, to say the least, somewhat sniffy about everything. It was as if those who had to struggle to make ends meet were of the opinion that Hector and Molly should have soldiered on with The Hall instead of losing face by taking in guests. It saddened her to think that status had taken on such importance with these people. As if the poorer they became the more status mattered until, presumably, that was all they would be left with.

'I'm sorry you're upset but something had to be done if the place isn't to fall about our ears.'

'I can't think what my friends in the City will say.' James was standing by the sink gloomily looking out at the yard which was chock-a-block with leaves. Molly felt that it would be more profitable if he went out to sweep them up rather than continuing this conversation, which was going to get them nowhere. But he looked so dejected that she had to go and put her arms about him, holding her hands at the angle of an Indian dancer so as not to get flour on his suit.

'If your friends judge you by what your parents are up to that seems a sad state of affairs to me. You're not responsible for our actions.'

'Come off it, Mother. You know damn well it matters.'

'But it shouldn't. Don't you see, James? What is the use of pretending that just because we have this huge house we are affluent. Anyone with any sense can see our life is one constant struggle.'

'But why won't the old man sell something?'

'Your friends wouldn't mind that then – seeing the family silver put up at Sotheby's? I really don't see the difference, at least your father is trying to hang on to everything.' She laughed, but still James looked dejected. 'Look, I'm sure if Shar loves you she'll forgive you your frightful parents.'

'I don't see her any more.'

'No? Might I ask why?' Molly was ashamed at how happy this news made her.

'She was too bossy and self-opinionated.'

'Really?' Molly pretended surprise, and had to bend her face over her pastry board to hide her self-satisfied grin. 'Anyone else?'

'Maybe . . .' James shuffled his feet and started to pick at the raw pastry. 'She's very sweet, actually. The complete opposite.'

'How nice . . .'

The door flew open and Tabby cannonballed into the room, but a transformed Tabby. Gone were the huge shoes, replaced by a smart pair of patent-leather pumps. She had on a short black miniskirt – but a neat and pressed one. She wore sheer black tights but, most surprising of all, a blue sweater with a coloured scarf around her neck. Molly could not remember the last time she had seen her daughter wear any colour to relieve the unrelenting black she always wore. The orange bits at the front of her hair were covered with a wide bandeau, the rest hung loose and shining down her back. She looked lovely. Molly could not help but wonder who or what had caused this transformation. But at least, at last she might ask to borrow her pearls, Molly thought happily.

'Hi! I've got a surprise, Mummy. You don't mind do you?' She was jumping from one foot to the other and Molly was struck at how like a little girl she could still be despite her outward sophistication.

'What sort of surprise?' she asked suspiciously, fully aware that Tabby's surprises should be treated with circumspection.

'Me, I'm afraid, Mrs Parminter,' and to her intense surprise and pleasure there stood Sebastian. 'I told Tabby it was a fearful cheek – Christmas and all that.'

'Good gracious, Sebastian, it's a pleasure.'

'We got engaged again. Look,' Tabby thrust her left hand out, waggling it about to show off a different ring. A very beautiful diamond had been chosen for this engagement.

'Again.' Molly realised she should have been making congratulating noises, but 'again' was all she could think of saying.

'Yes, Mrs Parminter. Last night. Aren't I the luckiest man alive?'

Molly was not too sure. Even though she loved Tabby to distraction she was not certain that marrying her was the best thing for Sebastian. He was too nice, too kind, too considerate. Tabby, she was certain, would make mincemeat of him. She had grown sufficiently fond of him to feel some concern. So, instead of agreeing, she merely smiled as happily as she could.

Introductions were made to James whose smile, to Molly, seemed the appallingly smug one of a person who felt himself in all ways superior to Sebastian, who was in his jeans and scruffy T-shirted uniform. But the smile was rapidly wiped off his face when he learnt who Sebastian was. After the previous conversation she feared he was over-impressed that Seb was heir to a viscountcy. On the other hand, she wondered if, in James' world, peopled by those who set such store by money, Sebastian's musical career was of even more importance, status-wise. Presumably because of the great wealth it generated he was acceptable on either score. But what if he had been a failed skiffle player – what then? Good gracious, what had made her think of skiffle of all things? She wondered what had happened to them, were they all defunct now with the advent of washing machines and the disappearance of the washboard? She must remember to ask Sebastian.

'And I want to give up art college, if you and Daddy don't mind. It's so drear . . .'

'You must do what you want, darling.' Molly was overjoyed at Tabby's decision. But what Tabby said next was like celestial music to her ears.

'I thought I'd like to do a secretarial course, Mummy.'

'Oh, yes?' Molly said, trying hard not to sound too enthusiastic, which would have been the kiss of death to the scheme. Life was always so much easier when Tabby decided what she wanted to do. When Molly made a suggestion it was always viewed with the utmost suspicion, and discarded.

'When we're married I can do all Seb's letters. There's masses of them you know. Do you like my new image?' Tabby gave a twirl. 'Don't I look like the perfect secretary?'

'Perfect, Tabby. I'm sure a secretarial course can easily be arranged.' Molly sounded as nonchalant as possible while brimming over with satisfaction. With the complete faith of all mothers of young daughters Molly believed implicitly that a secretarial course for daughters was a *good thing*.

'I hear you've got paying guests in for Christmas, Mrs Parminter.'

'Yes, six – all Americans.'

James shuffled about with so much embarrassment that even his feet seemed to have been affected by it.

'What fun!' Sebastian said. 'I've been telling my father to do the same for ages – at least it would help with the drains.'

'I'm sure Hector will give you all the details.' Molly glanced with pleasure at her level-headed future son-in-law.

The new hired staff arrived. They were in total contrast to the Musketeers. They were untidy, and both men could have done with a shave. Worse still, they had dirty shoes. This latter was of particular importance to Molly. Without fail, the state of a person's shoes revealed more than any psychiatrist's couch. Dirty and scuffed, then without doubt their owner's life would be disorganised. But polished and mended, no matter the age of the shoes, was an indication of an ordered life. And Hector set even greater store by the shoe test – what would he have to say? These three sets of shoes rang deafening alarm bells in Molly's mind. As if to prove the point, her sensitive nose detected a strong whiff of BO from Julian, the alleged butler.

She showed them their rooms and said pointedly that they would no doubt like to wash after their journey. Since they had come from Lynchester, all of seven miles away, it was not altogether surprising they looked at her as if she had a screw loose. Undaunted she persisted, showing them the bathroom and arranging to meet them downstairs in half an hour to show them where everything was.

They reappeared, and Molly gave Michael a tour of the kitchen and told him her ideas for dinner tonight. She was somewhat concerned by his total lack of interest in her suggestions. Florence, she suggested, should help Mrs Hodgson with cleaning the last of the silver. Molly was a great believer in *suggesting* rather than *ordering*. She doubted if Mrs Hodgson would still be with her if she *told* her to do anything. Finally she showed the butler his pantry.

An hour later she returned to give Mrs Hodgson her Christmas present since, understandably, she would not be in again until after the New Year. She walked into uproar. Both Julian and Florence were screaming abusively at Mrs Hodgson who, bristling with indignation, was putting on her coat, or at least trying to. In her agitation she had split the lining and kept losing her hand inside the coat.

'No one talks to my Julian like that, you evil old bag!' Florence shrieked.

'There's a word for the likes of you,' Julian thundered.

'Please, please everyone. What seems to be the matter?' Molly clapped her hands like a schoolteacher bringing an unruly class to order.

'I haven't come here to be insulted,' Julian said with almost grotesque dignity.

'Either they go, or I go.' Mrs Hodgson added her two penny-worth.

'But Mrs Hodgson, you're going anyway. It's your holiday.'

'Be that as it may, it's them or me,' she said, adding to Molly's confusion. Having sorted out the problem with the sleeve of her coat Mrs Hodgson now stood, legs slightly apart, arms akimbo, as if on the poop deck of a man-of-war.

'Would someone tell me what on earth's going on?' Molly's voice rose, not only with irritation but with concern as she sensed impending disaster.

'She said I stank,' Julian flared.

'So he does.' Mrs Hodgson still stood stolidly angry in the middle of the kitchen. 'You can't expect decent folk to work with a smell like that.'

'See, her's doing it again.' And Julian lunged towards her. That at least gave Mrs Hodgson a degree of mobility again.

'Don't you touch me . . . you . . . *stink-bomb*,' Mrs Hodgson hissed.

Molly was in a quandary. Mrs Hodgson was only speaking the

truth, even if it was unfortunate that she'd found it necessary to do so just at this moment.

'Well . . .' Molly began indecisively.

'Do you think I smell?' He was glaring at Molly now.

'Well . . . perhaps a little . . .' Molly said in almost a whisper.

'See. I told you so,' Mrs Hodgson crowed with triumph.

'That's done it Jules, come on. We're going.' Florence flounced.

'But you can't leave me . . .' Molly began.

'Oh yes we can. Stuff the lot of you,' and grabbing the malodorous Julian by the hand Florence dragged him out of the kitchen, only to pop her head round the door a second later. 'You coming Michael?'

'No, I need the dosh,' the chef, much to Molly's relief, replied.

'Sorry about that, Mrs Parminter, but you know me. I always speaks as I find.' Mrs Hodgson was buttoning her coat with the virtuous air of one who feels herself totally vindicated.

'Yes, Mrs Hodgson.'

'Have a Happy Christmas, Mrs Parminter, and . . .' she sidled over to Molly, 'I should keep an eye on him,' she whispered, nodding towards the chef. 'Drink,' she mouthed like Les Dawson, and with that picked up her present and marched out of the back door.

'*Now* what do we do?' Molly sat down at the kitchen table.

'Don't worry, Mrs Parminter, we'll muddle through.' The chef loomed over her and, from the smell on his breath, Molly realised that once again Mrs Hodgson had spoken the truth.

Chapter 18

Panic Is Forestalled

For the second time Sebastian came to the Parminters' rescue. He had listened silently to Molly's story of the staff's defection. Much to her disappointment, he said nothing. She had expected quite a lot of sympathy from him and was surprised when it wasn't forthcoming. Even more so when he suddenly announced he had to go out for a while.

Three hours later Sebastian appeared in the sitting-room resplendent in neatly pressed striped trousers, black jacket, white shirt, black tie and the shiniest shoes.

'Would you think of employing me as a butler?' he asked Molly, twirling around for all to see his splendour and laughing at the surprised expressions on both Tabby and Molly's faces.

'You look splendid, Sebastian. The perfect butler.' Molly admired the handsome young man.

'Where did you get that outfit from?' Tabby asked suspiciously, prowling around him as if looking for some defect.

'I went to my Uncle Felix's – he lives ten miles the other side of Lynchester. I borrowed this from his butler, it's his second-best suit.'

'You couldn't do it, though, not properly. You'd make a right prat of yourself,' Tabby said.

'Thanks for being so encouraging, Tabby, darling. Of course I could do it, I've seen butlers working all my life. It'll be easy as pie.'

'Am I to understand you want to work for me as a butler?' Molly asked, uncertain she was really witnessing this scene.

'Not work for you, Mrs Parminter, work with you. I don't want to be paid. It will be tremendous fun I'm sure.'

'Sebastian, you are so kind,' Molly said, marvelling that Tabby should have found a young man so perfect, and at the same time terrified that it would never last.

'Oh, Seb, you are spiffing!'

Molly looked up, astonished. Spiffing was a word that was out of date when she was young, yet here it was back in use by her daughter. At this rate Hector risked being trendy if he didn't watch out.

'On the drive back I had another idea, Mrs Parminter. Tabby here could take over as the maid.'

'Me?' Tabby managed, in that one syllable, to say exactly what she thought of Sebastian's idea.

'Yes. You. I'll help you with the beds, and things like that, and you can help me serve. This is an emergency, Tabby, and you should be helping your parents.'

'You're right, Seb. You're always right. And it'll probably be the most enormous fun.' Molly looked at Tabby closely, prepared to see an expression of disdain, sarcasm, cynicism or a combination of all three. Instead Tabby was almost purring with agreement. Molly felt nothing but awe at the effect Sebastian had on her daughter. If she were more religious, she would go down on her hands and knees and pray that they would marry. But Molly was a woman of principle and did not approve of the sort of person who prayed to the Almighty only when they wanted something.

Hector, upon his return from purchasing fresh supplies of wine in Lynchester, was more than pleased with the new arrangements. He was quick to see that with Sebastian and Tabby in their new roles the staff bill would be greatly reduced. He even began to wonder if they could sue the agency for incompetence and aggravation.

Molly had presumed that, since the six American guests had been booked in together by Mrs Carruthers, they were either friends or at least members of the same party. This was not so and, it transpired, a more varied group would have been difficult to imagine. Molly could not see how on earth everyone was going to get on and had to lock herself in the pantry and consume a whole Mars bar, she was so agitated.

Pip and Marilyn MacPherson were loud. Molly was sorry but there was no other way to describe them. Not only was their car noisy, so were their voices, and so were their clothes. They tumbled from the car in suspiciously high spirits. Pip, no doubt due to the Mac in his name, sported a tam-o'-shanter, and his scarlet trousers, a little tight on his generous behind, were more suitable for a golfing holiday. While Marilyn was the sort of woman who chose to fight the advance of age by ignoring it completely and was decked out in frills, a fur coat dyed shocking pink – Molly hoped that Cuckoo would not lay eyes on it – with hair so ferociously platinum that one wondered if it was real. She was wearing enough make-up to restock a whole counter at Boots. A collection of gold bangles on her wrists clanked and clattered as she moved, reminding those around of a manacled prisoner.

Pip nearly knocked Hector sideways with a friendly pat on the back that was more of a clout. He winced visibly when Pip suggested they go to Hector's 'den' for 'man talk'. As Hector said later, it was only a matter of time before Pip said 'a man's gotta do etc.'

Their noise and appearance was made even more incongruous by the setting of The Hall. Both were the sort of people that Molly normally referred to as bouncing through life. Undoubtedly, she thought wearily, these two would expect every minute of every day to be packed with activity.

Phillip and Mary Phillips were in total contrast. Dressed in a beautiful and understated style they moved with the calm assurance of the very rich. Molly feared that they had probably chosen to spend the Christmas holiday with them looking for peace and tranquillity. An unlikely commodity in the circumstances. They enthused knowledgeably about the house and its contents, Mr Phillips explaining he was a dealer in fine art in New York, which made Hector's ears prick up with interest. Molly made a mental note to tell him to leave the poor man alone on his holiday and not dare ask him about the Turner. They congratulated the Parminters on their wonderful home, were warmly appreciative of their bedroom and became, for them, wildly excited at sight of the bathroom.

All the same, kind and gracious as the others were, it was not surprising that Molly waited with bated breath for the arrival of the third couple, who, she was told, were a Franklin and Betty

Teepoint. At sight of Franklin Teepoint getting out of his car Molly's heart did not sink, it plummeted.

Towards her across the driveway moved a mountain of flesh which, with immense difficulty, began to mount the steps, wheezing and hissing as loudly as the village church organ when the churchwarden started the bellows.

'Mrs Parminter.' A deep voice, rich as molasses, rumbled out of the flesh reminding Molly, to a T, of Orson Welles.

They shook hands and were some moments into the small talk before Molly realised his wife Betty was lurking behind him. He was so huge that she was only aware of the wife when she peered shyly around the husband's bulk.

Molly hoped sincerely, for Mrs Teepoint's sake, that they no longer enjoyed a conjugal relationship for Betty was so small and Franklin so huge. Hector, after deep thought upon the subject later, said that he did not think Molly had to fear a suffocated house guest; considering Franklin's immense size, he doubted if it was physically possible. He began to embark on such flights of vulgarity that Molly had to speak to him quite sharply.

Given his size, which would make climbing the stairs an ordeal not only for him but for all those watching, the rooms had to be quickly rearranged and the Teepoints were given the ground-floor room for safety. Molly relaxed at that, but became rapidly unrelaxed when they rang the bell and Franklin ordered a bottle of Jack Daniels. Molly wondered whether they had a drink that sounded like a dog but Hector, with amazing foresight, had purchased several bottles telling Molly that it was well known that Americans drank little else. Hector never failed to amaze her with the amount of detail he knew.

'But at three o'clock in the afternoon?'

'Chap needs a booster, probably. It's not as if he's going to drink the lot, is it?' Hector laughed as he sent Sebastian off with the silver tray for his first butlering roll.

But he did drink it – all of it – so Tabby reported when she went in to turn the beds down for the night. As if Molly hadn't enough to worry about.

Unfortunately she had a considerable amount to worry her.

Entering the kitchen at six to check that Michael was coping she found him slumped against the Aga, a large whisky in hand, singing 'Land of Hope and Glory'.

'Oh Michael, how could you?' Molly swept across the kitchen, quickly removing the glass with one hand and with the other dragging a kitchen chair, which she adeptly slipped beneath him as he sank towards the floor.

He looked at her, head on one side, eyes seriously glazed. She waited patiently for him to say something since he looked as if he was about to. Instead he began a spirited rendition of 'Jerusalem'.

'Sebastian, what on earth shall we do with him?' she asked. Sebastian was entering the kitchen, practising a smooth sliding action which he was convinced was how a butler should walk. (That was how his father's butler had walked he'd explained, a mite huffily, to Tabby when she shrieked with laughter and asked him if his trousers were too small.)

'What a prat. He's completely trashed.' Sebastian looked down at the drunken Michael. 'Where's his room?'

'At the top of the house. We'll never get him up there, he's too drunk and too heavy.'

'Have you got a couple of blankets, Mrs Parminter? We can plonk him in the old pantry.'

James was summoned and he and Sebastian manhandled the now recumbent and loudly snoring Michael into the pantry.

By the time they returned Molly was already slipping on her overall about to set to cooking the dinner which, she discovered to her fury, Michael hadn't even started.

'I'm off now, Mother,' James informed her, looking as if he wished he didn't have to tell her as he sidled towards the door.

'Where?' Molly said with exasperation.

'A party. At the Fortescues. You know, they always have one, I always go.'

'I see.' For the first time Molly realised why Tabby so often spoke through her teeth; it gave a marked degree of satisfaction during such a frustrating episode as this.

She was flying round the kitchen, pink-faced with agitation and stress when Cuckoo stalked in.

'No one's been to see me,' she complained.

'Cuckoo, I'm sorry. But it's been one disaster after another – no one's had time.'

'That's it, isn't it? No one ever has time for me. You'll be sorry, you'll live to regret not caring for me. I'll change my will.'

'You do that, Cuckoo. You go now and change it. And while you're gone would you ask Hope if she could possibly give me a hand?'

'You don't employ her, I do. Of course you can't have her – get your own staff,' Cuckoo snapped and made Molly think longingly of Aunt Fifi. She wished she had accepted Molly's invitation to spend Christmas with them.

'As a matter of fact we do employ her since Hector pays her not inconsiderable wages. But as it is I'm asking her as a favour,' Molly said with studied slowness.

'What time's dinner?'

'Eight, if I'm lucky. But you're having yours in your room.'

'No I'm not. I'm having it downstairs with you, Hector said I could.'

'Oh, no,' Molly groaned, undecided whether she wanted to commit murder or suicide. 'Well, you can't and that's that – I've too much to do as it is already.'

'I hate you, Molly.'

'I'm not too keen on you at the moment.'

'I'm leaving.'

'Good.' Molly despised herself for being as childish and petulant as her mother-in-law. When Hector popped in to see how she was doing and to let her know half the guests were down for drinks, he received the full force of her anger.

'I never said any such thing. What I said to Mother was, we weren't having a proper Christmas. That we'd celebrate after the guests had gone.'

Molly looked at him with extreme loathing. At this rate she wouldn't be fit to cook baked beans on toast let alone a second turkey. But things were saved by the bell, or rather the back door slamming shut and Mrs Hodgson appearing.

'I thought you'd have trouble with that chef. I felt it in me water.'

Molly did not like to ask what she meant by this. It sounded incredibly personal. Instead she hugged Mrs Hodgson and welcomed her as if she was the Second Coming.

Amazingly the evening was not a total disaster. Molly's food was well received even if the guests had obviously been puzzled by her constant leaping in and out of the drawing-room during their pre-dinner drinks as she raced to the kitchen to check her cooking.

'Probably think you've got a weak bladder.' Hector's remark did nothing to help her equilibrium.

There was no question of them not eating with their guests since the guests had booked in to live with them *en famille* and not as in a hotel. Molly could see a time when Hector's initial enthusiasm for this idea was likely to wear thin. She could just imagine him if someone of the wrong political persuasion or someone who could not speak English sat beside him – he would drink too much and then nod off from boredom.

Molly had held her breath when Hector made a series of leaden comments on George III and colonies. These words were followed by a silence which seemed to go on for ever before from Franklin Teepoint came a great rumbling noise situated somewhere in the depths of his vast belly. The noise rolled and rippled upwards and finally tumbled forth as a loud, deep laugh. Once the others realised that they had just been witnesses to an example of the English humour they had all heard so much about, they too laughed. Molly thought the danger of such a thing recurring was over until she saw the cocky and self-satisfied expression on Hector's face – that of a man congratulating himself on his great wit. He was going to have to be spoken to, she decided.

Sebastian and Tabby worked wonderfully well, with Tabby only getting the giggles twice. Though Molly was horrified to discover afterwards that Pip had goosed her twice – once at the fish stage and once at the pudding.

There was one difficult moment when Marilyn insisted she knew Sebastian and would not believe him when he said she must be mistaken. There then followed a long inquisition by Marilyn as to where they had met. It would have been tedious but for the fact that it gave a fascinating insight into the social life of the MacPhersons.

'I never forget a face, do I Pip? I'm famous for my visual memory. I know you from somewhere, young man. It'll come to me later – perhaps much later tonight, I'll let you know,' she smiled over her glass of wine. Molly was afraid she had not been mistaken when she thought that Marilyn was flirting with Sebastian. While toy boys might be a good thing when restricted to people she did not know, it was entirely a different matter when it was her daughter's fiancé.

'I've a very common face,' Sebastian had said smoothly and Molly thought that Tabby was about to choke.

The seating at table had been a problem since Hector was too afraid of the Hepplewhite chairs to allow Franklin Teepoint to sit on one, so instead they put the large oak Jacobean chair, which normally stood in the hall, at his disposal. Molly was anxious that he might be offended but instead he sat without comment and she assumed that he was used to people guarding their more precious chairs.

Eating with him and Pip could not be called a pleasure. Pip entertained them with jokes, some of which verged on the blue – in the end Hector had had to stop him with a tactful 'There are ladies present.' This offended Pip who then sat in such a hurt huddle that Molly found herself feeling sorry for him.

The problem with Franklin Teepoint was even more aesthetic: he appeared to have difficulty in eating and breathing without the most alarming amount of noise. The hissing and gurgling from his lungs was bad enough but, coupled with the loud noises of masticating and the grunts and groans that the effort of eating cost him, it was not only unpleasant but also alarming to everyone around the table, all that is except Betty, who was obviously used to it all. The others feared that each mouthful might be his last. Their concern mounted at the amount he drank. When Sebastian had gone round the table with the wine a large hand shot out, removing the bottle and placing it very decisively in front of his position. Before dinner he had had four large whiskies, with dinner a good bottle and a half of wine. That, added to the bottle of Jack

Daniels, should have put him under the table. As Molly ushered the women away to the drawing-room for coffee she hoped that Hector would be mean with the port.

The women settled for the moment, Molly raced back to the kitchen to check things out. She found Mrs Hodgson, Sebastian and Tabby and, most surprising of all, James toiling away at the washing up.

'James! I thought you had gone to a party?'

'I got half-way then I thought I was being dreadfully selfish. In situations like this we should all pull our weight, shouldn't we?' Molly hugged him tightly, and felt a lovely glowing feeling which had nothing to do with the wine. He sounded so like Hector; if he was going to be like his father then all would eventually be well.

'You've got to get a dishwasher, Mummy.'

'If this goes on I will.'

'And you shouldn't be using this washing-up liquid. It's not *green*.'

'I know, I know, but it makes better bubbles.'

'Really, Mummy, you must think more ecologically.'

'Yes, dear,' Molly said obediently as she fiddled with the coffee cups. While understanding her daughter's concern for the planet, maintaining Tabby's standards was hard. It was so difficult in the supermarket to remember which items were sound and which weren't; which had been tested on animals, and which were cruelty free. Her one excursion to the Body Shop had resulted in a bag full of tubs and bottles. Now her bathroom was a clutter of bath oils and crystals, body creams and unguents, face scrubs and defoliants. Apricot, peppermint, avocado, lemon and lavender mingled into a heady *mélange* of smells. The mystery was that she had never felt the need for any of these things before. So she ended up using more rather than less, and surely that couldn't be ecologically sound either.

'I think you've all earned a drink,' she said, to sidetrack Tabby from her crusade for world survival. 'We could never have done it without all of you. Champagne? We've still got some of Colin Mann's.'

Mrs Hodgson did her usual 'I couldn't, to be sure', followed by

'No really', and finally, 'Oh well just a little one.' Which, from past experience, Molly knew always led to several more.

'What if Mr Teepoint kicks the bucket, Mummy? How will we get him out?'

'Tabby, what a dreadful thing to say,' Molly admonished, though the thought had crossed her own mind.

'Where would we get a big enough coffin from?' Tabby shuddered and giggled at the same time.

'Even if you got one how would you get it out of the room? The door's too narrow, I measured it,' Sebastian offered.

'You could always use the chain saw, cut him up,' Mrs Hodgson suggested seriously, reducing Tabby to a pathetic limp rag from laughter.

'It's not something to joke about. The poor man can't help it.'

'Can't help it? He's a pig. He had two of everything,' Tabby reported indignantly. 'And the noise he made, it was disgusting.'

'And the wine,' Sebastian added, still aggrieved at the interruption to his butlering efforts.

'I shan't let him die here. I shall think my hardest into keeping him alive,' Molly said emphatically. She was convinced that if one wanted something badly enough one had only to think it and it would happen. Not that she had any proof of this and certainly it had not worked for the flashings. 'I'll see to the coffee, Tabby.' She picked up the tray and returned to the waiting ladies in the drawing-room.

The women, surprisingly, were getting on well and Molly found they had an enormous amount in common. They had all read the same books – quite putting Molly to shame since she rarely had time to read anything and found she had not heard of half the authors they mentioned. They had seen the latest plays and musicals in London, which she hadn't, and talked knowledgeably about them all.

From these subjects they then moved into a very intelligent discussion of the history of the area, a lot of which was new to Molly. She had heard from Lulu, who often went to America, that the women were always well read and could speak with authority on a multitude of subjects. As she listened she thought of the rather inconsequential conversations which were the norm with most of her women friends – gossip really, not to put too fine a point on it. There and then she resolved to make it her New Year's resolution to learn more. If Americans were to be frequent guests she could not be constantly letting the side down.

Molly felt ashamed of her first reaction to Marilyn. None of the women she knew would have accepted Marilyn as easily as the other two Americans had. Not for the first time, since meeting Americans as her guests, she had to acknowledge that the Americans knew a lot more about manners than the Europeans gave them credit for. Despite always thinking she was not a snob, Molly had now to admit that she probably was. Unforgivable. But she comforted herself with the thought that as she was English she could not really help herself, could she?

She had planned charades at the end of the evening, but Franklin Teepoint's size put an end to that. It would have to be general conversation and she feared how Hector would fare if the men were as erudite as their women.

The problem hardly arose, however, for upon his arrival in the drawing-room Franklin Teepoint sat on a chair which immediately broke and sent him crashing to the floor. He lay stranded like a beetle, his fat legs waving impotently in the air, while from his nether regions issued a loud series of reports sounding like the rending of calico.

It took everybody's combined efforts to right him, after which everyone was so exhausted they all said they must go to bed. But not before they had thanked Molly and Hector fulsomely for a lovely evening. Molly could not help but worry that this might just be another example of American good manners.

By the time Molly got to bed she was exhausted. So much so that she could no longer cope with Hector's juvenile behaviour as he rolled about the bed laughing at Mr Teepoint's problems with wind.

'Hector, shut up. You're behaving like a nasty prep-school boy with a particularly nasty lavatorial sense of humour.'

But this only convulsed Hector further.

Chapter 19

Christmas Day

DESPITE THE STAFF problems, with Hope's added help in the kitchen Molly was able to arrange her morning so that she could attend morning service with everyone. Except Franklin Teepoint who, Betty explained, was feeling rather tired and had decided to spend the morning in bed to rest up for lunch. All of which sounded ominous to Molly.

Hector and Molly made a point of not going to church too regularly. Hector's logic was if they did it set a precedent, which would only lead to talk if they didn't go. Molly also felt he kept his attendance irregular just to keep the vicar on his toes; he could never be certain when Hector was going to turn up.

The living was in Hector's gift. Not that he had ever given it to anyone since Bertie Rumbelow had been installed by his father six months prior to his death. But Hector, she was sure, liked to nurse the idea that it was a gift he could take away again if he wanted. Molly was not sure what the ecclesiastical ruling was on this but without doubt the vicar believed it. Molly was certain it was this fear of losing his job which made the Reverend Rumbelow such a very nervous individual.

There really were some nasty nooks and crannies in Hector's character if one cared to probe, she thought. But it was an occupation she had decided against, for fear of what she might find. Far better to love him just as she found him. There was too much probing about in other people's minds these days and in her opinion all it led to was trouble.

She and Hector had never discussed his faith – it wasn't something she had felt the necessity to do. He said he was a Christian, and like herself always put C. of E. on forms, but she'd never known him pray or read the Bible outside their infrequent attendances at church. She often thought that it might be a Christianity of habit – a habit first instilled at prep school. If he had a God, undoubtedly He was white, spoke English, would have voted Tory and, Hector had once confessed in a weak moment, he was sure wore a dinner jacket. If she thought about Hector's God she imagined Him as a 1930s bandleader – the dinner jacket, she supposed.

For herself, Molly went to church because she liked the hymns, the organ, the angelic choirboys – sadly these days more often choirgirls – the smell of the place, the cosy familiarity of the services, the beautiful wording of the Book of Common Prayer.

She was no longer sure about the rest of it all, not after Vietnam. That had been the start of her slide from Grace. Before then, wars had been distant, seen only as a slot in the news at the cinema and duly sanitised and heavily censored by the authorities into a palatable offering for the man in the street. But television had brought the Vietnam war right into her sitting-room in all its brutalised horror. It was as if officialdom had decided that the populace could now see war as it really was. That was the beginning. After that she'd sat with cup of tea, tears pouring down her cheeks, and watched the ruins of earthquakes being bulldozed, burying the people who might still be alive in the ruins. She'd seen train crashes, people leaping from burning buildings. With gin and tonic in hand she'd sat in a comfortable chair and seen babes sucking at milkless breasts, and dying. All these images had built in Molly's mind and had made her faith wobble and finally collapse.

She still went to church for the hymns and the prettiness of it all. She still lived her life by the church's rules as she had been brought up to do. But at night she no longer prayed to *Him*. She couldn't, for He was no longer there.

All this she kept to herself. It was similar, really, to her loss of faith in the Conservatives. She thought it, but did not confide it to anyone, for it would only cause talk and trouble if she did.

No longer believing made her thoughts about the other worshippers easier on her conscience. For years she'd had serious doubts that the true spirit of Christianity beat in many of the village church's most stalwart supporters.

For a start she knew that Mrs Downs from Lower Cottages had thrown her daughter out for getting in the family way. She also knew, via Mrs Hodgson, that Jennifer Quinn who had the expression of an angel and was sanctimonious to boot, had had an abortion – the extent of Mrs Hodgson's knowledge of the more personal aspects of people's lives never failed to amaze her. Given their extreme views on homosexuals, black people, or the unemployed was she really to think that Christian hearts beat under Bat, Porky and Jib's immaculate suiting?

Previously such thoughts had made her feel guilt. The advantage now was that she could think such thoughts guiltlessly.

The church was packed, as it always was at Easter and Christmas, which made Molly glad Hector wasn't a man of the cloth. It must be very depressing, the other fifty or so Sundays, when the congregation was a handful.

Their guests had enjoyed the service enormously and raved about the 'quaint' church, and the 'ducky' choir, and the 'antiquity' of it all. They all walked back across the park. Molly had walked this way time without number. The difference in doing it with her American guests was the way their enthusiasm began to affect her. They admired and photographed everything with the excited exuberance of children. And she was told so many times how lucky she was to be privileged to live here that she was only half-way across the park when she was beginning to look at The Hall in a different light. It was beautiful. It was unique. Hector was right, it should be preserved, whatever the cost.

They arrived at the house to find Cuckoo on the steps, jumping up and down with excitement, a pink blur of agitation.

'It's that fat man,' she squealed without a thought for Betty Teepoint's feelings. 'His bed's collapsed. I can't lift him, he's too huge,' she said, in case anyone thought she should have done so.

Not stopping to remove coats and hats Hector, Molly, a tearful Betty, the concerned Phillips, and the highly amused MacPhersons trooped behind Cuckoo, who fluttered ahead of them like an exotic moth, to the new back bedroom.

Molly suddenly stopped dead in her tracks, making everyone else cannon into her. Everyone apologised to everyone else.

'How did you find him, Cuckoo?' Molly asked.

'I checked in to see if he was all right,' Cuckoo answered sanctimoniously. It was only when they reached the door that Molly found herself wondering how Cuckoo could possibly have known the man was there. Molly hadn't told anyone that he was not going to church. Cuckoo had been snooping, she reluctantly concluded. Hector must have one of his words with Cuckoo, something she knew he dreaded and which required a large fortifying whisky.

They found Franklin Teepoint in a tangle of bedding, patiently awaiting his rescuers. Once again it required everyone's concerted efforts to right him. The bed, a particularly fine Sheraton, was a wreck. They heaved him on to a sofa, where he meekly apologised for all the trouble and weakly asked for a Jack Daniels. Hector went to fetch the bottle; when Franklin asked for a drink he did not mean a measure. Molly could not help but think that his size was probably caused by his devotion to drink. But it wasn't her place to say anything, and she supposed that to Franklin the prospect of losing weight was so awesome that undoubtedly it needed another drink to get over such a depressing thought. Poor man.

Just before lunch Mrs Carruthers telephoned saying that although it was Christmas Day she liked to check that all was well. This was said with such self-satisfaction that it seemed she expected Hector to congratulate her for picking up the telephone.

'It isn't,' Hector barked. 'You sent this gross man, without warning us. He has, so far, broken a most valuable chair and now a bed. I'd like to know where you stand on your insurance, Mrs Carruthers.'

'I think it's more of a question of where you stand on yours, Mr Parminter. Such breakages are your responsibility and are no doubt covered by your house insurance. I'm sure. But while we're on the subject, I do hope you have had the foresight to take out public liability cover. Mr Teepoint would have every right to sue you for not having strong enough furniture. And being American –

a particularly litigious nation – I'm sure he will.' Mrs Carruthers' voice glowed with revenge.

Hector put the phone down, white-faced and speechless, and for a long time contemplated his uninsured state.

Molly was crossing the hall to check the dining table when she was stopped by Mrs Phillips.

'Molly, I don't quite know how to put this,' she started and Molly's stomach did a quick flip of nervous reaction.

'What?' she said weakly.

'It so silly but, before we went to church, I laid my clothes out – the ones I wanted to change into for your, no doubt splendid, lunch. It's not about the dress, that's fine, but I'd also put out a scarf, some beads and earrings, and, well, they're not there.'

'What colour are they?' Molly's heart was thumping so alarmingly that her only consolation was that it appeared to be in good condition or surely it would have stopped.

'The jewellery is not valuable, I wouldn't want you to worry on that score. But it's pretty, pink amethyst, and the scarf is . . .'

'Pink,' Molly said with a sigh. 'I'd appreciate it, Mary, if you said nothing about this. I'm sure I can return your possessions.'

'Of course, my dear Molly. I shan't breathe a word.' This was no consolation to Molly, for when people said that they usually rushed out and spread the information like a town crier.

Molly, face rigid with anger, went immediately to Cuckoo's apartment and stalked in without knocking.

'Give,' was all she said, her hand outstretched.

Cuckoo said nothing but looked insufferably pleased with herself. She sat silent, head on one side, black eyes gleaming with mischief. She looked like a little bird deciding whether to go for a worm or not. Suddenly she ducked her hand under the cushion she was sitting on and presented Molly with Mrs Phillips' jewellery and scarf.

'Why do you do this sort of thing, Cuckoo? Is it to annoy me?'

'I wanted them.'

'Don't be silly. You know you must not steal.'

'I was not stealing, I was borrowing,' the old woman said with a magnificent display of dignity, in the circumstances. 'I would have put them back. The trouble with you, Molly, is that you are an insufferable busybody.'

There was a lot Molly could have said but instead she left the room breathing deeply to calm herself. Time was, before Cuckoo had got as bad as this, when Molly had regarded with censure people who put their old folks into homes. These days she could think of nothing she would like better than for Cuckoo to be safely away in a nice residential home somewhere. Funny how easy it was to change one's views. Molly realised she was lucky. They had space, Cuckoo had her own quarters, she had Hope looking after her and waiting on her twenty-four hours a day. What must it be like living in a small house, no help, no one to turn to when an aged person was being difficult? How did those daughters cope? She'd read recently about a spate of granny bashing. She had been shocked but even as she read it she could understand. Babies got battered, now the elderly; it was sad. At the beginning and the end of life one was at risk – the young and the old, but so were those who had care of them.

'My mother-in-law took them,' she said simply to Mary Phillips, thinking that the truth was the best thing in such trying circumstances. 'I can't apologise enough.' Molly found herself imagining the subsequent phone call from Mrs Carruthers and she and Hector being drummed out of Aristocratic Homes Inc.

'Please, Molly, don't you worry. I understand completely. My mother's the same, only it's blue with her.'

Molly spent a very happy ten minutes with Mary, comparing notes on the respective motherly crosses they bore. Then seeing the time, she felt the surge of panic which never seemed to leave her these days, excused herself and raced for the kitchen, aware that the ability to walk normally seemed to be deserting her.

Once in the kitchen she wondered why she flapped so. Not only was it injurious to her health but it was, undoubtedly, rude to those who were helping her so efficiently. Lunch, in Hope's care, was well advanced. Sebastian, Tabby and James had laid the table, done the drinks trays, dusted the rooms, lit the log fires. All of them were calmly sitting round the table enjoying a coffee.

Last night Mrs Hodgson had volunteered to come in too.

Reluctantly Molly had turned the offer down, saying Mrs Hodgson must be with her family. From her expression it was evident that she was disappointed that Molly had not jumped at the chance of having her help.

'You see, Mrs Parminter, we don't normally have drink in the house. It's not a good idea, if you get my drift?'

Molly did not get the drift so Mrs Hodgson explained.

'My hubby gets at it, that's why. You know, makes him go — funny.' Mrs Hodgson mouthed the last word.

'Well . . .' Molly began, not wanting Mrs Hodgson to suffer unduly.

'You're probably right, Mrs Parminter. I'd best be at home.'

But today Molly could look around her kitchen and see that, truthfully, Mrs Hodgson's help would have been superfluous.

Hope, it transpired, was a wonderful cook. Molly gritted her teeth when she thought of the meals she had cooked for Hope and Cuckoo and carted upstairs on trays. The Cuckoo problem was neatly solved by sitting her in the kitchen in a supervisory capacity and where she would lunch with Hope, Sebastian and Tabby when the guests had been served. After the little episode with the amethysts Cuckoo, in any case, could not face the Phillips and so settled down to make everyone's life in the kitchen hell — a ploy which failed miserably. No one took any notice of her.

James had come to terms fully with the guest problem and had thrown himself into the show with amazing good grace. He was finally heard to say 'you know this is rather good fun.' Molly used him to see to the drinks tray, to serve the guests' drinks and to help Sebastian when necessary.

Everyone entered into the spirit of things by wearing their best bibs and tuckers, submitting to paper hats and Hector's insistence that everyone read the silly jokes from the crackers out loud. As the wine flowed the noise from the dining-room reached a grand crescendo.

Molly felt she should receive a round of applause at the end of the meal for the smoothness of the whole operation. But no one said anything, and she had to acknowledge that, as the professional caterer she supposed she now was, she should not expect it. So she had to be content with congratulating herself on her calmness and perfect hostessing qualities.

After lunch and the Queen's speech, Hector surprised the Americans by insisting they stand for the national anthem – all that is except Franklin Teepoint. Because of the wear and tear on his furniture, Hector felt it prudent if he stood up and sat down as infrequently as possible. Then it was time for the presents round the tree.

Molly had thought she should buy small presents for their guests – an almost impossible task when she did not know them. She was surprised but mortified when all three couples produced the most beautifully wrapped and expensive presents for herself and Hector. It made her soap and Nan Carter's *History of Lynshire*, wrapped in paper from Woolworth's, look not only stupid but mean.

After all the food and excitement, half opted to sleep and the other half went for a long walk around the village. Molly kicked off her shoes, curled up and watched the television. She would never normally have watched on Chrstmas Day, in fact had never allowed the children to do so, but today was different. It was not a normal Christmas and besides, Hector had hired the largest available colour TV for the guests. Used as she was to her black-and-white set, Molly was transfixed and hoped Hector would allow it to stay once everyone had gone.

That evening Molly had asked Lulu, Annie English, Porky and Hyacinth for drinks and moral support. Since the rest had been so po-faced about Hector's venture, Molly enjoyed not inviting them.

Lulu, on arriving, flung her arms round Tabby and Sebastian, immediately letting the cat out of the bag as to who they really were. But her new friends – for that was how she now thought of the guests – thought it all a delightful wheeze. And Marilyn was vindicated, for she had been to see Sebastian and the Drones twice. Molly, full of euphoria, even relented sufficiently to allow Cuckoo in, mainly because she felt Hope should receive the enthusiastic thanks from the Americans for her superb cooking.

They finally played charades, and although Franklin Teepoint could not participate by acting he proved brilliant at guessing.

Once the contented guests had gone to bed the family sat in the kitchen for a post-mortem. There it transpired that Marilyn, admittedly before she knew Sebastian's true identity, had leapt upon him in the butler's pantry and offered him $200 to do *it* there and then. But he had manfully fought her off. Pip, having mauled Tabby once too often, had got a quick clip round the chops for his effort.

That apart, it had been a good day. Even the electrical supply had obliged. Molly went to bed with less worry than before. She was aware that if she had nothing genuine to worry about she would undoubtedly invent something, but tonight she had a couple of worries in reserve. First there was the furniture that Teepoint had broken. If it was to be restored it would no doubt wipe out any chance of a profit again. But the worry uppermost in her mind was Tabby, standing in the drawing-room, shiny eyed with excitement and flushed with her success at charades saying,

'You know, I think I might like to be an actress.'

Chapter 20

Phillip Phillips Consults Molly

Hector had arranged for the whole party to go to Lulu's son's estate for the Boxing Day Lawn Meet. Franklin Teepoint opted to stay in bed, a cast-iron one that Hector had found in the stables.

Molly, using a multitude of fairly lame excuses, did not go: she had seen enough meets to last her a lifetime, and with the guests away for the whole day she could catch up on a myriad tasks. So she was not too pleased when Sebastian searched her out in the kitchen where Hope was making stock for soup, and Molly was clearing out the refrigerator, shocked at the mould that she found – why was her refrigerator always reminiscent of a penicillin factory? – to tell her that Mr Phillips would like a word with her.

'Didn't he go with the others?'

'No, he's got an allergy to horses.'

'Oh really! I wonder what people had wrong with them before allergies were invented,' Molly said crossly, slipping off her apron and glancing at herself in the small mirror that she had hung on the kitchen wall so that she could check her make-up before swanning out to see her guests. She patted her hair straight, quickly powdered her nose, and went to find him.

'You wanted to see me, Phillip?' she asked tentatively, for *en route* she had suddenly wondered if, perhaps, his wife had broken her promise and had told him about the theft of her jewellery. If so, would he be as understanding as his wife over Cuckoo's little habit? Maybe he would insist on suing them or, worse, calling in the police.

'Molly, I *do* want to see you badly,' he said a shade eagerly for him, she thought. 'It's about the pictures in my room.'

'Yes? Which ones?'

'The Huxtable Rivers.'

'You know his work?' she said, surprised, for apart from Hector and his *Children's Illustrated Bible* she knew of no one else who had ever heard of this particular Victorian artist.

'But of course. If you remember, I mentioned I'm a dealer in fine art in New York. Huxtables have become highly sought after during the past five years or so.'

'Are they? What a pity then, that they're not by him.'

'I hate to appear to contradict a lady but you're wrong, Molly. Those three are some of the finest I've ever seen.'

'They're copies.' Molly launched into her explanation of how and why she had these pretend Huxtables on her walls.

'You have another nine?' Phillip said with astonishment.

'Yes, but I haven't had time to unpack them, what with one thing and another.'

'Might I see them?'

'But of course.' She led him to the back of the house and through the kitchen, relieved that everything was reasonably neat and tidy, to the back pantry where Aunt Fifi's crate still stood, half-unpacked.

With deference, and handling each painting as if it were a holy relic, Phillip removed the pictures one by one. He studied them carefully, holding them up to the poor light from the single bulb, moving them back and forth in the weak glow.

'Would you like to take them to a better light?' she asked helpfully.

'If it's not too much bother.'

She helped him carry the remaining pictures to the kitchen table, where he perused them one by one under the strip light, this time using a pocket magnifying glass.

'There's no doubt about it, Molly. These are genuine Huxtables,' he pronounced finally.

'I can't believe that. No, you see we all knew they were copies. The whole family has always known.'

'I'd stake my reputation on them.'

'I wouldn't if I were you,' Molly laughed and then, seeing his serious expression, stopped short. 'I'm sorry Phillip, I'm sure you're a wonderful expert but this time . . . It's probably the light . . .' she said as kindly as she could. He was a nice man and a guest, so she did not want to offend him.

But it made no difference how sweet she was, or how patient, Phillip would not accept her explanation and there, in her kitchen, with Hope an interested listener as she made a hollandaise sauce, he launched into a lecture. Molly listened, fascinated, as he told them about brush strokes, tonal values. He explained that each artist's technique was peculiar to him, like a fingerprint almost, and was recognisable to one, such as he, who had made a study of this particular artist. Molly found it all most interesting. 'At a conservative estimate I would say each one must be worth in the region of $48,000. That's . . .' he quickly produced a pocket calculator, 'about £30,000,' he concluded.

Molly looked at him and then at the paintings, wouldn't it be nice . . . ? She shook her head. 'How sad then that they're not what they seem,' said Molly, sticking to her guns. She could not make out if Phillip's expression was one of annoyance or exasperation. She hoped she was not offending him. She must think of something else to distract him. 'If you're an expert, I've another painting which might interest you. Have you had a look at our possible Turner? We've had experts galore looking at that, no one seems to be sure.'

'Oh that's not a Turner – it's good but no, I'm sorry Molly, it's not by the master.'

This news cheered Molly for if Phillip could be so wrong about the Huxtables then undoubtedly the Turner was genuine. If so, she would have to have a long talk with Hector about it, try all she could to get him to sell it. They would not really miss it, it was not one of their favourites. It was very small and not particularly pleasing, Turner or not. She supposed all artists had their off days and undoubtedly this picture was the product of one of his.

Phillip looked as if he had no intention of leaving the kitchen so Molly suggested he went to the library. He might find a book on Huxtable Rivers there, she told him. She doubted if there was, but at least it would get him out from under her and Hope's feet.

Molly stacked the pictures against the wall; she hadn't time to move them back to the pantry now. And she began, with Hope's now invaluable assistance, to prepare dinner. That's what should have happened but instead, Molly realised, she was assisting Hope.

'Mrs Parminter. If you're going to continue to have guests you wouldn't consider allowing me to do the cooking, would you?'

'Are you serious, Hope?'

'Totally. I love to cook, you see, but I've never had anyone to cook for. I nearly got married once but he didn't appreciate food, so I couldn't go through with it, could I?' Hope said, with an expression of such sadness flitting across her face that Molly felt ashamed of all the jokes she and Hector had made about 'Hope giving up Hope', and fairly lame things like that. Cuckoo's companions came and went and they had never really given a thought to why these women chose such a lonely and difficult job. Molly was always lecturing Tabby to think of others, without much success admittedly. But how much thought had she herself given Hope? Of course the woman must have a past of sorts but Molly had never even considered it, or whether Hope had been happy or sad or damaged. She put her hand out to touch her, as if by making physical contact she could make up for past neglect.

'Oh, poor Hope. No, you couldn't even have considered him, not when you're such a good cook. If you are game, then I can't think of a better solution.'

'What about Cuckoo?' Hope asked, looking over her shoulder as if she expected the old woman to be eavesdropping.

'Whatever Hector says about this business, I fear it will be very intermittent. I can't exactly see armies of tourists making their way to our door. When we have a booking we could get a temporary companion in for Cuckoo. But then, if Hector's right and this business booms, we'll find someone permanently for her.'

'Thank you, Mrs Parminter. You've made me incredibly happy. There's just one thing, I don't think we should tell her right away, do you?'

Molly wholeheartedly agreed as she thought of the monumental paddy that would ensue. And they did not say a word half an hour later when Cuckoo swanned into the kitchen, complaining she was being neglected. Hope became flustered and Molly made soothing noises. She finally sat Cuckoo down with the pile of Brussels sprouts she needed trimmed for dinner. This task made Cuckoo as happy as a sandboy for it gave her an ideal vehicle for complaint. As she attacked the vegetables, she asked of everyone generally what her late husband would say if he could see her now. How low she had sunk. How wicked it was to make an old woman work . . . and so on. Cuckoo was cruelly exploited and blissfully happy. This allowed the other two to get on with their jobs.

Phillip was pacing the hall when the party returned from the meet. Immediately he collared Hector and, with his words falling over one another, excitedly told him he was sitting on a small fortune in Huxtables.

Hector happily careered into the kitchen with a suspiciously high flush, undoubtedly caused by the brandy in his hip flask. 'For the cold' he always said when he filled it even though Molly had never said one word against it. Such emergency supplies were reasonable in the bitter cold but since the last few Boxing Days had been as warm as spring, Molly was amused that he still used the same excuse.

'Calm down Hector, do. There's nothing to get excited about. They're fakes. I'm getting sick to death of saying it.'

'But Phillip Phillips says . . . .'

'I don't care what Phillip said. He's wrong. Everyone makes mistakes.'

'If they were though, we could sell them.'

'If they were I wouldn't sell them, I couldn't. Uncle Basil left them to me, what would Aunt Fifi say?'

'When she's dead, then – then you could.'

'Really, Hector, sometimes you can be intolerably insensitive. And who are you to tell me to sell or not? Good gracious, we could sell a couple of sticks of furniture belonging to you and a lot of worries would disappear.'

'That's different.'

'What's different about it?'

'Those are Parminter treasures.'

'Well mine are Pigeon treasures.'

'It's not the same.'

'It damn well is.'

They glared at each other across the kitchen table. Hector slumped on to one of the chairs. Throughout, Cuckoo had been swivelling her head, looking first to one then the other.

'You're a selfish woman, Molly. I've always said you were. I've never been taken in by you for one moment,' Cuckoo said, incapable of keeping her nose out of others' business.

'Mother, please . . .' Hector said, emphasising each word.

'I'm only looking after your interests, Hector.'

'Well, you're not helping at all, Mother. So if you wouldn't mind just keeping quiet?'

'Really! That I should have such an ungrateful son. You'll regret this, Hector.' She pushed her chair back, Brussels sprouts cascading on to the floor. Without a backward glance she swept angrily from the room.

'Oh, dear, she's going to change her will again,' Molly pushed her hair back from her eyes.

'I'm being unfair, aren't I?' Hector looked at her with shame in his eyes and Hope, seeing the expression, quietly left the room.

'Yes you are.'

He began pulling the crust off a loaf of bread on the table. She slapped his hand.

'Stop that, it'll look as if the mice have been at it.'

'Phillip wants an expert from Wellbrookes to see them.'

'How much will that cost?'

'Nothing. They'll value free in the hopes you'll sell through them.'

'But I keep telling you . . . .' She realised she was speaking through her teeth again, she must stop it.

'I can't tell Phillip we don't want him to now. He's only trying to help.'

'It'll be a waste of the man's time.'

'Tell you what, Molly. If the cove from Wellbrookes says they're originals then I'll sell something from the house as well.'

'You would?' She looked at him with suspicion. That was something she would believe when she saw.

'I would,' he said, but she sensed distinct uncertainty in his voice.

'Do what the hell you want.' She was fed up with the whole topic. Molly wished she had the time to make some bread to get rid of some of the serious venom she was feeling.

The next morning the house party left, and Molly was genuinely sad to see them go – even Franklin Teepoint. Maybe most of all Franklin. For that morning he had asked to speak to Hector and had pressed upon him £1,000 to cover all the damage.

Hector had made rumbling noises, looking hungrily at the pile of banknotes. His upbringing told him he should refuse; the state of his bank balance made him want to grab the money and run.

'I'm sorry for all the trouble I've caused, Hector – please take it. I'm used to it. I always make allowances for breakages in my holiday budget.'

All along Molly had felt sorry for the poor man, and had found the jokes about his size distasteful. Now she felt even sorrier, if inwardly relieved that he had not decided to turn up his toes at The Hall. That thought had been haunting her the whole time he had been there. The children had been right, the logistics of dealing with his enormous corpse would have proved almost insurmountable.

It was another fortnight before the man from Wellbrookes, a Crispin Heald, arrived. He was dressed in a smart grey suit, with a waistcoat of bright scarlet and gold brocade. His voice was piping high and his manner so epicene that she could see Hector putting on his guard as if lowering a portcullis on his nether regions. Much to Hector's distress – indicated by raised eyebrows, frantically nodded head, and a mouthing of words which would have done Mrs Hodgson proud – Molly refused point blank to accompany Crispin and her husband to study the paintings. Crispin Heald spent over two hours closeted with a nervous Hector. He emerged to congratulate Molly fulsomely: she was the lucky owner of twelve Huxtable Rivers RA, a once greatly renowned Victorian master and now fashionable again. He lectured them both at great and tedious length, as if having started he was so riveted by the sound of his own voice and the depth of his knowledge that he could not stop. He disagreed with Phillip Phillips on only one thing – the price. In his opinion each painting was worth nearer £50,000, given the excellence of the work.

'I do wish everyone would listen to me.' Molly wished she could stamp her foot, she felt so annoyed, as she once again trotted out the history of the pictures.

'I am the world's leading authority on Huxtable Rivers,' the smart young man said, his smoothness beginning to fray around the edges.

'Then I suggest you start looking for another career,' Molly said so sharply that she quite took herself by surprise.

'Molly!' Hector said, awed at his wife's rudeness, while Crispin Heald suddenly took an inordinate interest in his highly polished fingernails.

'Perhaps Mrs Parminter would feel happier if I took one of her paintings with me for a couple of my colleagues to verify my findings.'

'As you wish, Mr Heald. But I have to say I think it's all remarkably silly.'

She left the room but heard Hector saying, 'While you're here, Heald, perhaps you'd like to look at my Turner – in inverted commas, so to speak.' And she heard him give his silly laugh, the one he reserved for whenever he was embarrassed, combined with the one he used when being a creep and trying to get something for nothing.

Chapter 21

Hostilities Are Resumed

MOLLY PACKED ALL the paintings away in their box; they were causing too much trouble on the walls. Often she walked into Hector's study to find him scribbling on scraps of paper which he hastily scrunched up and threw into the waste-paper basket, with the guilty expression of a naughty boy caught writing notes in school. For some time she ignored this until, one day, curiosity got the better of her. One Thursday when he had gone to Lynchester, she crept in and smoothed out one of the papers, to find he had been working on a list of calculations concerning the money he still dreamt would be hers soon. She frowned.

'We'll see about that!' she snorted as she read the first item on Hector's list – a new BMW. She agreed with his listing of the flashings next, and the building of four bathrooms *en suite*. She had to wipe a tear away when she read 'A David Shilling hat for Molly'. But she quickly stopped being sentimental when she saw 'vintage port' underlined three times. She might love Hector dearly but there were times when he was exasperating in the extreme.

Molly decided to forget all about the pictures and found she wished Uncle Basil hadn't even remembered he had promised them to her. Forgetting was made easy when, a few days later, she received a telephone call from James to say he would be home at the weekend and was bringing a friend. Molly went into her usual whirl of excitement and was glad that no one was booked in for that particular weekend.

The guest situation, she admitted, had surprised her. Despite it being the early months of the year a trickle still booked in. Not just

Americans either. They had had Germans, two Belgians and a honeymoon couple from Bristol – they had been the easiest guests of all; they only wanted to be left alone. This state of affairs was primarily because Hector had now joined another four agencies. He had had the most enormous pleasure in telling this to Mrs Carruthers. She was not pleased, she had blustered and threatened to take them off her books, a bit like having their epaulettes stripped, Hector had joked. 'You must do what you want, Mrs Carruthers,' he had said boldly, with the confidence of the other agencies behind him. But she had done nothing, and in two weeks they had six booked in from Aristocratic Homes Inc.

The memory of the weekend with James' last girlfriend, Shar, was still fresh in Molly's mind, so it was not surprising that she was apprehensive about the weekend.

Emma Trowbridge, however, appeared to be perfect. She was everything any mother-in-law dreamed of, and certainly Molly had, time without number, in her bath. She wasn't the blonde blue-eyed girl she had imagined but grey-eyed and Titian haired – a bit like the young Bette Davis, she thought. Within an hour of her arrival Molly was wondering, in view of her colouring, what her grandchildren would look like.

Everyone was taken with her. Cuckoo virtually purred when the girl was in the room and behaved impeccably as the young woman fussed over, and fetched and carried for her. Hector was totally smitten and looked set to spend the whole weekend making his harrumphing noise. The dog fell in love. James no longer appeared nearly as pompous and glowed with pride. And it was about this time that Molly began to worry.

Could anyone be this perfect? She wondered. She had often noticed while watching television how deeply suspicious she always felt of certain people – usually female – who glowed with sweetness and goodness. Often she and Hector had disagreed; invariably he accused her of being jealous. She wasn't, she just, like most women, could recognise saccharin when she saw it. Whereas Hector was frequently besotted; one only had to watch him drooling over certain women TV presenters to see he was in no fit state to judge. Logically, the way she was thinking wasn't fair.

Sebastian was equally faultless and she didn't doubt him, so why did she feel this about Emma? Was she being sexist, or wise?

That evening Lulu had invited them all to dinner since she was bursting with curiosity to meet the new girlfriend. Molly had thought the evening perfect and so was surprised when she went to collect her coat from Lulu's bedroom to have her friend gallop up behind her.

'My God, Molly, James certainly chooses them, doesn't he?' And she lifted her hands in mock horror.

'I don't know what you mean,' Molly said a shade frostily as she searched for her coat in the pile on the bed.

'Pure saccharin, *nobody* is that nice.'

'You're such a cynic, Lulu.'

'No I'm not, I'm just realistic.'

'Bitchy, more like.'

'Molly!' Lulu exclaimed, surprised by the irritability in Molly's voice. Of course what Lulu did not realise as she looked at Molly with consternation was that Molly was finding this conversation, with its echoes of her own thoughts, extremely uncomfortable. 'S-o-r-r-y . . .' Lulu enunciated, pulling a face as she did so.

But the damage had been done and Molly found it difficult to sleep that night. Was she jealous? Was that the simple explanation – jealous not, as Hector and most men would have thought, of the girl's youth and beauty, but jealous that she was being usurped in James' affections. She did not think so, she was not a possessive mother. But Lulu had said . . . but then, should she listen to her women friends? Women were always too hypercritical of each other. When was the last time she had heard a fair assessment of a woman, by a woman? Unable to sleep, Molly finally got up, went downstairs and made herself a cup of hot chocolate. As she sat at the kitchen table she finally resolved there was nothing she could do even if she was right about Emma. It was James' life and he must do what he wanted with whom he chose. His life was no longer her business. Her job now was to be there to pick up the pieces if things went wrong – but then only if he wanted her to. She felt better and padded back to bed, curled up close to a gently snoring Hector and thanked the God she no longer believed in for giving her such a husband whom she loved, warts and all.

Tabby appeared unexpectedly the following morning with two friends, Murdo and David. They had, it transpired, been to an all-night party across the county and were looking for breakfast.

Molly was getting the breakfast. Tabby, for once unasked, was helping. Molly did not feel happy. Normally, young men like Murdo and David as companions for her daughter would have pleased her – they were smart, polite, intelligent. But what was Tabby doing careering around Lynshire with two young men when she was engaged to another? And what bothered her most was the way Tabby spoke and acted, with Murdo in particular, it smacked of too marked a degree of friendship for Molly's comfort.

'Where's Sebastian?' Molly asked as nonchalantly as she chould muster.

'Recording,' Tabby replied without looking up from the bread she was slicing into doorsteps.

'Are Murdo and David friends of his?'

'Mummy, you're snooping,' Tabby waggled the bread knife at her and laughed.

'I'm not, I'm concerned,' Molly said with righteous indignation.

'Murdo and David are friends of a girl I met at secretarial college. They don't know Sebastian. I like them and that's that.' Tabby reeled off this information as if it had been learned by rote; her expression of pained boredom was a warning to Molly to mind her own business. Only Molly chose not to heed the warning.

'Would Sebastian like you out with other young men?'

'Do you know, Mummy, shorthand is the most boring subject on earth.'

'Don't change the subject, Tabby. I'm worried. I don't think you should flirt with Murdo as you do when engaged to Sebastian. It's not nice and might give the wrong impression.' Molly turned from the Aga in time to catch Tabby pulling faces at her. 'And you can stop that,' Molly snapped.

'Whenever I come here it's Sebastian this and Sebastian that. I get sick to death of the sound of his name.'

'Have you had a row with Sebastian? What's going on? Honestly, I don't understand you at all.'

'You don't, do you? All you want for me is a nice, safe husband who wouldn't say boo to a goose. You don't care about me, only what people will say.' Tabby's voice was rising dangerously.

'That's not fair, Tabby, and you know it.'

'All I know is you've always preferred James to me and now it's Sebastian you're all over.'

'Don't talk such utter rubbish,' Molly said with ill-concealed anger at this all too familiar and totally unjustifiable wail. 'I don't like what I see and I would appreciate it if you would behave yourself under your father's roof.'

'God, what a hypocrite you are, Mother. It was all right for saintly Sebastian to sleep with me . . .'

'It was not all right, if you must know. I did not approve, but what was I to do? You'll do exactly as you want, you always have. My main concern was to prevent your father from finding out.'

'See what I mean – hypocritical.'

'If protecting your father from a truth that would hurt him is hypocritical, then yes I am and can see no fault in it.'

'*And* bourgeois.' Tabby hurled the worst insult she could think of at her mother.

'If it's bourgeois to be offended by your behaviour over Sebastian; to want you to marry a decent, honest, man; then I am. If it's bourgeois to try and maintain some standards of morality in a world I no longer understand, OK I am. And you know what? I'm proud to be, I'm not insulted by your taunt. And I can tell you now, Tabby. When you have a daughter, and you have to sit back and watch her being stupid, you will be just as bourgeois as I am.'

Tabby looked at her mother, aghast. She was used to Molly changing the subject or leaving a room, not facing her head on.

'I don't plan to do anything with Murdo,' she mumbled. 'And Sebastian knows where I am and he didn't mind.'

'That's fine then,' Molly said quietly and resolved to tell Hector that they must stop admiring Sebastian so much or the engagement would be off again.

*

By mid-morning all thoughts of Emma, Tabby, James and Sebastian were wiped away when the household was alerted to the sound of a shotgun being fired, followed quickly by the buzz of a large crowd of people moving up the High Street with a determined stride. Hector looked at Molly and she at him and without exchanging a word they raced down the drive and joined the throng which was marching to Farmer Feather's fields.

They arrived to find Gussie, shotgun in hand and surrounded by all her dogs, holding at bay a sizeable group of men with chain saws and a large digger.

'I'm not pretending!' she shouted, waving the shotgun in the direction of the workmen who, to a man, ducked. 'You take one step towards that copse and I'll fire.'

'Good gracious,' said Hector. 'Gussie, put that gun down or you'll be in trouble with the law.'

'Whose side are you on?'

'If you'd explain, Gussie.'

'These men here have been sent by the Mann creature to cut down the copse, haven't you? She glared angrily at the workmen, who looked sheepishly at their feet.

'We're only doing our job, Guv,' one of them pleaded to Hector.

'Murderers!' Gussie shouted before Hector could intervene in the capacity of arbitrator, one he rather fancied his skills at. 'There's a badger's sett up there. Woodpigeon, partridge . . . do you know how rare partridge are now? Nearly extinct.'

The crowd was beginning to mutter and they too were glowering at the workmen who started to shuffle nervously. It was then Molly realised that Gussie was made up to the nines. In her tight breeches and hacking jacket – which Molly had never seen before – she looked even more beautiful than ever.

It was at this point Colin Mann appeared, just as it looked as if the workmen were going to slide away. His appearance gave them new heart and they bent down to pick up their saws as if arming themselves with pikes and staves.

'I would like to point out, Mrs Ford, that you are trespassing on my land.'

Gussie gave him such a look of loathing that Molly was amazed he still stood. 'Stop them!' Gussie shrieked. 'There's been a Hunter's Copse since Domesday. Are you lot going to stand there and let this man cut your inheritance down?' From the crowd's reaction it was obvious that they were not going to allow it to happen. Colin, sensing the mood, stepped forward and held up his hand.

'My dear Mrs Ford . . .' Colin began but stopped short when he found himself looking down the muzzle of Gussie's gun.

'Don't you "dear" me, you patronising oaf,' Gussie flared back to cheers from the more feminist elements in the crowd.

'But, Gussie, there's a preservation order on that copse. It's the first thing we did when we heard about these shenanigans,' Hector said reasonably.

'Do you think the derisory fines the courts hand out will stop him? That's nothing to him and the money he's set to make. But the trees will be gone for ever. Defend them – encircle them . . .' Gussie pointed dramatically to the copse with her gun and Molly was convinced that at any moment she was likely to launch into Henry V's speech at Agincourt. The villagers let out a deafening cheer and began to scramble across the field. Holding hands they started to encircle the copse.

Now the reason for Gussie's appearance became apparent. Across the field bumped a large lorry with HTV painted on the side – the television people had arrived. Molly felt certain it was only a matter of minutes before the BBC would be here as well. Here were two stories, the environment, and Gussie, famous film star, coming out of her Greta Garbo phase for the first time in years.

Gussie was a true professional. Her interview went smoothly, she had marshalled her arguments well, she knew her best angle. She appealed direct to camera, the limpid eyes begging the viewers to take her side. Everyone began to congratulate each other – no one would resist that.

And then Colin asked to be interviewed. He was so handsome, so charming and reasonable, that several feminine hearts in the crowd, despite themselves, began to flutter alarmingly, and many faltered.

'Stop! Stop everything . . .' Across the field, her grey hair streaming behind her, a raincoat hastily thrown over her pyjamas, her wellington boots slipping and sliding on her feet, raced their local historian, Nan Carter. 'Stop this desecration. This field must not be touched,' she shouted, everything about her, hair, clothes, head, wobbling with agitation. 'Down there is a large colony of wild *Orchis sercina*.'

'*Orchis sercina*?' the crowd echoed.

'Oh, yes. Without doubt this is the happiest day of my life. It was thought to be extinct, you see. But there's dozens of plants.'

'How do you know?' Colin demanded. The cameras had already swung to Nan, and Colin was now busily manoeuvring his body back into shot.

'Because, young man, I am an expert on wild flowers. That's how I know.'

'But it's winter, there are no flowers.'

'No, but after the extremely hot summer and mild autumn there's foliage. I would stake my reputation on it. The moment the officials from Kew come this field will be protected forthwith. What do you say, Mr Parminter?'

Hector did not say anything really but made the sort of noises that he used when out of his depth and was not sure what to say but which, to everyone except Molly, always sounded very wise.

'It looks as if you've done the village a favour, Colin. We'd never have known they were there but for you.' Gussie was smiling her largest smile, and speaking in her sexiest husk.

'Very well,' he said, his face dark with anger. 'But it was an orchid that beat me. There's still my Elizabethan Village development,' he said menacingly, indicating to his workmen to follow him.

Everyone else clustered round Gussie and Nan in congratulation before racing home to set their videos so that they could see themselves time and again on TV.

Chapter 22

Solutions

I T TOOK THE village some time to settle after the excitement of the television cameras. There was after all a marked kudos in appearing on the box, if only as a figure in the crowd. Videos had duly been sent to Sydney, Adelaide and even Vancouver, where past inhabitants of Sarson Magna now lived and pined for a village which had only ever existed in their imagination.

Nan Carter was right. The experts from Kew verified her discovery and, to her great excitement, she was asked to write a paper on the find – more impressive, she felt, than local history.

Colin Mann sulked. There was no other word for it. He and Sue took themselves off on a round the world cruise which at least gave everyone three months' breathing space before the next battle.

Sybil Potter-Smythe had been elected to the Council, having quickly jumped on the orchid bandwagon, so to speak. And she was also now a valued committee member of the Conservative Association.

Molly was busy. Hector had been right, there was a market for their sort of entertainment. The only regret she had was that her free time now was negligible – no more popping down to Lulu, she had to rely on her friend to call on her. Thus, from Lulu and Mrs Hodgson, she culled the latest gossip.

It was from them that she heard one of the choicest pieces of gossip to hit Sarson Magna in a long time. The schoolteacher, Miss Truro, had disappeared while on holiday in Morocco – white slave traffic was out of the question, was the consensus, since she was fifty if she was a day and it would not have been kind to a bus to compare them. A temporary teacher had been installed but was having to lodge in Churchill Drive since all Miss Truro's things were in the schoolhouse cottage. It was a fine legal tangle to be sure and one which was likely to finish the vicar off with worry, since it was a church school.

No one had seen Annie English for weeks, ever since she had embarked on a trilogy of lust in the Middle Ages. Although the books were not yet written, let alone published, there was already a waiting list at the mobile library, for Annie's books went down well in the village, sexy as they were, or probably because they were, as Lulu said.

Sybil and Hyacinth were still not speaking, Lulu reported, but that wasn't surprising really. The Trotters had sold their shop but were being very mysterious about the new owners who would take over in June. And Lulu thought she might be in love again – for once with someone suitable, a consultant from Lynchester General. At least he was the right age, Molly was happy to report to Hector.

There was no doubt about it, Molly was missing the village and yet there was a time when she had thought it restrictive and boring. It was strange living in the village yet not, nowadays, really being part of it.

It was some time before Molly realised that the strange discontent she'd been feeling, before the advent of the guests, had disappeared. She no longer gave a fig what people might think about her defection from the Conservative Association, and with the added confidence acquired from having a proper job, she even went as far as to tell Hector how she felt.

'I've been meaning to have a word with you about that,' Hector said, which sounded ominous. 'I'm fed up myself – everyone takes me for granted. I'm disillusioned with everything.'

'Oh Hector!' she said, eyes shining as if he had just reasserted his love for her.

'I didn't know how to tell you, I thought you'd be upset.'

'Isn't it strange how we so often think the same things – like twin souls.'

'I don't know about that . . .' Hector looked a little taken aback at such metaphysical thinking. 'I blame that woman for everything. I'd go as far as to say that damn woman is ruining the party.'

'Mrs Thatcher?'

'Good God, no, Sybil Potter-Smythe. She's hijacked the whole of the Association. I can't work with her – too bossy. We'll resign together, shall we?'

A month later they again heard from Wellbrookes. The paintings had been authenticated.

Hector and Molly's battle was a royal one: he frustrated by what he saw as her obduracy, and she angry at what she regarded as his insensitivity. The war raged all day and into the night. Neither had ever experienced anything like it. Molly was seriously thinking of moving into a spare bedroom, if hostilities did not cease. The problem was eased only when Aunt Fifi finally came to stay.

Hector, Molly noticed to her disgust, was charming almost beyond endurance to the old lady.

When Aunt Fifi heard the story of the paintings she laughed so much that Molly became seriously concerned for her well-being.

'You've got to sell them, Molly, don't be so silly. So much money, think what you could both do with it. You could fix those annoying flashings at last and still have a comfortable income for life.'

'But it would be fraudulent. And secondly Uncle Basil left them to me, I couldn't do it. One can't give away or sell a present.'

'Now you listen to me, Molly. The first person to sell them would have been my darling old horror, Basil. If he hadn't died of laughing first. And what is more, if all these so-called experts can't see a fake when it's staring them in the face – that's their problem not yours. You've been completely honest with them.'

Molly sat silent.

'And have you thought, Molly,' Fifi continued, 'perhaps we are wrong and the experts are right?'

'But the family always said.'

'Maybe it was a joke.'

'Oh, surely not, Fifi.'

'I wouldn't put anything past the Pigeons – a mischievous lot, Hector, but then you never really knew them, did you?'

'No, I can't imagine why not,' he said, and had the grace to blush. At least Molly thought it might be one.

'If we did sell them then we share the money with you, Fifi.' Molly looked at her aunt.

'Good gracious no, I don't want any money. What on earth for? I've all I want. Basil left them to you, my dear – you do as you want.'

Hector, through all this, was sitting on the edge of his chair nodding his head vehemently in agreement whenever Aunt Fifi spoke and looking doleful when it was Molly's turn. There was no point in asking his opinion, it was written all over his face.

'What about our bargain then, Hector?' She looked sternly at her husband.

'What bargain?' he asked, with an insufferable air of innocence.

'That if I sell, you'll sell.'

He pretended surprise. 'Did I say that?'

'You know you did.'

'Well perhaps I could let the Turner go. It obviously isn't.'

'And?'

'You never liked the Serpentine desk in the inner hall, you always said it collected too much dust.'

'Done.' Molly put out her hand to shake his and Fifi glowed with satisfaction.

'I've an idea, Molly. Why don't you have them copied? Then you'll still have them,' her aunt suggested.

And that's what Molly did. Tabby recommended a friend of hers who had actually completed his art course. Molly was a little wary, doubtful whether any artist Tabby knew was likely to be suitable. She was pleasantly surprised to find this young man only painted representational pictures and was not in the habit of raiding skips to compose his paintings. He copied the Huxtables beautifully; it was difficult to tell the difference. But Molly insisted that each picture bore his signature, plus an explanation on the back of the canvas – she couldn't go through this again, ever.

Having made the decision to go ahead with the sale, it was irritating to find that there were further delays. But the pictures had to be fitted into the right sale, the brochure printed, and experts the world over informed.

During this period Molly felt she was walking around waiting for a bomb to explode, terrified that someone somewhere in the world would bounce up to announce they had the originals and Molly would be arrested. She spent many hours wondering what clothes she should wear for her trial at the Central Court of the Old Bailey. Meanwhile Hector blithely went about dreaming of all the money they were going to have.

But nothing happened, no one popped up with the originals. Still not satisfied, Molly wrote to the chairman of the auctioneers to say that she did not believe in her pictures' authenticity. She received a letter couched in the most soothing tones, written by a man who obviously thought he was dealing with a creature of pathetic intelligence.

Molly would not go to the sale. She was too scared, too embarrassed, and too frightened. But Hector went.

Molly spent that afternoon tidying up in the back pantry – the crate the paintings had come in still stood there. It was a good sturdy wooden box and might come in handy. She pulled out the straw packing, stuffing it in plastic sacks. At the bottom of the box was an envelope yellow with age, the ink browned with the years. Gingerly she opened it, fearful that the fragile paper might disintegrate. Inside was an invoice. In beautiful copperplate handwriting she read *'To Jonathan Disney, artist, of 62 Philomel Terrace, £50.00 for the copying, in oils, of twelve pictures for Walter Pigeon Esq.'*

Molly sat back on her heels and rocked with laughter. She scrambled up and went into the kitchen and then to Hector's study. On his desk she scrabbled about amidst the chaos searching for a letterhead of the auctioneers. She finally found one and put out her hand to the phone just as it rang.

It was an almost incoherent Hector. 'They sold, all of them, the whole bang shoot, way above estimate. Molly my love, you're rich . . .'

'But . . . ? She started to speak and then stopped. What was the point? She had tried and no one would listen. All it proved was that the art world was mad. And didn't it just show how difficult it was to say what was art and what wasn't. She only wished Jonathan Disney, artist, whoever he was, was still alive to hear how highly the world's art experts thought of his work.

As instructed by Hector, she went down to the cellar to get two bottles of Colin's champagne to put on ice ready for Hector's rapid return. They were the last two bottles – saved in the nick of time, she said to herself as she turned the cellar light off.

Then Molly did two things. First she called a travel agent and booked a trip, first class, for Fifi and a companion of her choice, to India including a tour in a maharajah's train. She had remembered that when she was a child Fifi had told her she longed to see the Himalayas before she died.

Finally she picked up the phone again. 'Mr White, It's Molly Parminter here. About my flashings . . .'

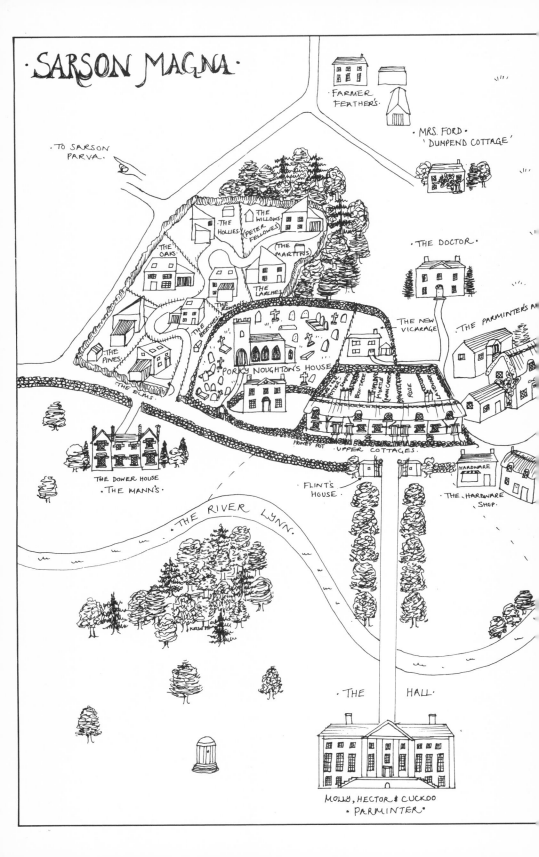

Keto Diet for Weight Loss

A cookbook of Tasty recipes to lose weight easily while continuing to eat the foods you love!

Dana Roberts

Table of contents

Dana Roberts

Quick Recipes

Quinoa Bowls

Preparation time: 10 Minutes

Cooking time: 1 Minute

Servings: 4

Ingredients:

- 1 and ½ Cups quinoa
- 2 Tablespoons honey
- 2 and ¼ Cups of water
- ¼ Teaspoon pumpkin pie spice
- 2 Cups strawberries, chopped

Directions:

1. In your instant pot, mix quinoa with honey, water, spice, and strawberries, stir, cover, and cook on high for 1 minute.
2. Leave quinoa aside for 10 minutes, stir a bit, divide everything into bowls and serve.
3. Enjoy!

Nutrition:

- Calories: 162
- Fat: 3
- Fiber: 3
- Carbs: 6
- Protein: 3

Cornmeal Porridge

Preparation time: 10 Minutes

Cooking time: 20 Minutes

Servings: 4

Ingredients:

- 1 Cup cornmeal
- 1 Cup milk
- 4 Cups of water
- ½ Teaspoon nutmeg, ground
- ½ Cup sweetened condensed milk

Directions:

1. In a bowl, mix 1 cup water with cornmeal and stir well.
2. In your instant pot, mix the rest of the water with milk and cornmeal mix and stir.
3. Also, add nutmeg, stir, cover, and cook on high for 6 minutes.
4. Add condensed milk, stir, divide into bowls, and serve.
5. Enjoy!

Nutrition:

- Calories: 241 Fat: 4
- Fiber: 6 Carbs: 12
- Protein: 6

Breakfast Rice Pudding

Preparation time: 10 Minutes

Cooking time: 20 Minutes

Servings: 6

Ingredients:

- 2 Cups nut milk
- 1 and ¼ Cups water
- 1 Cup basmati rice
- 1 Cup coconut cream
- ¼ Cup maple syrup

Directions:

1. In your instant pot, mix nut milk with water, rice, cream, and maple syrup, stir well, cover, and cook on high for 20 minutes.
2. Stir pudding again, divide into bowls and serve.
3. Enjoy!

Nutrition:

- Calories: 251
- Fat: 5
- Fiber: 3
- Carbs: 6
- Protein: 5

Breakfast Tortillas

Preparation time: 10 Minutes

Cooking time: 13 Minutes

Servings: 6

Ingredients:

- 2 Pounds red potatoes, cubed
- 4 Eggs, whisked
- 6 Ounces ham, cubed
- ¼ Cup yellow onion, chopped

For the instant pot:

- 1 Cup water

For Serving:

- 6 Tortillas

Directions:

1. In a bowl, mix eggs with ham, onion, and potatoes and whisk well.
2. Add this to a baking dish and spread.
3. Add water to your instant pot, add trivet, add baking dish inside, cover and cook on high for 13 minutes.
4. Arrange tortillas on a working surface, divide eggs, mix on each, wrap and serve for breakfast.
5. Enjoy!

Nutrition:

- Calories: 212
- Fat: 3
- Fiber: 7
- Carbs: 9
- Protein: 12

Special Pancake

Preparation time: 10 Minutes

Cooking time: 45 Minutes

Servings: 4

Ingredients:

- 2 Cups white flour
- 2 Eggs
- 1 and ½ Cups milk
- 2 Tablespoons sugar
- 2 and ½ Teaspoons baking powder

Directions:

1. In a bowl, mix flour with eggs, milk, sugar, and baking powder and whisk really well.
2. Add this to your instant pot, spread, cover, and cook on Manual for 45 minutes.
3. Leave your pancake to cool down, slice, divide between plates, and serve.
4. Enjoy!

Nutrition:

- Calories: 251
- Fat: 5
- Fiber: 2
- Carbs: 6
- Protein: 3

Millet and Oats Porridge

Preparation time: 10 Minutes

Cooking time: 13 Minutes

Servings: 8

Ingredients:

- 1 Cup millet
- ½ Cup rolled oats
- 3 Cups water
- ½ Teaspoon ginger powder
- 2 Apples, cored and chopped

Directions:

1. Set your instant pot on sauté mode, add millet, stir and toast for 3 minutes.
2. Add oats, water, ginger, and apples, stir, cover, and cook on high for 10 minutes.
3. Stir porridge again and divide it into bowls to serve.
4. Enjoy!

Nutrition:

- Calories: 200
- Fat: 2
- Fiber: 3
- Carbs: 4
- Protein: 5

Dana Roberts

Lunch Recipes

Eggs Benedict Deviled Eggs

Preparation time: 15 Minutes

Cooking time: 25 Minutes

Servings: 16

Ingredients:

- 8 Hardboiled eggs, sliced in half
- 1 Tablespoon lemon juice
- ½ Teaspoon mustard powder

- 1 Pack Hollandaise sauce mix, prepared according to the directions in the packaging
- 1 lb. Asparagus, trimmed and steamed
- 4oz. Bacon, cooked and chopped

Directions:

1. Scoop out the egg yolks.
2. Mix the egg yolks with lemon juice, mustard powder, and 1/3 cup of the Hollandaise sauce.
3. Spoon the egg yolk mixture into each of the egg whites.
4. Arrange the asparagus spears on a serving plate. Top with the deviled eggs.
5. Sprinkle remaining sauce and bacon on top.

Nutrition:

- Calories: 80 Total Fat: 5.3g
- Saturated Fat: 1.7g Cholesterol: 90mg
- Sodium: 223mg Total Carbohydrate: 2.1g
- Dietary Fiber: 0.6g Total Sugars: 0.7g
- Protein: 6.2g Potassium: 133mg

Spinach Meatballs

Preparation time: 20 Minutes

Cooking time: 30 Minutes

Servings: 4

Ingredients:

- 1 Cup spinach, chopped
- 1 ½ lb. Ground turkey breast
- 1 Onion, chopped
- 3 Cloves garlic, minced

- 1 Egg, beaten
- ¼ Cup milk
- ¾ Cup breadcrumbs
- ½ Cup Parmesan cheese, grated
- Salt and pepper to taste
- 2 Tablespoons butter
- 2 Tablespoons Keto flour
- 10oz. Italian cheese, shredded
- ½ Teaspoon nutmeg, freshly grated
- ¼ Cup parsley, chopped

Directions:

1. Preheat your oven to 400 degrees F.
2. Mix all the ingredients in a large bowl.
3. Form meatballs from the mixture.
4. Bake in the oven for 20 minutes.

Nutrition:

- Calories: 374 Total Fat: 18.5g
- Saturated Fat: 10g Cholesterol: 118mg
- Sodium: 396mg
- Total Carbohydrate: 11.3g
- Dietary Fiber: 1g Total Sugars: 1.7g
- Protein: 34.2g Potassium: 336mg

Bacon Wrapped Asparagus

Preparation time: 10 Minutes

Cooking time: 20 Minutes

Servings: 6

Ingredients:

- 1 ½ lb. Asparagus spears, sliced in half
- 6 Slices bacon

- 2 Tablespoons olive oil
- Salt and pepper to taste

Directions:

1. Preheat your oven to 400 degrees F.
2. Wrap a handful of asparagus with bacon.
3. Secure with a toothpick. Drizzle with the olive oil. Season with salt and pepper.
4. Bake in the oven for 20 minutes or until bacon is crispy.

Nutrition:

- Calories: 166 Total Fat: 12.8g
- Saturated Fat: 3.3g Cholesterol: 21mg
- Sodium: 441mg Total Carbohydrate: 4.7g
- Dietary Fiber: 2.4g Total Sugars: 2.1g
- Protein: 9.5g Potassium: 337mg

Buttered Cod

Preparation time: 5 Minutes

Cooking time: 5 Minutes

Servings: 4

Ingredients:

- 1 ½ lb. Cod fillets, sliced
- 6 Tablespoons butter, sliced
- ¼ Teaspoon garlic powder

- ¾ Teaspoon ground paprika
- Salt and pepper to taste
- Lemon slices - Chopped parsley

Directions:

1. Mix the garlic powder, paprika, salt, and pepper in a bowl.
2. Season codpieces with seasoning mixture.
3. Add two tablespoons of butter in a pan over medium heat. Let half of the butter melt. Add the cod and cook for 2 minutes per side. Top with the remaining slices of butter.
4. Cook for 3 to 4 minutes.
5. Garnish with parsley and lemon slices before serving.

Nutrition:

- Calories: 295 Total Fat: 19g
- Saturated Fat: 11g Cholesterol: 128mg
- Sodium: 236mg Total Carbohydrate: 1.5g
- Dietary Fiber: 0.7g Total Sugars: 0.3g
- Protein: 30.7g Potassium: 102mg

Chicken and Rice Congee

Preparation time: 10 Minutes

Cooking time: 35 Minutes

Servings: 1

Ingredients:

- 90 Grams of rice, brown
- 2 Cups cold water
- 2 Chicken drumsticks
- ½ Tablespoon ginger, sliced into strips
- Salt, to taste

Directions:

1. First, rinse the rice under tap water by gently scrubbing the rice.
2. Drain any milky water. The next step is to add ginger, rice, chicken drumsticks, and water to the instant pot.
3. Do not add salt at this stage.
4. Now close the lid of the pot and cook on high pressure for 30 minutes.
5. Then, naturally, release the steam.
6. Open the lid carefully; check if the congee looks watery. Heat up the instant pot by pressing the sauté button.
7. Cook until the desired thickness is obtained. Season it with salt and then use a fork to separate the meat from the bone.
8. Remove the congee from the pot. Serve and enjoy.

Nutrition:

- Calories: 493 Total Fat: 6g
- Sodium: 248mg
- Total Carbohydrate: 73.9g
- Protein: 32g

Steamed Cod with Ginger

Preparation time: 15 Minutes

Cooking time: 15 Minutes

Servings: 4

Ingredients:

- 4 Cod fillets, skin removed
- 3 Tbsp. lemon juice, freshly squeezed
- 2 Tbsp. coconut aminos
- 2 Tbsp. grated ginger
- 6 Scallions, chopped

Directions:

1. Place a trivet in a large saucepan and pour a cup or two of water into the pan. Bring to a boil.

2. In a small bowl, whisk well lemon juice, coconut aminos, coconut oil, and grated ginger.

3. Place scallions in a heatproof dish that fits inside a saucepan. Season scallion's mon with pepper and salt. Drizzle with ginger mixture. Sprinkle scallions on top.

4. Seal dish with foil. Place the dish on the trivet inside the saucepan—cover and steam for 15 minutes.

5. Serve and enjoy.

Nutrition:

- Calories: 514 Fat: 40g
- Carbohydrates: 10g Protein: 28.3g

Flounder with Dill and Capers

Preparation time: 10 Minutes

Cooking time: 15 Minutes

Servings: 4

Ingredients:

- 4 Flounder fillets
- 1 Tbsp. chopped fresh dill
- 2 Tbsp. capers, chopped
- 4 Lemon wedges

Directions:

1. Place a trivet in a large saucepan and pour a cup or two of water into the pan. Bring to a boil.
2. Place flounder in a heatproof dish that fits inside a saucepan. Season snapper with pepper and salt. Drizzle with olive oil on all sides. Sprinkle dill and capers on top of the filet. Seal dish with foil. Place the dish on the trivet inside the saucepan—cover and steam for 15 minutes.
3. Serve and enjoy with lemon wedges.

Nutrition:

- Calories: 447 Fat: 35.9g
- Carbohydrates: 8.6g Protein: 20.3g

Chili-Garlic Salmon

Preparation time: 10 Minutes

Cooking time: 15 Minutes

Servings: 4

Ingredients:

- 5 Tbsp. sweet chili sauce
- ¼ Cup coconut aminos

- 4 Salmon fillets
- 3 Tbsp. green onions, chopped
- 3 Cloves garlic, peeled and minced

Directions:

1. Place a trivet in a large saucepan and pour a cup or two of water into the pan. Bring to a boil.
2. In a small bowl, whisk well sweet chili sauce, garlic, and coconut aminos.
3. Place salmon in a heatproof dish that fits inside a saucepan. Season salmon with pepper. Drizzle with sweet chili sauce mixture. Sprinkle green onions on top of the filet.
4. Seal dish with foil. Place the dish on the trivet inside the saucepan. Cover and steam for 15 minutes.
5. Serve and enjoy.

Nutrition:

- Calories: 409 Fat: 14.4g
- Carbohydrates: 0.9g Protein: 65.4g

Chili-Lime Shrimps

Preparation time: 5 Minutes

Cooking time: 10 Minutes

Servings: 4

Ingredients:

- 1 ½ lb. Raw shrimp, peeled and deveined
- 1 Tbsp. chili flakes
- 5 Tbsp sweet chili sauce

- 2 Tbsp. lime juice, freshly squeezed
- 1 Tsp. cayenne pepper

Directions:

1. In a small bowl, whisk well chili flakes, sweet chili sauce, cayenne pepper, and water.
2. On medium-high fire, heat a non-stick saucepan for 2 minutes. Add oil to a pan and swirl to coat the bottom and sides—heat the oil for a minute.
3. Stir fry shrimp, around 5 minutes. Season lightly with salt and pepper.
4. Stir in sweet chili mixture and toss well shrimp to coat.
5. Turn off fire, drizzle lime juice and toss well to coat.
6. Serve and enjoy.

Nutrition:

- Calories: 306 Fat: 19.8g
- Carbohydrates: 1.7g Protein: 34.9.g

Tuna Patties

Preparation time: 10 Minutes

Cooking time: 10 Minutes

Servings: 8

Ingredients:

- 20oz. Canned tuna flakes
- ¼ Cup almond flour
- 1 Egg, beaten
- 2 Tablespoons fresh dill, chopped
- 2 Stalks green onion, chopped

- Salt and pepper to taste
- 1 Tablespoon lemon zest
- ¼ Cup mayonnaise
- 1 Tablespoon lemon juice
- 2 Tablespoons avocado oil

Directions:

1. Combine all the ingredients except avocado oil, lemon juice, and avocado oil in a large bowl.
2. Form 8 patties from the mixture.
3. In a pan over medium heat, add the oil.
4. Once the oil starts to sizzle, cook the tuna patties for 3 to 4 minutes per side.
5. Drain each patty on a paper towel.
6. Spread mayo on top and drizzle with lemon juice before serving.

Nutrition:

- Calories: 101
- Total Fat: 4.9g
- Saturated Fat: 1.2g
- Cholesterol: 47mg
- Sodium: 243mg
- Total Carbohydrate: 3.1g
- Dietary Fiber: 0.5g
- Total Sugars: 0.7g
- Protein: 12.3g
- Potassium: 60mg

Grilled Mahi Mahi with Lemon Butter Sauce

Preparation time: 20 Minutes

Cooking time: 10 Minutes

Servings: 6

Ingredients:

- 6 Mahi mahi fillets
- Salt and pepper to taste
- 2 Tablespoons olive oil
- 6 Tablespoons butter
- ¼ Onion, minced

- ½ Teaspoon garlic, minced
- ¼ Cup chicken stock
- 1 Tablespoon lemon juice

Directions:

1. Preheat your grill to medium heat.
2. Season fish fillets with salt and pepper.
3. Coat both sides with olive oil.
4. Grill for 3 to 4 minutes per side.
5. Place fish on a serving platter.
6. In a pan over medium heat, add the butter and let it melt.
7. Add the onion and sauté for 2 minutes.
8. Add the garlic and cook for 30 seconds.
9. Pour in the chicken stock.
10. Simmer until the stock has been reduced to half.
11. Add the lemon juice.
12. Pour the sauce over the grilled fish fillets.

Nutrition:

- Calories: 234 Total Fat: 17.2g
- Saturated Fat: 8.3g Cholesterol: 117mg
- Sodium: 242mg Total Carbohydrate: 0.6g
- Dietary Fiber: 0.1g Total Sugars: 0.3g
- Protein: 19.1g Potassium: 385mg

Shrimp Scampi

Preparation time: 15 Minutes

Cooking time: 10 Minutes

Servings: 6

Ingredients:

- 2 Tablespoons olive oil
- 2 Tablespoons butter
- 1 Tablespoon garlic, minced
- ½ Cup dry white wine
- ¼ Teaspoon red pepper flakes
- Salt and pepper to taste
- 2lb. Large shrimp, peeled and deveined
- ¼ Cup fresh parsley, chopped

- 1 Teaspoon lemon zest
- 2 Tablespoons lemon juice
- 3 Cups spaghetti squash, cooked

Directions:

1. In a pan over medium heat, add the oil and butter.
2. Cook the garlic for 2 minutes.
3. Pour in the wine.
4. Add the red pepper flakes, salt, and pepper.
5. Cook for 2 minutes.
6. Add the shrimp.
7. Cook for 2 to 3 minutes.
8. Remove from the stove.
9. Add the parsley, lemon zest, and lemon juice.
10. Serve on top of spaghetti squash.

Nutrition:

- Calories: 232 Total Fat: 8.9g
- Saturated Fat: 3.2g Cholesterol: 226mg
- Sodium: 229mg Total Carbohydrate: 7.6g
- Dietary Fiber: 0.2g Total Sugars: 0.3g
- Protein: 28.9g Potassium: 104mg

Dana Roberts

Dinner Recipes

Quick Pumpkin Soup

Preparation time: 10 Minutes

Cooking time: 20 Minutes

Servings: 4-6

Ingredients:

- 1 Cup of coconut milk
- 2 Cups chicken broth
- 6 Cups baked pumpkin
- 1 Tsp. garlic powder
- 1 Tsp. ground cinnamon
- 1 Tsp. dried ginger
- 1 Tsp. nutmeg
- 1 Tsp. paprika
- Salt and pepper, to taste
- Sour cream or coconut yogurt, for topping
- Pumpkin seeds, toasted, for topping

Directions:

1. Combine the coconut milk, broth, baked pumpkin, and spices in a soup pan (use medium heat). Stir occasionally and simmer for 15 minutes.
2. With an immersion blender, blend the soup mix for 1 minute.
3. Top with sour cream or coconut yogurt and pumpkin seeds.

Nutrition:

- Calories: 123 Fat: 9.8g
- Carbs: 8.1g Protein: 3.1g

Fresh Avocado Soup

Preparation time: 5 Minutes

Cooking time: 10 Minutes

Servings: 2

Ingredients:

- 1 Ripe avocado
- 2 Romaine lettuce leaves, washed and chopped
- 1 Cup coconut milk, chilled
- 1 Tbsp. lime juice
- 20 Fresh mint leaves
- Salt, to taste

Directions:

1. Mix all your ingredients thoroughly in a blender.
2. Chill in the fridge for 5-10 minutes.

Nutrition:

- Calories: 280 Fat: 26g
- Carbs: 12g Protein: 4g

Creamy Garlic Chicken

Preparation time: 5 Minutes

Cooking time: 15 Minutes

Servings: 4

Ingredients:

- 4 Chicken breasts, finely sliced
- 1 Tsp garlic powder

- 1 Tsp. paprika
- 2 Tbsp. butter
- 1 Tsp. salt
- 1 Cup heavy cream
- ½ Cup sun-dried tomatoes
- 2 Cloves garlic, minced
- 1 Cup spinach, chopped

Directions:

1. Blend the paprika, garlic powder, and salt and sprinkle over both sides of the chicken.
2. Melt the butter in a frying pan (choose medium heat). Add the chicken breast and fry for 5 minutes on each side. Set aside.
3. Add the heavy cream, sun-dried tomatoes, and garlic to the pan and whisk well to combine—Cook for 2 minutes. Add spinach and sauté for an additional 3 minutes. Return the chicken to the pan and cover with the sauce.

Nutrition: Calories: 280 Fat: 26g

- Carbohydrates: 12g Protein: 4g

Garlicky Pork Shoulder

Preparation time: 15 Minutes

Cooking time: 6 Hours

Servings: 10

Ingredients:

- 1 Garlic head, peeled and crushed
- ¼ C. fresh rosemary, minced
- 2 Tbsp. fresh lemon juice
- 2 Tbsp. balsamic vinegar

- 1 (4-lb.) Pork shoulder

Directions:

1. In a bowl, add all the ingredients except pork shoulder and mix well.
2. In a large roasting pan, place the pork shoulder and generously coat with the marinade.
3. With a large plastic wrap, cover the roasting pan and refrigerate to marinate for at least 1-2 hours.
4. Remove the roasting pan from the refrigerator.
5. Remove the plastic wrap from the roasting pan and keep it at room temperature for 1 hour.
6. Preheat the oven to 2750 F.
7. Place the roasting pan into the oven and roast for about 6 hours.
8. Remove from the oven and place pork shoulder onto a cutting board for about 30 minutes.
9. With a sharp knife, cut the pork shoulder into desired size slices and serve.

Nutrition:

- Calories per serving: 502
- Carbohydrates: 2g Protein: 42.5g
- Fat: 39.1g Sugar: 0.1g
- Sodium: 125mg Fiber: 0.7g

Rosemary Pork Roast

Preparation time: 15 Minutes

Cooking time: 1 Hour

Servings: 6

Ingredients:

- 1 Tbsp. dried rosemary, crushed
- 3 Garlic cloves, minced
- Salt and freshly ground black pepper, to taste
- 2lb. Boneless pork loin roast
- ¼ C. olive oil
- 1/3 C. homemade chicken broth

Directions:

1. Preheat the oven to 3500 F. Lightly grease a roasting pan. In a small bowl, add rosemary, garlic, salt, black pepper, and with the back of a spoon, crush the mixture to form a paste.
2. With a sharp knife, pierce the pork loin at many places.
3. Press half of the rosemary mixture into the cuts.
4. Add oil in the bowl with the remaining rosemary mixture and stir to combine.
5. Rub the pork with rosemary mixture generously. Arrange the pork loin into the prepared roasting pan. Roast for about 1 hour, flipping and coating with the pan juices occasionally.
6. Remove the roasting pan from the oven. Transfer the pork to a serving platter.
7. Place the roasting pan over medium heat.
8. Add the broth and cook for about 3-5 minutes, stirring to lose the brown bits from the pan. Pour sauce over pork and serve.

Nutrition:

- Calories per serving: 294
- Carbohydrates: 0.9g Protein: 40g
- Fat: 13.9g Sugar: 0.1g
- Sodium: 156mg Fiber: 0.3g

Persian Chicken

Preparation time: 10 Minutes

Cooking time: 20 Minutes

Servings: 6

Ingredients: 1/2 Small sweet onion,

- 1/4 Cup freshly squeezed lemon juice
- 1 Tablespoon dried oregano
- 1/2 Tablespoon of sweet paprika,
- 1/2 Tablespoon of ground cumin
- 1/2 Cup olive oil
- 6 Boneless, skinless chicken thighs

Directions:

1. Put the vegetables in a blender. Mix it well.
2. Put the olive while the motor is running.
3. In a sealable bag for the freezer, place the chicken thighs and put the mixture in the sealable bag. Refrigerate it for 2 hours, while turning it two times. Remove the marinade thighs and discard the additional marinade. Preheat the barbecue to medium. Grill the chicken, turning once or until the inner part is well done.

Nutrition: Fat: 21g Carbohydrates: 3g

- Potassium: 220mg Sodium: 86mg
- Protein: 22g

Pesto Pork Chops

Preparation time: 20 Minutes

Cooking time: 20 Minutes

Servings: 3

Ingredients:

- 3 (3-ounce) Top-flood pork chops, boneless, fat
- 8 Tablespoons Herb Pesto (here)
- 1/2 Cup bread crumbs
- 1 Tablespoon olive oil

Directions:

1. Preheat the oven to 360 ° F. Cover a foil baker's sheet; set aside.

2. Rub one tablespoon of pesto evenly across each pork chop on both sides.

3. Every pork chop in the crumbs of bread is lightly dredged.

4. Heat the oil in a medium-high heat large skillet. Brown the pork chops for about 6 minutes on each side.

5. Place on the baking sheet the pork chops. Bake until the pork reaches 136 ° F in the center for about 10 minutes.

Nutrition: Fat: 8g Carbohydrates: 10g

- Phosphorus: 188mg Potassium: 220mg
- Sodium: 138mg Protein: 23g

Roasted Red Pepper and Eggplant Soup

Preparation time: 20 Minutes

Cooking time: 40 Minutes

Servings: 6

Ingredients:

- 1 Small sweet onion, cut into quarters
- 2 Small red peppers, halved
- 2 Cups of eggplant
- 2 Garlic cloves, crushed
- 1 Cup of olive oil
- 1 Cup of Easy Chicken Stock
- Water
- 1/4 Cup of chopped fresh basil

Directions:

1. Preheat the oven to 360 ° F. In a large ovenproof baking dish, place the onions, red peppers, eggplant, and garlic.
2. Add the olive oil to the vegetables.
3. Roast the vegetables. For about 40 minutes or until slightly charred and soft.
4. Slightly cool the vegetables and remove the peppers from the skin.
5. In a food processor (or in a large bowl, using a handheld immersion blender), purée the vegetables with the chicken stock. Move the soup to a large pot and add sufficient water to achieve the desired thickness. Heat the soup and add the basil to a simmer. Season and serve with pepper.

Nutrition: Fat: 2g Carbohydrates: 8g

- Phosphorus: 33mg Potassium: 188mg
- Sodium: 86mg Protein: 2g

Cilantro-Lime Flounder

Preparation time: 20 Minutes

Cooking time: 6 Minutes

Servings: 3

Ingredients:

- 1/4 Cup homemade mayonnaise
- 1 Lime juice Zest
- 1 1/2 Cup fresh cilantro
- 3 (3-ounce) Flounder fillets

Directions:

1. Preheat the oven to 300 ° F. Stir the mayonnaise, lime juice, lime zest, and cilantro in a small bowl.

2. Place three pieces of foil on a clean work surface, about 8x8 inches square. In the center of each square, place a flounder fillet.

3. Top the fillets with the mixture of mayonnaise evenly. Season the flounder with the pepper. Fold the foil sides over the fish, create a snug packet, and place on a baking sheet the foil packets. Bake the fish for three to six minutes. Unfold and display the boxes.

Nutrition: Fat: 3g Carbohydrates: 2g

- Phosphorus: 208mg Potassium: 138mg
- Sodium: 268mg Protein: 12g

Dana Roberts

Dessert Recipes

Snickerdoodle Muffins

Preparation time: 10 Minutes

Cooking time: 12 Minutes

Servings: 6

Ingredients:

- 6 2/3 Tbsp. coconut flour
- 1/2 Egg
- 1 Tbsp. butter, unsalted, melted
- 1 1/3 Tbsp. whipping cream
- 1 Tbsp. almond milk, unsweetened

Others:

- 1 1/3 Tbsp. erythritol sweetener and more for topping
- 1/4 Tsp. baking powder
- 1/4 Tsp. ground cinnamon and more for topping
- 1/4 Tsp. vanilla extract, unsweetened

Directions:

1. Turn on the oven, set it to 350 degrees F and let it preheat.
2. Meanwhile, take a medium bowl, place flour in it, add cinnamon and baking powder. Stir until combined.
3. Take a separate bowl, place the half egg in it, add butter, sour cream, milk, vanilla, and whisk until blended.
4. Whisk the flour mixture until a smooth batter is obtained, divide the batter evenly between two silicon muffin cups, and then sprinkle cinnamon and sweetener on top.
5. Bake the muffins for 10 to 12 minutes until firm, and then the top has turned golden brown and then serve and enjoy!

Nutrition:

- Calories: 299 Fat: 13.2g
- Fiber: 10.5g Carbohydrates:4.1g
- Protein: 3.8g

Egg Custard

Preparation time: 15 Minutes

Cooking time: 55 Minutes

Servings: 8

Ingredients:

- 5 Organic eggs
- Salt, as required
- ½ Cup Yacon syrup
- 20 Ounces unsweetened almond milk
- ¼ Teaspoon ground ginger
- ¼ Teaspoon ground cinnamon
- ¼ Teaspoon ground nutmeg
- ¼ Teaspoon ground cardamom
- 1/8 Teaspoon ground cloves
- 1/8 Teaspoon ground allspice

Directions:

1. Preheat your oven to 325ºF.
2. Grease 8 small ramekins.
3. In a bowl, add the eggs and salt and beat well.
4. Arrange a sieve over a medium bowl.
5. Through a sieve, strain the egg mixture into a bowl.
6. Add the Yacon syrup to the eggs and stir to combine.
7. Add the almond milk and spices and beat until well combined.
8. Transfer the mixture into prepared ramekins.
9. Now, place ramekins in a large baking dish.
10. Add hot water in the baking dish about 2-inch high around the ramekins.
11. Place the baking dish in the oven and bake for about 30–40 minutes or until a toothpick inserted in the center comes out clean.
12. Remove ramekins from the oven and set aside to cool.
13. Refrigerate to chill before serving.

Nutrition:

- Calories: 77
- Fat: 3.8g
- Carbs: 6g
- Cholesterol: 102mg
- Sodium: 116mg
- Fiber: 0.5g
- Sugar: 3.7g
- Protein: 3.8g

Mocha Ice Cream

Preparation time: 15 Minutes

Cooking time: 15 Minutes

Servings: 2

Ingredients:

- 1 Cup unsweetened coconut milk
- ¼ Cup heavy cream
- 2 Tablespoons granulated erythritol
- 15 Drops liquid stevia
- 2 Tablespoons cacao powder
- 1 Tablespoon instant coffee

- ¼ Teaspoon xanthan gum

Directions:

1. In a container, add the ingredients (except xanthan gum), and with an immersion blender, blend until well combined.
2. Slowly add the xanthan gum and blend until a slightly thicker mixture is formed.
3. Transfer the mixture into the ice cream maker and process according to the manufacturer's instructions.
4. Now, transfer the ice cream into an airtight container and freeze for at least 4–5 hours before serving.

Nutrition:

- Calories: 246 Carbs: 6.2g
- Fat: 23.1g Cholesterol: 21mg
- Sodium: 52mg Fiber: 2g
- Sugar: 3g
- Protein: 2.8g

Dana Roberts

Condiment Recipes

Thai Peanut Sauce

Preparation time: 5 Minutes

Cooking time: 0 Minutes

Servings: 3

Ingredients:

- 2 Tbsp. Apple Cider Vinegar
- ¼ Cup Thai Red Curry Paste
- 1 Cup Peanut Butter
- 1 ½ Cup Coconut Milk
- 1 Tbsp. Lime Juice
- ¼ Cup Brown Sugar
- 2 Tbsp. Soy Sauce

Directions:

1. For a quick and easy sauce, simply place everything into a food processor and meld until soft. Be sure you keep any sauce and dressing in the fridge to keep fresh!

Nutrition:

- Calories: 100 Carbs: 9g
- Fat: 7g Protein: 1g

General Tso Sauce

Preparation time: 5 Minutes

Cooking time: 10 Minutes

Servings: 4

Ingredients:

- ¼ Cup rice vinegar
- ½ Cup water
- 1 ½ tablespoon sriracha sauce
- ¼ Cup soy sauce
- 1 ½ Tablespoon corn starch
- ½ Cup sugar

Directions:

1. General Tso Sauce is a classic, and you can now make a healthier version of it! All you have to do is take out your saucepan and place all of the ingredients in.
2. Once in place, bring everything over medium heat and whisk together for ten minutes or until the sauce begins to get thick.
3. Finally, remove from the heat and enjoy!

Nutrition:

- Calories: 80 Carbs: 11g
- Fat: 3g Protein: 2g

Dana Roberts

Smoothies Recipes

Tropical Green Paleo Smoothie

Preparation time: 15 Minutes

Cooking time: 0 Minutes

Servings: 5

Ingredients:

- Spinach. 3 cups (Kale, or a blend of small leafy greens, packed)
- Whole Banana. 1 (Peeled)
- Whole Orange. 1 (Peeled)
- Pineapple. 1-½ cup (Cubed)
- Coconut Milk. 1 cup

- Whole Avocado. ½ (pitted and skin removed)
- Crushed Ice. 2 cups
- Wild Orange Essential Oil. 3 drops (optional)
- Dried Coconut Chip. 10 pieces (optional)
- Dried Coconut Chips for Topping (optional)
- Pure Maple Syrup. 1 Tablespoon (optional, depends on the sweetness of fruit)
- Chia Seeds for Topping. One teaspoon (optional)

Directions:

1. Add all the ingredients minus the chia seeds and coconut chips in a high-speed blender. Blend for about 2 minutes, until creamy and smooth.
2. Transfer mixture to serving glasses and top with the chia seeds and coconut seeds. It can be refrigerated for up to 3 days. Stir quickly to recombine if placed in the fridge.

Nutrition:

- Calories per serving: 33
- Carbohydrates: 8.5g
- Protein: 2.2g
- Fat: 0.4g
- Sugar: 4.3g
- Sodium: 225mg
- Fiber: 1.9g

Vegan Banana Avocado Green Smoothie Bowl with Blueberries

Preparation time: 5 Minutes

Cooking time: 0 Minutes

Servings: 1

Ingredients:

For the Smoothie:

- Fresh Baby Spinach. 60 grams
- Whole Avocado. ½
- Whole Peach. 1
- Whole Banana. ½
- Rolled Oats. 2 Tablespoons
- Peanut Butter. 1 Tablespoon
- Coconut Water. 3 Tablespoons

For the Topping:

1. Whole Blueberries. 12
2. Cacao Nibs. 1 teaspoon

Directions:

1. Add all the smoothie ingredients to your blender. Blend until creamy and smooth, about 30 seconds.
2. Pour into a bowl and add toppings.
3. Enjoy!

Nutrition:

- Calories per serving: 414
- Carbohydrates: 10.8g
- Protein: 12.5g
- Fat: 35.7g
- Sugar: 0.6g
- Sodium: 188mg
- Fiber: 4.8g

Kale Strawberry Green Smoothie Bowl

Preparation time: 8 Minutes

Cooking time: 0 Minutes

Servings: 1

Ingredients:

For the Smoothie:

- Whole Strawberries. 2
- Zucchini. 2 ounces
- Kale. 1 cup
- Sliced Cucumber. 1.4 ounces

- Whole Banana. ½
- Dairy-Free Milk. 4 tablespoons

For the Topping:

- Whole Strawberry. 1
- Hemp Hearts. ½ Tablespoon
- Shredded Coconut. 1 Tablespoon
- Whole Oats. 2 Tablespoons

Directions:

1. Add all the smoothie ingredients to a high-speed blender. Blend for about 2 minutes, until it is creamy and smooth.
2. Transfer the mixture to serving bowls and add the toppings.

Nutrition:

- Calories per serving: 326
- Carbohydrates: 8.2g
- Protein: 7.8g Fat: 29.4g
- Sugar: 0.3g Sodium: 126mg
- Fiber: 4.1g

Dana Roberts

Salad Recipes

Potluck Lamb Salad

Preparation time: 20 Minutes

Cooking time: 10 Minutes

Servings: 4

Ingredients:

- 2 Tbsp. olive oil, divided
- 12oz. Grass-fed lamb leg steaks, trimmed
- Salt and freshly ground black pepper, to taste
- 6½oz. halloumi cheese, cut into thick slices
- 2 Jarred roasted red bell peppers, sliced thinly

- 2 Cucumbers, cut into thin ribbons
- 3 C. fresh baby spinach
- 2 Tbsp. balsamic vinegar

Directions:

1. In a skillet, heat one tablespoon of the oil over medium-high heat and cook the lamb steaks for about 4-5 minutes per side or until desired doneness. Transfer the lamb steaks onto a cutting board for about 5 minutes. Then cut the lamb steaks into thin slices.
2. In the same skillet, add halloumi and cook for about 1-2 minutes per side or until golden. In a salad bowl, add the lamb, haloumi, bell pepper, cucumber, salad leaves, vinegar, and remaining oil and toss to combine. Serve immediately.

Nutrition:

- Calories: 420 Carbohydrates: 8g
- Protein: 35.4g Fat: 27.2g
- Sugar: 4g Sodium: 417mg Fiber: 1.3g

Spring Supper Salad

Preparation time: 15 Minutes

Cooking time: 5 Minutes

Servings: 5

Ingredients:

For the salad:

- 1 lb. Fresh asparagus, trimmed and cut into 1-inch pieces
- ½ lb. Smoked salmon, cut into bite-sized pieces
- 2 Heads red leaf lettuce, torn
- ¼ C. pecans, toasted and chopped

For dressing:

- ¼ C. olive oil - 2 Tbsp. fresh lemon juice
- 1 Tsp. Dijon mustard
- Salt and freshly ground black pepper, to taste

Directions:

1. In a pan of boiling water, add the asparagus and cook for about 5 minutes.
2. Drain the asparagus well. In a serving bowl, add the asparagus and remaining salad ingredients and mix.
3. In another bowl, add all the dressing ingredients and beat until well combined.
4. Place the dressing over salad and gently toss to coat well. Serve immediately.

Nutrition:

- Calories: 223 Carbohydrates: 8.5g
- Protein: 11.7g Fat: 17.2g
- Sugar: 3.4g Sodium: 960mg Fiber: 3.5g

Chicken-of-Sea Salad

Preparation time: 15 Minutes

Cooking time: 5 Minutes

Servings: 6

Ingredients:

- 2 (6-oz.) cans olive oil-packed tuna, drained
- 2 (6-oz.) cans water-packed tuna, drained
- ¾ C. mayonnaise
- 2 Celery stalks, chopped
- ¼ of onion, chopped
- 1 Tbsp. fresh lime juice

- 2 Tbsp. mustard
- Freshly ground black pepper, to taste
- 6 C. fresh baby arugula

Directions:

1. In a large bowl, add all the ingredients except arugula and gently stir to combine.
2. Divide arugula onto serving plates and top with tuna mixture.
3. Serve immediately.

Nutrition:

- Calories: 325 Carbohydrates: 2.7g
- Protein: 27.4g Fat: 22.2g
- Sugar: 0.9g Sodium: 389mg Fiber: 1.1g

Sweet Potato Salad

Preparation time: 10 Minutes

Cooking time: 10 Minutes

Servings: 3

Ingredients:

- 2 Teaspoons olive oil
- 1 Sweet potato, spiralized
- 1 Apple, cored and spiralized
- 3 Tablespoons almonds, toasted and sliced
- Salt, to taste
- 3 Cups spinach, torn

For the salad dressing:

- 1 Teaspoon apple cider vinegar
- 2 Tablespoons apple juice
- 1 Tablespoon almond butter, melted
- ½ Teaspoon ginger, minced
- 1½ Teaspoons mustard
- 1 Tablespoon olive oil

Directions:

1. In a bowl, mix the vinegar with the apple juice, almond butter, ginger, mustard, and one tablespoon oil and whisk.
2. Heat a pan with the two teaspoons oil over medium-high heat, add the sweet potato noodles, stir, cook for 7 minutes and transfer to a bowl.
3. Add the rest of the ingredients and the dressing, toss and serve.

Nutrition:

- Calories per serving: 500
- Carbohydrates: 7g
- Protein: 8g
- Fat: 2g
- Sugar: 0.3g
- Sodium: 434mg
- Fiber: 0g

Dana Roberts

Appetizers and Snacks

Spiced Jalapeno Bites with Tomato

Preparation time: 10 Minutes

Cooking time: 0 Minutes

Servings: 4

Ingredients:

- 1 Cup turkey ham, chopped
- 1/4 Jalapeño pepper, minced
- 1/4 Cup mayonnaise
- 1/3 Tablespoon Dijon mustard
- 4 Tomatoes, sliced

- Salt and black pepper, to taste
- 1 Tablespoon parsley, chopped

Directions:

1. In a bowl, mix the turkey ham, jalapeño pepper, mayo, mustard, salt, and pepper.
2. Spread out the tomato slices on four serving plates, then top each plate with a spoonful turkey ham mixture.
3. Serve garnished with chopped parsley.

Nutrition: Calories: 250 Fat: 14.1g

- Fiber: 3.7g Carbohydrates: 4.1g
- Protein: 18.9g

Coconut Crab Cakes

Preparation time: 20 Minutes

Cooking time: 25 Minutes

Servings: 4

Ingredients:

- 1 Tablespoon of minced garlic
- 2 Pasteurized eggs
- 2 Teaspoons of coconut oil
- 3/4 Cup of coconut flakes
- 3/4 Cup chopped spinach
- 1/4 Pound crabmeat
- 1/4 Cup of chopped leek
- 1/2 Cup extra virgin olive oil
- 1/2 Teaspoon of pepper

- 1/4 Onion diced
- Salt

Directions:

1. Pour the crabmeat into a bowl, then add in the coconut flakes and mix well.
2. Whisk eggs in a bowl, then mix in leek and spinach.
3. Season the egg mixture with pepper, two pinches of salt, and garlic.
4. Then, pour the eggs into the crab and stir well.
5. Preheat a pan, heat extra virgin olive, and fry the crab evenly from each side until golden brown. Remove from the pan and serve hot.

Nutrition:

- Calories: 254 Fat: 9.5g
- Fiber: 5.4g Carbohydrates: 4.1g
- Protein: 8.9g

Tuna Cakes

Preparation time: 15 Minutes

Cooking time: 10 Minutes

Servings: 2

Ingredients:

- 1 (15-ounce) can water-packed tuna, drained
- 1/2 Celery stalk, chopped
- 2 Tablespoon fresh parsley, chopped
- 1 Teaspoon fresh dill, chopped
- 2 Tablespoons walnuts, chopped

- 2 Tablespoons mayonna.
- 1 Organic egg, beaten
- 1 Tablespoon butter
- 3 Cups lettuce

Directions:

1. For burgers: Add all ingredients (exce, and lettuce) in a bowl and mix until well ∪
2. Make two equal-sized patties from the mixtɩ
3. Melt some butter and cook the patties for abou minutes.
4. Carefully flip the side and cook for about 2-3 minutes.
5. Divide the lettuce onto serving plates.
6. Top each plate with one burger and serve.

Nutrition:

- Calories: 267 Fat: 12.5g
- Fiber: 9.4g Carbohydrates:3.8g
- Protein: 11.5g

Preparation time: 15 Minutes

Cooking time: 15 Minutes

Servings: 4

Ingredients:

For Tempura zucchinis:

- 1 1/2 Cups (200 g) almond flour
- 2 Tbsp. heavy cream
- 1 Tsp. salt
- 2 Tbsp. olive oil + extra for frying
- 1 1/4 Cups (300 ml) water
- 1/2 Tbsp. sugar-free maple syrup
- 2 Large zucchinis, cut into 1-inch thick strips

For Cream cheese dip:

- 8oz. Cream cheese, room temperature
- 1/2 Cup (113 g) sour cream

- 1 Tsp. Taco seasoning
- 1 Scallion, chopped
- 1 Green chili, deseeded and minced

Directions:

Tempura zucchinis:

1. In a bowl, mix the almond flour, heavy cream, salt, peanut oil, water, and maple syrup.
2. Dredge the zucchini strips in the mixture until well-coated.
3. Heat about four tablespoons of olive oil in a non-stick skillet.
4. Working in batches, use tongs to remove the zucchinis (draining extra liquid) into the oil.
5. Fry per side for 1 to 2 minutes and remove the zucchinis onto a paper towel-lined plate to drain grease.
6. Enjoy the zucchinis.

Cream cheese dip:

1. In a bowl or container, the cream cheese, taco seasoning, sour cream, scallion, and green chili must be mixed,
2. Serve the tempura zucchinis with the cream cheese dip.

Nutrition:

- Calories: 316 Fat: 8.4g
- Fiber: 9.3g Carbohydrates: 4.1g
- Protein: 5.1g

Bacon and Feta Skewers

Preparation time: 15 Minutes

Cooking time: 10 Minutes

Servings: 4

Ingredients:

- 2 lb. Feta cheese, cut into 8 cubes
- 8 Bacon slices
- 4 Bamboo skewers, soaked
- 1 Zucchini, cut into 8 bite-size cubes
- Salt and black pepper to taste
- 3 Tbsp. almond oil for brushing

Directions:

1. Wrap each feta cube with a bacon slice.
2. Thread one wrapped feta on a skewer; add a zucchini cube, then another wrapped feta, and another zucchini.
3. Repeat the threading process with the remaining skewers.
4. Preheat a grill pan to medium heat, generously brush with the avocado oil and grill the skewer on both sides for 3 to 4 minutes per side or until the set is golden brown and the bacon cooked.
5. Serve afterward with the tomato salsa.

Nutrition:

- Calories: 290 Fat: 15.1g
- Fiber: 4.2g
- Carbohydrates: 4.1g
- Protein: 11.8g

Avocado and Prosciutto Deviled Eggs

Preparation time: 20 Minutes

Cooking time: 10 Minutes

Servings: 4

Ingredients:

- 4 Eggs
- Ice bath
- 4 Prosciutto slices, chopped
- 1 Avocado, pitted and peeled
- 1 Tbsp. mustard
- 1 Tsp. plain vinegar
- 1 Tbsp. heavy cream
- 1 Tbsp. chopped fresh cilantro
- Salt and black pepper to taste
- 1/2 Cup (113 g) mayonnaise

- 1 Tbsp. coconut cream
- 1/4 Tsp. cayenne pepper
- 1 Tbsp. avocado oil
- 1 Tbsp. chopped fresh parsley

Directions:

1. Boil the eggs for 8 minutes.
2. Remove the eggs into the ice bath, sit for 3 minutes, and then peel the eggs.
3. Slice the eggs lengthwise into halves and empty the egg yolks into a bowl.
4. Arrange the egg whites on a plate with the hole side facing upwards.
5. While the eggs are cooked, heat a non-stick skillet over medium heat and cook the prosciutto for 5 to 8 minutes.
6. Remove the prosciutto onto a paper towel-lined plate to drain grease.
7. Put the avocado slices into the egg yolks and mash both ingredients with a fork until smooth.
8. Mix in the mustard, vinegar, heavy cream, cilantro, salt, and black pepper until well-blended.
9. Spoon the mixture into a piping bag and press the mixture into the egg holes until well-filled.
10. In a bowl, whisk the mayonnaise, coconut cream, cayenne pepper, and avocado oil.
11. On serving plates, spoon some of the mayonnaise sauce and slightly smear it in a circular movement. Top with the deviled eggs, scatter the prosciutto on top, and garnish with the parsley.
12. Enjoy immediately.

Nutrition:

- Calories: 265 Fat: 11.7g
- Fiber: 4.1g Carbohydrates: 3.1g
- Protein:7.9g

Chicken Club Lettuce Wraps

Preparation time: 15 Minutes

Cooking time: 15 Minutes

Servings: 1

Ingredients:

- 1 Head of iceberg lettuce with the core and outer leaves removed
- 1 Tbsp. of mayonnaise

- 6 Slices of organic chicken or turkey breast
- Bacon (2 cooked strips, halved)
- Tomato (just 2 slices)

Directions:

1. Line your working surface with a large slice of parchment paper.
2. Layer 6-8 large leaves of lettuce in the center of the paper to make a base of around 9-10 inches.
3. Spread the mayo in the center and lay with chicken or turkey, bacon, and tomato.
4. Starting with the end closest to you, roll the wrap like a jelly roll with the parchment paper as your guide. Keep it tight and halfway through, roll tuck in the ends of the wrap.
5. When it is completely wrapped, roll the rest of the parchment paper around it, and use a knife to cut it in half.

Nutrition:

- Calories: 179
- Fat: 4.1g
- Fiber: 9.7g
- Carbohydrates: 1.3g
- Protein: 8.5g

About the author

Dana Roberts is an author, nutritionist and mom of three beautiful princesses.
At the age of 38 she discovered that she had breast disease and this brought her a big hormonal imbalance.
At the age of 43 she noticed a gradual weight gain that prompted her to try different diets.
So many of these had little or no effect on her. After a few years, her body underwent drastic changes.
She gained a lot of weight, her breasts collapsed and a lot of stretch marks appeared. Not wanting to risk serious health problems, she discovered the ketogenic diet and decided to try it.
She began to notice that some foods gave her more energy and others weighed her down. Food addiction also influenced her diet because when she didn't bring awareness to her emotions, she reacted by eating.
She spent years fighting this addiction and finally found a way to overcome it and rediscover her former beauty, creating recipes that could fill both her stomach and her soul.
The book "Keto Diet Cookbook for women after 50" offers to all women the possibility to lose weight with a program based not only on diet, but also on the addiction that sometimes food creates.

CPSIA information can be obtained
at www.ICGtesting.com
Printed in the USA
BVHW062037010321
601387BV00007B/520